DEMON BLOOD

SHADOW CITY: ROYAL VAMPIRE

JEN L. GREY

on that dream. The thing needed to get to the point. I was already losing interest.

"Are you sure about that?" The shadow sighed. "Because once you learn everything, you can't forget it."

The threat hung between us. If my heart were still beating, it would be pounding.

A loud, unnerving laugh escaped the shadow, and my sanity teetered.

Just tell me, I demanded.

The shadow inched closer, its eyes darkening to crimson. "It's better if I show you."

Its hands grabbed the edge of the hoodie.

I braced myself. No doubt, this would be the most terrifying thing I'd ever seen. All the horror shows my sister, Annie, had ever forced me to watch flashed through my mind, but when I tried to settle on one image, my brain would flash to another.

The shadow hesitated, enjoying my inner turmoil. It had reveled in my panic since I was a child.

When I thought I couldn't take it anymore, the shadow inched the hoodie back. The light revealed the creature's chin, illuminating pink-toned fair skin that reminded me of someone, though I couldn't say who.

"Everything will make sense." The shadow cackled. "And that's when everything will change."

As the shadow revealed more of its face, the red eyes morphed into emerald eyes identical to my own.

Something shifted inside me.

Even though I didn't understand my desperation, my gut wanted the shadow to stop.

"Too late," the shadow said, removing the hoodie completely.

Long, straight copper hair cascaded past her shoulders, and I took in her face in shock. Even the heart shape face and rosy lips were exactly like mine.

It was like looking in a mirror.

This wasn't possible.

"But it is," the shadow told me. Could I even call her a shadow anymore? "You see, I'm the hidden part of you that you know nothing about. The part your human side has concealed."

Alarm rang through me. *I don't understand.* But I wasn't sure I wanted to.

She reached toward me and whispered, "But you're about to. Everything I've wanted to show you is moments away. It's finally time."

Before I could scream *no*, the shadow leaped at me. I tried to grab her, but my body was still paralyzed. I had no way to hold her off.

Our bodies merged, and coolness shivered into me. Her consciousness melded with mine as we became one, and the world flashed bright and dark like a strobe light.

I wasn't sure what to do, but then the most amazing thing happened.

A thumping started in my chest.

Was it possible? My heart had stopped, but I could hear my blood whooshing through my veins.

"Is her heart beating again?" someone asked with disbelief.

Something warm squeezed my hand, and a slight

buzzing passed between us as his skin touched mine. I grimaced, waiting for my blood to boil again, but nothing uncomfortable happened, just my lungs expanding and emptying.

Fingertips brushed my cheek.

Alex.

I knew it was him, though his touch felt different.

He leaned over me. "You need to go. She almost died because of you."

I wasn't dead? But how was that possible? I was in that weird place with the shadow—no, wait ... with me.

The person sighed, and I realized it was Roman, one of the shifters who held me captive to make sure I didn't leave Shadow City. "I didn't mean—"

"Save it for someone who cares," Alex hissed.

Ugh, I wished Alex wouldn't talk to Roman that way. Roman managed the cops here at the warehouse, but he'd seemed like a good guy. He'd dropped information to me about the shifter turmoil, and he had to have done it on purpose.

Veronica? Alex connected.

Warmth slammed into me as our bond reestablished. All of his emotions—fear, love, concern, anger—engulfed me like torrential rain. If I thought I'd felt his feelings before, it didn't compare to now. I couldn't tell where I began, and he ended. It was as if we were one being. *Yeah.*

His relief flowed into me. *Oh, thank the gods.*

Moisture hit my face—his tears. The scent of metal combined with salt overloaded my nose.

How in the world could I smell someone's tears? But that wasn't the only odd thing. Not only could I hear my heartbeat but Alex's and Roman's too, each faster than mine due to a mix of emotions.

My eyes fluttered open ... and the world looked completely different. Colors I'd never seen before exploded within my vision, each even more beautiful than teal, my favorite color. I had no clue what to call them. The overwhelmingly colorful lights of Shadow City's atmosphere had nothing on these. No matter how many times I blinked, the world was different.

More crisp, more vivid, more ... everything.

Something brushed against my mind—a new sensation. Darkness clung to my skin then spread throughout my body. I sat up, moving faster than ever before. The room blurred. I considered it a small blessing that the room was no longer spinning.

"Careful," Alex said, and I stared in wonder. His soft blue eyes had flecks of crystal inside them. "What's wrong?"

Cold ran through me, and I realized exactly what the sensation was. I sucked in a breath. "The shadow. It's here." And I had to get it out of me. *Now.*

CHAPTER TWO

ALEX SCANNED THE ROOM. "WHERE?"

"Inside me."

"Shadow?" Roman stepped from the doorway into the room. His dark olive skin appeared paler than when I'd met him. His shaggy, toffee-colored hair hung in his lime-green eyes, which were filled with concern. "What is she talking about?"

Alex's normally sun-kissed skin turned a shade of pink as anger coursed between us. His nostrils flared as his head snapped in Roman's direction. "It's none of your business."

Hey. I touched his hand and pushed calmness toward him. I took a moment to breathe in the sweet syrupy scent that was uniquely his, and tears threatened to spill from my eyes.

I'd thought I'd never feel his touch or smell him again. Having him here beside me was like a dream come true.

Yes, it was that cliché, but I couldn't contain my joy even in a bad situation.

He smelled better than I remembered, and my body warmed in a very inappropriate way.

Down, girl. We were still in danger, in a special storage room that contained something that had cut me, causing my blood to boil until I'd died.

Death.

How the hell was I alive?

Everything that had happened in the hours before my heart had stopped flitted through my mind. How Matthew and Azbogah had used the shifter attack outside the council building to warrant a quick vote for the cops to capture me at Sterlyn and Griffin's condo and bring me to this artifact warehouse. How the fight had been brutal, and when I'd gone down to the ground floor of the condominium to escape, I'd run straight into the arms of the guards who had brought me here.

It wasn't bad enough that Matthew had forced Alex's and my hands to get me into Shadow City—he'd then done all he could to turn me into a vampire.

But we had to focus on one thing at a time, and right now, we had to get out of here before Matthew created more problems. *Be nice to him.*

His attention turned to me, and I noticed his golden-brown hair was slightly longer than normal, the tips brushing his forehead. *Why? He's holding you prisoner.*

He felt like he had no choice. I couldn't judge Roman when I understood what it felt like not to have any good options. You chose the best one to protect yourself and did what was expected of you.

Growing up in foster homes and an orphanage, I'd bitten my tongue and done what I could to get by. I'd been a prisoner, and I'd bet that many residents in Shadow City felt the same way.

Most were locked in a city with no escape. Everyone had their own agendas, especially the individual races. Their leaders used anything they could to gain leverage. *Hasn't Matthew put you in the same position? Like the way he's trying to force the council to make me change into a vampire.*

Noises from afar caught my attention, reminding me that Sterlyn, Griffin, Rosemary, and Matthew were in the foyer.

"If you don't let us back there, I will kick your ass," Rosemary threatened, her usual calm demeanor gone. "Our friend is being held captive, and it sounds like something is wrong."

"You aren't authorized." Matthew's tone sounded more pretentious than usual, like a toddler getting ready to throw a tantrum.

I moved to stand, and before I realized it, I was on my feet. Blinking, I wiggled my fingers. The coolness of my blood reminded me of the shadow. "Everything is different. It's the shadow. I need to get it out of me."

"Veronica, it's not the shadow." Alex stepped in front of me and placed his hands on my shoulders. "You were dying—"

My mind raced as I comprehended things quicker

than usual. "No, I died. My heart stopped, and I went to a dark place." A chill ran down my spine. Not from the shadow but from my memory. "Then, as I got acclimated to the absence of color, it was like someone flicked on all the lights, and the shadow appeared. That's how I came back—the shadow climbed inside me." The severity of the situation weighed on my chest. How could I remove the very thing that had brought me back to life? The presence inside me affected me in ways I didn't understand, giving me enhanced speed, sight, and hearing.

"I'll give you two a minute alone." Roman pulled at the collar of his black shirt, which displayed the Shadow City police symbol—a paw print from the city emblem—on the right side.

"No, you'll get into more trouble." I'd already caused enough problems between him, Matthew, and the council. My escape through the air ducts would become a problem, but I had made the best decision I could at that moment: buying time until Alex and my friends could get here.

One option could work for him. "Maybe you should lock me back up in the room you left me in."

"No need for that." Roman cleared his throat uncomfortably. "You were brought here because you were a human and causing havoc with the vampires who can't control their urges. That's no longer a problem."

I stilled. Alex's words from before I'd died replayed in my mind. *I hope you meant what you said earlier.* I glanced at my hands. My skin was smoother, and the scar on my forearm that I'd gotten while playing basketball as a child was gone.

Unable to believe my eyes, I inspected my elbow, expecting to see the gaping wound from when Cody, another guard, had pushed me to the ground outside the condominium, but there was no evidence I'd ever been hurt.

My fingers instinctively went to my face, which had been scabbed over as well, while my gaze flicked to my knee. Again, I noted no injuries, just smooth skin. Had the shadow healed me? "How?"

Unless—

"Veronica." My name rolled off Alex's tongue in a way that quickened my heart. Trepidation wafted off him. "Remember when you said you wanted to be turned?"

I touched my neck, remembering the pain I'd felt seconds before my heart had stopped. "Am I ..." I trailed off as numbness spread through me.

"A vampire?" Alex finished and nibbled on his bottom lip. He exhaled. "Yeah. You're going to move quicker, and you may be very hungry."

The sensations and feelings I was experiencing weren't due to the shadow but from me becoming something different. Had everything in the dark void been a nightmare? Part of me hoped so, but it had felt so real. There was no way it could've been a figment of my imagination.

The shadow ... no.

"Did I mess up?" Alex asked with concern. "I thought ..."

Great, I had my soulmate doubting himself.

Soulmate.

How funny. I'd thought that sounded weird, but it was the best way to describe us.

Our souls were connected.

Intermingled.

"*No.*" I let the magnitude of my feelings surge through me and into him. I didn't want him to doubt himself, me, or us. "I didn't feel the change." I'd imagined that a human body changing into a supernatural one would have caused some powerful sensations.

"When your heart stopped, it was because of my bite." Alex took my hand and watched my reaction to his words. "The change happens while your heart isn't beating. It takes about a minute. Though, for a moment, I wasn't sure if it had stopped because of my bite or because of whatever you were going through." He placed his forehead against mine as fear ran between us. "I was scared when it took so long for your heart to start again. I thought I'd lost you."

"I was out for only a minute?" I had figured it was hours. It was as if time had ceased to exist while I'd been in the void.

Alex cupped my face. "Close to two minutes, and it felt like an eternity."

Yeah, I agreed with him there. "This is what being a vampire is like?" He'd made it sound horrible, but other than the disorientation, it wasn't bad at all.

"Okay, I'm going in," Griffin said from another room. "I don't give a damn if you forbid it."

"Veronica," Roman said regretfully. "Can we go out there before things escalate?"

I nodded and grinned, realizing Matthew would see me in this form.

Alex hissed, *I don't like him calling you Veronica.*

I about laughed at the odd statement. *That's my name. Only my friends call me Ronnie. What should he call me?*

He may not be your friend, but you're my Veronica, Alex growled. *I don't like anyone else using it.*

I'd noticed that Alex only called me by my full name. I'd come close to asking him to call me Ronnie, but it hadn't felt right. I liked him using my full name, which had never happened before, but he was my first in all the ways that counted, including that one. *You do realize your siblings call me Veronica.*

Yeah, and I thought I hated that, Alex complained. *But that was before that prick used your full name.*

I snorted, and Roman inspected me like I had two heads. That was saying something since I'd just come back from being quasi-dead.

"If you take one step into that hallway, I will call the council and inform them that, not only did you attack the cops who came to take Veronica into custody for her own safety, but that you came here, to one of the most heavily guarded places in Shadow City, and demanded entry without full council consent," Matthew said from the front of the building to Sterlyn, Rosemary, and Griffin.

"And since you haven't been granted access, you can't enter that hallway without triggering spells," he gloated. "Go ahead and try. It'll just make my case."

That jackass was something. I was ready to wipe the smug expression off his face, and I couldn't even see it.

Things would only get tenser the longer we stayed back here. I didn't mind if that stressed Matthew out, but I didn't want to cause the others more headaches.

"Let me put this back." I walked to a box on the floor —the one the shadow had dragged me to and forced me to open. I'd reached into it earlier, and something had cut me. I picked up the box to put it back on the shelf but didn't find anything inside it.

Strange.

"That's odd. I've never noticed that box before." Roman shook his head and waved for us to follow him.

Eager to leave the room, I put the box on the shelf. My surroundings blurred as I hurried out the door. The abrupt change caught me off guard, and I placed a hand on the wall to steady myself.

Hey. Alex appeared beside me. *Are you okay?*

I thought once I transitioned, you wouldn't have to ask me that anymore. I laughed without humor. I hated that even in supernatural form, I was struggling.

He kissed me and stared deep into my eyes. *You just went through a huge change. It'll take time to adjust. Lean on me. I want to be your rock just like you've become mine.*

I'd never imagined that I could love this man more, but my heart grew two sizes with feelings just for him.

The urge to take him right there in the middle of the hallway sank into my bones.

"You're full of shit," Sterlyn said. "Alex got back there without any issues, so the cops must have disabled the spell. We're heading back there now."

Though it was the last thing I wanted to do, I forced myself to step away from Alex. I took his hand and turned to find Roman standing at the door to the hallway. He bounced on his feet, wanting me to hurry along.

See. I had to point things out to Alex. *Roman obviously wants us to go out there, but he's giving me time to get my shit together and allowing us to have a moment. He's been considerate the entire time I've been here.*

Alex intertwined our fingers and tugged me toward the door. *I still don't trust him, but I'll trust your judgment unless he does something suspicious.*

I wouldn't complain.

As we marched down the beige hall, our shoes squeaked on the tile the way mine had when I'd arrived here in human form. The "no sneaking" spell was still locked in place.

We stepped through the doorway into the building's foyer, and Matthew's teak eyes focused on me. His mouth dropped open.

CHAPTER THREE

MATTHEW'S light brown hair was ruffled from whatever scuffle had gone on out here. He tugged at his fitted charcoal shirt, which clung to his slender frame and made his vanilla-cream complexion seem paler. "What the hell happened?"

"Don't play games," Alex said, tensing beside me. "You heard us back there."

Roman grunted. "Actually, he didn't. I took the spell down temporarily for you to get through, but then it went back into place. It blocks noise one-way and protects warehouse employees so we can strategize out loud, since we all aren't the same race and can't pack-link."

I tried to follow the conversation, but the scents of everyone, mixed together, was overwhelming. It reminded me of walking through the perfume section at the mall. My head ached from the over-the-top aromas of Matthew's sweet apple, Sterlyn's musky freesia, Griffin's musky myrrh and leather, the scents of the two other shifters, and Rosemary's rose scent.

Add in the whooshing of blood and the pounding of hearts, and my focus was shot. This had to be how a drug addict felt on a high. I wanted to close my eyes and cover my ears, but I refused to let Matthew see me in that state. He already thought I was weak, and I didn't want to add to his perception.

"Hey." Sterlyn's silver-purple eyes fixed on me. "How are you feeling?" Her long silver hair was more breathtaking than I remembered. All the various shades of silver wove together and contrasted against her olive skin. She wore black, her standard, but her skin glowed.

Now that my attention was on her, something inside me recognized her, and she seemed more familiar than before. Pureness radiated from within her, and part of me wanted to be in her presence while another part wanted to run. Again, I had two sides at odds.

"Ronnie?" Rosemary stepped toward me, her hands lifted in surrender. Her dark purple, stardust eyes surveyed me as if assessing risk.

I couldn't help but stare at her. The same pure essence pulsed from her as well. Though her skin didn't glow, goodness wafted off her, and her magic felt similar to mine, more so than Sterlyn's.

I couldn't make sense of it.

Alex wrapped an arm around my waist to anchor me. "She's acclimating."

"You two head back to the warehouse and finish up,"

Roman instructed the two shifters I didn't know. They quickly exited the room, desperate to get away.

Rosemary pushed her mahogany hair over her shoulders and straightened, gesturing at me. "Is this going to be a problem?"

Hurt coursed through me. I'd caused trouble for them since I'd gotten here, but she'd never made me feel like a burden.

Until now.

Perhaps my transition into a vampire had changed her opinion of me. "Not unless you make it one." I couldn't hide the pain in my voice.

When he shook his head, Griffin's honey-brown hair didn't move an inch due to all the gel in it. His hazel eyes darkened as he pinched the bridge of his nose, making his bicep bulge. "She didn't mean it like that."

At least my sense of him was still normal. I didn't feel drawn to him like I did with Rosemary and Sterlyn, although goodness swirled around him too.

"What are you talking about?" Rosemary scoffed. "Of course, I did. Newly turned vampires are desperate for blood even if our blood makes them sick. It's a desperate hunger inside them. All of us could be at risk."

Maybe being a vampire wouldn't be a problem after all. "I'm fine. Truly." I hadn't known that could be a problem, but I wasn't starving or craving blood.

"That's not what we thought you meant." Sterlyn chuckled, but her brows furrowed in question.

You and me both. But I knew not to say anything.

"When did this happen?" Matthew waved a hand at me. "I thought she didn't want to turn."

I regarded him and froze. Something strange radiated from him—like I could sense his soul. It wasn't vile, but it definitely wasn't good. I couldn't define the sensation, but it made my skin crawl.

I focused on the threat in front of me because that was exactly what he was.

"Why would you think that?" I didn't want him to assume he knew my wants and desires. Only Alex was allowed to know them. "Because I didn't want to be turned the moment you tried to force me?"

"Be careful how you speak to me," Matthew hissed, his fangs descending slightly. "I am your king."

I bit the inside of my cheek to keep from laughing. He'd caused enough problems for us all—the last thing I needed to do was antagonize him.

Alex scowled. "She's my mate and your soon-to-be sister-in-law, which will officially make her part of the royal family in all ways."

Wait, sister-in-law?

Matthew wrinkled his nose in disgust. "You're going to *marry* her despite her not being vampire-born?"

"That's a given." Griffin snorted, not even trying to hold in his amusement. "They're soulmates. What did you expect? In every way that matters, they're one. Marriage is just a formality."

"One that you have not observed," Matthew snapped, his hands fisted.

Whoa, that was not cool. He wanted to cause problems between Sterlyn and Griffin.

"That question, dear brother, proves you don't know me." Alex's fingers dug into my skin as bitterness rolled through him. "I'm not sure you ever did."

"Don't play that game." Matthew rubbed his arms. "You were always on the same page as me."

"Only because our father said that standing behind you should be my first priority." Alex frowned. "I always backed you up because that's what he wanted, but my priorities changed the moment Veronica walked into Thirsty's Bar."

"Always loyal until an unclaimed human girl came along." Matthew thrust a finger at me. "What would Father think? Ever since he died, you've been changing into someone I don't know."

With every word, their relationship grew more tenuous. *Maybe we should have this conversation elsewhere, like at the mansion.* I had to force those words out because the mansion was the last place I wanted to go. Between the attacks on me there and Matthew always being around, I'd rather jump into the fiery pits of Hell. But this was Alex's brother. Even though my foster mother, Eliza, and foster sister and best friend, Annie, weren't my blood relatives and we were no longer living in the same normal world, I'd do anything for them.

That would never change.

They'd been there for me when no one else had—until Alex. Now, my family had grown by leaps and bounds, but the fact that Annie and Eliza had been first was immutable.

You're right. Now isn't the time. Alex stood tall, towering over my five-foot-five frame. He easily had seven inches on me. "There is nothing we can say or do to reverse the damage between us. And right now, I need to get Veronica settled after the hellacious day she's had because of you."

"Because of me?" Matthew mocked, his nostrils flaring. "She got locked up because your *friends* don't have control over the shifter race and because you brought her around other supernaturals, causing the vampires to lose control and risk losing their humanity. None of that was my fault."

From what the others had said, I would know when someone lied. Supernaturals could smell it in the air, but I smelled only the same scents that had been assaulting my nose. *Am I missing the lie?* I sniffed discreetly, hoping no one would notice.

Humor floated into me from Alex. *No. From his perspective, he didn't lie. Ezra coordinated the shifter attack, and Sterlyn and I brought you to the council building. Even though he might have influenced the situation, he didn't outright lie. Supernaturals like to dance around the line without going over.*

Great. So, the council was more political than I'd realized.

"I agree with Alex." Sterlyn lifted her chin. "We've all had a rough day, and it's time to get some rest, especially since a council meeting has been called for the morning."

"Fine." Matthew crossed his arms. "Since Veronica is now—"

"Ronnie," Alex snapped. "She's Ronnie to everyone but me."

A smile spread across my face before I could hold it back. I loved that he wanted to be the only one to call me by my full name. I used to only want my friends to call me Ronnie, but that had changed when Alex had said my full name.

"Whatever." Matthew rolled his eyes. "Since *Ronnie* is now turned, you two will come back to the mansion with me."

And there it was. I'd expected it, but that didn't stop the dread from rolling through my chest.

"No," Alex said with resolve. "We will not be going back to the mansion."

Thank God. I'd thought Alex would want us there too, not necessarily for himself but for Gwen, his sister.

"You have nowhere else to go." Matthew smirked and arched a brow. "It's not like there are many vacant places in Shadow City, and technically Ver—*Ronnie* can't leave until the council agrees."

"Of course, they have somewhere else to go." Sterlyn placed a hand on her mate's arm and batted her eyes at the vampire king. "Our home."

"They already have a room, and all their stuff is there," Griffin said and kissed Sterlyn's cheek. "We're more than happy to have them stay with us for as long as they wish."

"And if they don't want to stay there," Rosemary interjected, walking to my other side, "they're more than welcome at my home, too."

Yet again, they were reaffirming that they were on our side, proving what I'd known all along. They were more than my friends.

They were my family, and I'd been stupid to consider, for even a second, that they wouldn't be my friends because I'd become a vampire.

Matthew exhaled and scrutinized his brother. "Is that what you want? To stay with *a silver wolf* or an *angel?*"

"Yes," Alex said with conviction. "I trust them, which is more than I can say for you."

Matthew's chest heaved. "What the hell does that mean?"

It was like a dog chasing its tail. We went round and round, having the same conversation multiple times and adding to the hurt and anger. My skin buzzed as coolness floated through my body, the sensation similar to how I felt when the shadow appeared, but this time, it was inside me. "You can't be serious." I was sick and tired of Alex fighting my battles.

Matthew glared at me. "I was talking to my—"

"Your brother," I said with annoyance. Matthew always wanted to dictate the conversation and the story-line, and I was sick of it. "Yes, I know, but *you're the problem now.* Not me."

He moved menacingly toward me. "Now listen here—"

Alex moved to block me, but I pivoted around him. Matthew would never respect me if I didn't stand my ground. "No. I'm talking."

Sterlyn beamed and laid her head on Griffin's shoulder, watching the show.

"Right. *I'm* a horrible person. I came to Shadow Terrace looking for my sister, who'd been brainwashed by a soulless vampire. Because *you* didn't keep a tight rein on your kingdom and your people, Alex and I found each other." If he wanted to play the blame game, I was all in. "Despite my being human, fate refused to keep Alex and me apart. So, what did you do? Instead of supporting our relationship, you forced our hand and made me come to Shadow City to stay in a mansion full of vampires who'd never been around a human before."

"That's very true," Griffin whispered and laughed. "He did."

Alex leaned over and whispered, knowing everyone could hear him, "And don't forget he was supposed to warn our staff that a human was coming, and he didn't." *By the way, I find you very sexy right now.*

You can show me how sexy I am when we get back to the condo, I flirted back before returning my focus to Matthew. "Poor Sergio attacked me as soon as I entered the mansion. Had Alex and I not completed our bond so he'd know when I was in trouble, Sergio would've killed me."

Matthew opened his mouth, but dammit, I wasn't

done, so I kept going without taking a breath. "After all that, you made it a point to get to the council meeting earlier than us to force me into becoming a vampire. You didn't even attempt to discuss that option with Alex or me." That was the part that hurt so much. I'd never imagined I'd find someone I'd want to spend my life with. Every time I'd thought I might be interested in someone, they'd get too clingy, or something had just felt off. Now I had Alex, who had a family I would've loved to be part of. Instead, *this* was where we'd wound up.

Alex turned so we were facing down his brother together. "So, please, tell me, why in the world would we ever trust you again?"

The vampire king stood there for a second, silent, before inhaling sharply. "This is how you want our relationship to go?"

"I'm at a complete loss." Rosemary rubbed her temples. "How can someone so slow be a king?"

Unlike our friend Sierra, whom I missed fiercely, Rosemary wasn't being a smartass. The angel was truly confused.

"Ronnie just pointed out that they aren't the ones creating the tension—you are," Rosemary said. "I don't know how much clearer they can be."

"This isn't over." Matthew stalked to the door. He turned back toward us, his face red. "Gloat tonight. I dare you. Because tomorrow, everything you know will change."

CHAPTER FOUR

MATTHEW MARCHED out the door as if that would make his threat scarier. I'd been through hell, and I'd been turned into a vampire. There wasn't much more he could threaten me with.

"I thought we had another day before the council meeting." Maybe I'd been in that room longer than I realized?

"When Ezra informed the council of everything that happened today, they scheduled the meeting a day early." Sterlyn examined me. "Which we were okay with because we weren't sure we could get you out before then."

"But the shifter issue ..." The shifter attack had put Sterlyn and Griffin under scrutiny as the shifter representatives. Ezra too, but the council seemed focused on discrediting Sterlyn. From what I'd gathered, that was due to her rare silver wolf heritage—she was part wolf and part angel.

Griffin glanced at Alex. "It'll be fine. We should have enough votes to put a bandage on the issue while we dig into Ezra and his involvement."

Alex connected, *We need to get you home and continue this conversation away from prying ears. You need rest and something to eat.*

Even though I trusted Roman, the more he overheard, the more of a compromised position we put him in. We'd caused him enough problems to last a lifetime.

I turned to the jaguar shifter and smiled. "Thank you for all your help."

Roman smiled sadly then glimpsed at Sterlyn and Griffin. He lowered his head slightly. "I wish I could give you more information, but that's all I know. But as I told Ver—Ronnie, you have enemies working against you, more than you realize. Dick made promises to several shifters, telling them if they backed him to take you down, Griffin, things would be different. When you stepped up with a silver wolf mate, you angered a lot of people."

"How so?" Griffin leaned toward Roman. "The alpha power transferred to me and is rightfully mine, and Sterlyn is helping me take down corruption."

"I believe that." Roman placed a hand on his chest and lowered his voice. "But many see it as you deciding you're mated to someone powerful enough to force people into line. The silver wolves aren't viewed as protectors anymore, but betrayers. They ran off when the shifters put their trust in them to lead."

Sterlyn tilted her head, taking in the police officer

before us. "How do you see it?"

"Atticus helped my mother when we were struggling after Dad's death." He pointed to the emblem on his black shirt. "And gave me a job here four years ago. If it hadn't been for his direction and kind hand, I wouldn't have pulled through. Atticus helped us, and because of that, I was able to help my mother when my own leader caused his death."

"Your leader killed your dad?" I probably should've remained silent, but the brutality of this world—of my new world—was still shocking. And bizarrely, killing someone wasn't necessarily viewed as a bad thing, as long as it was within your own race. "Why?"

"He thought Dad was trying to take over as leader, though that wasn't true. He just didn't agree with our leader's decision to appoint a new director of training. He said the director was too brutal and the new methods of torture forced us to forget that we were part human too." Roman averted his gaze and rolled his shoulders. "People are preparing for civil war. It's been going on behind the scenes longer than you know. Your father had hoped that opening the gates would eliminate some of that pressure."

"Everything you said will be kept confidential." Griffin held out a hand to the police officer. "And thank you for telling us."

Roman shook his hand. "It's not much. Ever since then, Mom and I have been ostracized, especially because I got this job from Atticus, so I don't know much beyond that. I do know your dad fired the director to ensure our race didn't become ruthless, creating a bigger rift between the jaguars and the wolves. I don't know who's involved, but if you have allies, I'd recommend keeping them close."

"If Matthew is watching, he'll grow more curious the longer we stay here." Rosemary opened the front door, waving us out. "We need to get moving."

I couldn't get out of there fast enough. I'd been desperate to leave Sterlyn and Griffin's condo earlier today, and now I was eager to get back. That proved how much could change in the blink of an eye.

"Thank you," I told Roman one last time before stepping out of the building.

The unique Shadow City colors danced around in the air, but they weren't as stunning in the darkness as they were during the day. My vision acclimated, but my head still spun as if a virtual reality game were swirling around me.

No one milled in front of the warehouse, and I was surprised to see one vehicle parked off to the side, and it wasn't Griffin's. "How did you get here?"

Alex took my hand. "By foot. It takes about the same amount of time but allows us to stay under the radar more." *Unlike my brother, for example.* He gestured to the vehicle. *We didn't want to alert the council to our presence, not that it mattered in the end, since Matthew was already here.*

Ah, the candy-red Porsche made sense, especially since the red was similar to blood. Matthew must have chuckled when he'd picked out the color.

Douchebag.

I hated that they'd been put in a position to cause more turmoil with Ezra, Azbogah, and Matthew. "I'm sorry. No matter what I do, I become more of a problem for everyone here."

"You're not the problem," Sterlyn said as she and Griffin caught up and turned down the road toward the busy part of the city. The buildings in this area were close together and made of something that resembled brick. They were about twenty stories high, many with lights on, and a few windows held flickering lights as if someone inside was watching television, making me think they were residential.

The five of us walked in silence.

Are they upset with me? They'd come here to protect me, but Griffin and Sterlyn had lost a lot since I'd dropped into their lives. The shifter attacks had ramped up, and cops had burst into their home uninvited. I wouldn't blame them if they weren't thrilled to know me.

Alex's hand tightened on mine. *Why would you ask that? They were practically as desperate as I was to get to you.* He winked at me, his blue irises lightening to sky blue. *Almost.*

Despite the hell I'd gone through, being with him—especially with him teasing—made me smile. *But no one is saying anything.*

We turned a corner, and people came into view. I steadied myself against the onslaught of sounds and smells.

That's because we can't talk about all the things we need to discuss until we get back to the condo. Alex's thumb gently stroked my hand, making me tingle. *You never know who might be listening. Think about Kira.*

Kira, the fox shifter who'd identified Ezra as the traitor in our midst. I hadn't even considered what had happened to her after all hell had broken loose at the condo. The last I'd seen, she'd been wailing on her cousin, Grady, whom her father planned on naming the next fox leader. *What happened to her?*

She went home to her father with Grady. His shoulders stiffened. *I have a feeling they'll be at the hearing tomorrow to stand against us.*

Kira? That surprised me. She wanted Griffin and Sterlyn's support to take over leadership of the foxes, so going against them didn't make sense.

He nodded. *Yeah, but she's sly. If we play our cards right, we might have an ally there.*

As we reached the hordes of people, I noticed that those who smelled similar were grouped together and kept apart from others. Our group was the only one with intermingled races.

The vampires had a pale undertone to their skin, even those with darker complexions. Their skin looked muted, which I'd never noticed until now.

There were groups with the underlying musk that I'd noticed on Sterlyn, Griffin, and Roman.

The angels were the easiest to identify because they flew overhead, along with a few birds that were also shifters.

The groups even dressed differently. The vampires wore more revealing clothing as if to enhance their alluring features. The shifters wore jeans or khakis with informal shirts, probably so they could fight if needed or undress easily to shift.

The angels wore the dressiest clothes, like they were superior in every way.

As we walked past the groups, the people who weren't vampires stiffened, not wanting any of us to touch them but also not wanting to show signs of submission.

We glided easily through the groups, but Alex tightened his grip on me through larger crowds.

Is something wrong? I blinked, trying to gain my bearings through the sounds bombarding me. I could hear every heartbeat, inhalation, and whisper.

He glanced at me. *No, but you haven't eaten and are newly turned. Even though vampires don't feed from other supernaturals for many reasons—one being they taste extremely bitter—when you turn, the cravings don't care about the source of blood.*

Out of the corner of my eye, I saw the other three nervously glancing my way. They all expected me to snap.

I'm hungry, but I don't want blood. The thought of drinking blood didn't disgust me like it had before, which kind of unnerved me, but an egg sandwich or steak was on top of my list.

Alex's brows furrowed, but he didn't respond.

We reached the forty-story-high condominium tower with its signature golden gloss and gigantic sign out front that proclaimed it as THE ELITE WOLVES' DEN in cursive writing. A wolf print was stamped underneath in midnight black.

"Let's go in through the garage. I don't want to talk to anyone in the main entrance," Griffin said and bore left toward the gate that led down to the attached garage.

At the glass-enclosed elevator, Griffin scanned his badge and waved us all inside. Sterlyn hit the button to the top floor, and the silver doors slid closed.

Within seconds, we were walking into their beautiful modern living room. The dark platinum tile floors contrasted against the stratus shade walls, while the outer walls were all glass, offering a breathtaking view of the entire city.

The entire room was in disarray.

A woman in navy yoga pants and a lavender shirt was scrubbing blood off a white leather couch lying on its side. Ulva glanced at us, her striking sapphire blue eyes dimmer, and her golden hair hanging limply around her worry-lined face. The woman who'd seemed ageless suddenly appeared well into her forties.

The entire room had looked like a page from a catalog, with white leather couches sitting perpendicular to one another and a white coffee table sitting in the center. But everything had been overturned, and the table was broken.

The only thing that seemed the same was the sliding glass door that led to the balcony. Roughly as big as the living room, the balcony had two gold chandeliers hanging over black lounge chairs and a black-topped bar on one side.

"Mom, I told you we'd take care of this." Griffin rushed to his mother and helped her to her feet. "You should get some rest."

"Do you think I could fall asleep knowing my dear, sweet—" She glanced at me, and her mouth dropped open. "Dear gods, what happened?"

Rosemary lifted a hand. "I'd like to know the same thing."

That was a good question. I'd figured out a lot since the police had taken me. "First off, while I was held at the artifact warehouse, I decided I wanted to become a vampire. But I didn't plan on it going down like it did. When Alex connected with me to tell me Matthew was on his way and you were trying to catch up, I had to do something other than sit there. I was so sick and tired of feeling like a victim."

"Yeah, Alex said you climbed through the air ducts." Sterlyn lifted a couch by herself and put it back in place. "I'm assuming that started whatever trouble you got in."

Griffin lifted a chair and studied his mother. "Sit."

Ulva wrinkled her nose as she stared at her son. "Why don't you talk to Sterlyn that way?"

He laughed. "I've tried. She won't let me."

"You've trained him well." Ulva winked at Sterlyn.

Rosemary glared. "I want to hear what happened. We can joke after."

"I'm with her," Alex said as he took my arm and led me to the couch away from the shifters. We sat next to each other, and I placed my hands in my lap.

All five stared at me. I hated being the center of attention, so it was best if I got it all out fast. "I made too much noise in the air duct. Every move I made was like a drumbeat, and that was before I had supernatural hearing. When I reached the room next to mine, I dropped inside, not realizing it was a room for secret artifacts."

I expected one of them to ask a question, but they all remained quiet. Well, okay then. "Matthew arrived, and Roman and the guards figured out where I was. As he was trying to get into the room, I was drawn to a box. I reached inside, and something cut me. It burned like boiling water had been poured over my skin." I shivered at the memory.

"That's how I found her." Alex placed an arm around my shoulders. "She was muttering that her skin was hot, and her heartbeat was erratic. She'd told me earlier that she wanted to become a vampire, so I bit her and used my venom."

"What was in the box?" Rosemary asked.

"I don't know. After I turned, I looked in the box, and nothing was inside. Whatever cut me had vanished."

Griffin sighed. "Thank goodness Alex got there. You might have died."

"Guys, I need to head home and talk to Mom and Dad." Rosemary's wings protruded from her back, and she expanded them, getting ready to fly. With my new vision, I could make out each dark feather and see flecks of silver in them. "I want to tell them everything that went down, so I'll meet you back here in the morning."

"That sounds good." Sterlyn smiled at her.

Griffin nodded. "If they want to join you, that would

be fine too."

I liked Griffin the more I was around him. Once you proved you were loyal to him and Sterlyn, he would do anything for you. He didn't even mind Alex anymore.

"No, that wouldn't be smart," Alex interjected. "The council could turn our dependency on allies against us. They already don't like how close Rosemary and I are becoming with all of you. Adding Yelahiah and Pahaliah to the mix could lead to disaster. There is a reason I haven't pushed Gwen to join us, despite her being partial to Veronica."

Griffin smirked. "Other than her being a vampire and me not wanting her here?"

I pointed at myself. "I'm a vampire now."

Griffin's face softened. "You're different."

"And me too?" Alex smiled cockily. "You don't threaten me regularly any longer."

"I don't like where this conversation is heading," Griffin growled, gazing at Sterlyn. "He's getting way too comfortable."

She smacked his arm playfully. "Oh, stop."

"I'll see you guys at the council meeting," Rosemary said. She opened the glass door and headed outside. She took off into the sky like a rocket.

Something solid and cold brushed my leg, and I turned to find Alex holding his phone with both hands, meaning it wasn't him.

Strange.

I reached between the cushions and felt the coolness of metal. My blood began to boil again.

CHAPTER FIVE

ALEX TENSED, feeling the discomfort racking through me. His attention shifted to my side. "What's wrong?"

I looked beside me but didn't see anything. The coolness persisted, and I knew my body's reaction wasn't a figment of my imagination. I blinked and unfocused my eyes then noticed the outline of a dagger between the couch cushions. The area around it was hazy, letting it blend in with the shadows. It wasn't fully visible, but it was there.

"I don't know," I whispered, worried that the dagger would disappear if I spoke at normal volume.

I reached for it, hoping I was grasping the handle. I paused, waiting for a pinprick, but warmth surged through my body, reminding me of how I'd felt the first time Sterlyn had touched me.

The outline filled in, and the dagger materialized in my hand. I lifted it in wonder. The blade and handle were black, the blade an oblong triangle with fluting that blended in with the black leather handle. At the end of the handle, a dark purple stone stood out faintly.

A silver pentagram sat in the center of a circle outlined by another circle that resembled a sun with flames flickering away from the edges. There was something both sinister and pure about the dagger, which accounted for the combination of warmth and coolness I felt handling it.

Sterlyn stood and leaned over me, examining the dagger. "Where did you get that?"

That was the million-dollar question. "I ... I don't know. But I think it was in the box back at the artifact building."

"You snuck it out?" Griffin pursed his lips, not seeming angry or upset ... more stunned.

"No!" I didn't want anyone to think I'd stolen it. "There was nothing in the box when I put it back on the shelf. This dagger just appeared beside me. I don't know how."

"I was there. She didn't pick up anything." Alex reached for the dagger, and it disappeared from my hand before he could touch it, but I still felt its warmth and weight in my palm. He jerked back. "How...?"

I was at a loss for an explanation. "I don't *know*. This is insane. How did it get here?"

"It has to be magic." Ulva moved next to Sterlyn and inspected my hand. She said with awe, "I've never seen anything like this before."

"Do you think it's witch magic?" Griffin asked,

joining the circle around me. "They're known for hiding items."

The little I knew about this world mocked me once more. "But it's not completely hidden. There's an outline of it."

Griffin squinted. "I don't see anything. It's like you're holding nothing."

"You don't see the hazy outline of it?" Sterlyn narrowed her eyes. "It's faint, but I can see it."

"I don't think this has anything to do with a witch." Alex turned his head from side to side as if changing positions would help him see it. "If a witch bespelled the dagger, it would remain hidden, not appear and hide again. And no one would be able to see it, so both Veronica and Sterlyn being able to makes that less plausible."

Griffin sniffed. "I don't smell anything out of the ordinary, and we checked the whole place when the shifters left to make sure no one was hiding or snooping around."

"I don't smell or hear anyone either." Sterlyn touched the handle and jerked back. "Ouch." She shook her hand and hissed.

"What happened?" I hadn't felt anything.

She put her fingers into her mouth. "It shocked me."

"Are you okay?" I could never live with myself if something happened to her because of me.

"Yeah, the pain ended once I stopped touching the handle." Her face was etched with worry. "But I have no clue what it means."

Alex reached for it, but I moved my hand. I didn't want him to get hurt.

"Let me try." He touched my shoulder. "If it hurts, I won't hold on to it, but I'm curious to see what will happen to me, since I'm neither wolf nor hybrid."

Frowning, I moved my hand back near him.

He reached for the dagger but halted as unease filtered through our bond.

If you aren't comfortable ... I started, but he reached for the handle again like one of us might change our minds.

Half an inch from the handle, his hand stopped.

Hey, don't worry. After seeing Sterlyn's reaction, I didn't blame him for not wanting to touch it. *It's probably better that way.*

He cut his eyes to me and arched a brow. *I didn't stop —I can't reach it.* He strained as he tried to touch it again, but his hand didn't get any closer. "Whatever is hiding it won't let me touch it."

"Interesting." Sterlyn's eyes lightened. "Another puzzle."

"If I didn't love you so much, I would think you were insane." Griffin shook his head with an adoring smile. "We have enough puzzles already. Another one just adds to my frustration."

Sterlyn rolled her eyes. "At the moment, this one doesn't seem too threatening."

"Let me try," Ulva said and reached for it, but Griffin grabbed her wrist.

"It's bad enough that Sterlyn got hurt. I won't let you

get hurt too." Griffin released his hold. "I'm a full wolf too, so I'll try." He rolled his shoulders and moved to touch the dagger, but like Alex, he couldn't get there.

How strange.

"You and Sterlyn must have something in common." Griffin frowned. "I have no clue what."

Ulva chuckled. "There's one thing they clearly have in common, along with me."

After a second, I understood her meaning. "We're all female."

"So, Griffy, I get to try after all." Ulva straightened her shoulders, proud to be involved.

Griffin opened his mouth, but Sterlyn glared at him firmly. They had to be using their connection to speak. When I'd first met them, I'd thought they just knew each other so well that they could communicate via expressions, but now I knew it was the supernatural connection between soulmates, or rather what wolves called fated mates. I wasn't sure what the difference was.

He huffed but didn't say anything as Ulva darted for the dagger, but her hand stopped half an inch from the handle, the same as Alex and Griffin.

"We know it's not because they're females." Alex rubbed his chin. "I think I would've preferred that to whatever *this* means."

I had to agree with him.

Sterlyn pursed her lips and tilted her head at me.

My phone rang with Eliza's ringtone.

Shit, I hadn't spoken to her in a couple of days, and

even though I didn't know what to say to her, I couldn't brush her off.

"Here." Alex leaned over and picked my phone off the floor from between the two couches. "You must've dropped it during the scuffle."

Eliza was probably beside herself, thinking I was doing what Annie had done not too long ago—losing my head over a boy. "I'm going to our room to talk with her in case you all need anything else." A yawn escaped me.

"No, it's fine." Sterlyn snorted. "I'm exhausted, and we have the council meeting at nine in the morning. It's best if we all get some rest. We should get there early. I have a feeling Matthew, Ezra, and Azbogah will already be there, ready to work the members."

"Sounds good." I was dreading tomorrow, but not as much as the phone call I was about to take. Putting off answering would only upset Eliza more and increase the tension between us.

I hurried down the hallway with my phone and the dagger. Passing Griffin and Sterlyn's room, Atticus's former office on the right, and Ulva's room on the left, I reached the room at the end of the passage that I shared with Alex.

I answered the phone just before the voicemail could pick up. "Hello."

"Veronica Bonds!" Eliza said. "Why have you not been answering my calls?" Her voice held an edge that I'd never heard before.

Trying to figure out what to say, I took in the room. It was three times the size of my bedroom back home in

Lexington with Eliza and Annie. A king-sized bed abutted the center of the left wall, its gorgeous black canopy accented with white netting that cascaded from the top and was tied back at the corners. The coffee-toned sheets always appeared ironed, no matter how many nights we'd slept in them, and the glass outer wall showcased another spectacular city view.

"Are you there?" Eliza bit out.

"Yes, sorry." She deserved better than my silence. I made my way to the nearest end table and placed the dagger on it. "The past few days have been hectic."

"Something feels ..." She paused. Searching for the right word. "... off. Are you okay?"

She'd always had a sixth sense when it came to Annie and me. "Yeah, just ... going through a lot of changes is all."

"Changes?" Her voice went low. I wasn't sure I could have heard her if I'd still been human. She cleared her throat. "What kind of changes? You're still yourself, right?"

What a strange question. It seemed a little passive-aggressive, which irritated me. "Who else would I be?" Great, now I was deflecting, but I *had* changed significantly. I believed my essence was the same, but my outlook would change now that I could see and hear things in new ways.

"Did *that boy* do something to you?" Eliza asked. "It's time you come home. Now."

"Alex has been amazing to me." Her tone and implications pissed me off, but she wanted to protect me. I had to remember I'd be acting the same way in her shoes. She didn't know what he'd sacrificed for me, and I couldn't tell her. Even if I could, she would freak out and not understand. "He's the love of my life, Eliza," I murmured.

She breathed and swallowed before speaking again. "Why don't you bring him home so I can meet him? Annie says he's nice, but you're my daughter, and I need to make sure you're all right."

The problem was her request was reasonable. She and Annie were family, and the fact that my life had changed so drastically in the past few weeks didn't negate that. Refusing to come home would be the equivalent of a slap in the face. "You know what? You're right."

"I am?" she asked, then coughed. "I mean, of course, I am."

"I'll talk to Alex about coming home for a visit." I had to make sure I could leave Shadow City without issue and that my bloodlust was under control. I would protect them, even if it meant hurting them more. "I'll call you soon with a plan."

Her pause indicated surprise. "Sounds good. Make sure you do."

The phone line went dead.

I still hated that she hung up whenever she'd said her piece, but that was classic Eliza.

A deep ache tugged at my heart from missing Eliza, Annie, Killian, and Sierra. In moments like these, Sierra had an uncanny way of making a situation feel not quite as dark. I was ready to get back to Shadow Ridge so our whole group could be together again.

I examined the city, looking at the varied buildings that were so unlike Shadow Terrace and Shadow Ridge. The taller buildings appeared golden, while the smaller buildings resembled brick or the whitewashed Grecian style, but this place was breathtaking in its own right.

The door behind me opened, and Alex stepped inside and shut it behind him. My heart fluttered, thankful we had more time together. Forever wouldn't be long enough with him. He held a glass in his hand. *Is everything all right? You seemed upset.*

Even though I loved our connection, I wished I could keep some feelings to myself. I didn't want to talk about Eliza. It'd been a crappy day, and I wanted to take solace in his arms.

I walked over to him, and he wrapped his arms around me. I connected. *I just want to focus on you.* I needed to be close to him, to feel safe in his arms.

Drink something first. He held the cup out. *You just turned, and it's important.*

I wanted to argue, but his jaw was set in determination, so I obliged. I took the glass and grimaced.

He placed his hand over the top. "Just drink. Don't look at it." He bit his bottom lip. "It might be easier that way."

I nodded, and when he removed his hand, I tipped the glass back and drained the contents. The metallic taste of blood wasn't repulsive—there was a subtle sweetness to it like a red wine I'd once snuck a sip of at Eliza's. The liquid hit my stomach and eased a pang I hadn't realized was from hunger. I'd figured it was from the fight.

"There." I smiled and set the glass on the dresser behind us. I stepped closer so his chest touched mine, needing to feel him. I'd been afraid I'd never see him again. In fact, I'd been certain of it, so being with him was a dream come true. Before he could argue, I lifted onto my tiptoes and kissed him.

He moaned as desire wafted through our connection. *Damn, the combination of blood and you is better than I imagined.*

His syrupy sweetness tasted better than I remembered, probably because I was a vampire. I slipped my tongue inside his mouth to taste more of him.

Veronica, you transitioned tonight. A low growl emanated from his chest as he pushed his love toward me. *You need to rest.*

Rest was the furthest thing from my mind. I slipped my hand down his boxers and stroked him, enjoying the way he felt and responded to my touch. *Are you saying you aren't in the mood?* I teased, already feeling his reaction.

I'm trying to take care of you. He groaned and moved his hips, quickening the speed.

Normally, he took care of me first, but I wanted to make it about him tonight. I trailed kisses down his neck to the base where I could feel his heartbeat. Something swirled inside me. I hadn't realized my teeth had extended until they bit into my lip. I flinched, and Alex tensed.

What's wrong? He pulled away, and his eyes darkened to navy as he took in my face. "Veronica ..." he said with a tone of frustration.

"Do I look different?" Slowly, I withdrew my hand from his waistband and glanced in the mirror.

I stumbled back in fear.

CHAPTER SIX

THE PERSON in the mirror was identical to me. She had the same wavy copper hair, the same heart-shaped face, and the same skin tone, albeit slightly paler. However, there were two noticeably different things: emerald eyes infused with light red and a crimson circle outlining the irises, and long, sharp teeth jutting from her mouth.

Logic said I should have expected this but seeing it had taken me by surprise.

"Hey," Alex murmured as he placed a hand on my cheek and turned my head in his direction. His eyes were still dark as he rested his forehead against mine. "It's okay."

"How can you say that?" Part of me felt right in this form, as if I'd been destined to be this way, but another part viewed myself as a monster. "I'm different."

"No," he said sternly. "A wise woman once told me

we are who we are. You are still the woman I fell in love with."

"I've only been like this for a couple of hours." For him to say that this soon was silly. We wouldn't be able to gauge the effects of my change for a while. "You can't know that."

"I beg your pardon." He used his formal dialect, enhancing his slight accent that wasn't quite British. "I do know that for a fact."

"Oh, really?" I appreciated his efforts to comfort me, but we had to call things as they were. "It has nothing to do with the fact that we're soulmates?"

"It does partly," he admitted and ran his fingers through my hair. "It helps because I sense you, and you feel like the same person as earlier today, just stronger."

"But I could change." Maybe I'd been wrong before. "All this—"

"The first thing you did when you woke up as a vampire was stand up for a guard I wanted to kill for keeping you hostage." As Alex spoke, his sweet breath hit my face. "Most people who'd just turned would have been focused on feeding."

"He was trying to help us." I couldn't let Roman get hurt for doing what he had to do, especially when he hadn't wanted to. Letting Alex come to me while I'd been in pain and telling us about the shifters put him at risk but letting me go would've declared war on the council.

Alex nodded. "Then, when we got back to the condo and Eliza called, you answered the phone despite not wanting to."

"She'd have been worried." Again, I couldn't will-ingly put Eliza through that. She was struggling enough without me ignoring her calls.

A grin peeked through, and he kissed my forehead. "That's my point. From everything I've seen and heard, the worst part of a person is unleashed right after they turn. All the sensations are overwhelming, and the blood-lust is so strong, but you woke up protecting and taking care of everyone. You are *amazing*."

No foul smells were whirling around; his emotions were sincere and full of love, and his heartbeat was steady. In other words, there was no reason I shouldn't believe him. He meant everything he'd said. "You have to believe that because we're mates."

"Yes, we're soulmates." He intertwined our fingers. "But sometimes even love isn't strong enough to keep two people together, even the ones fate has blessed. Though rare, there are some things that happen that even fated love can't overcome. But seeing you like this proves you won't become someone I can't stand beside. This proves you'll always be someone I want beside me."

"Same." My heart was so full I was afraid it might burst with all my love for him. The magnitude of my feel-ings was so strong it should have been impossible. "Though you might have started out a little ornery, you've become the man who was always inside you."

"Only because of you." He smiled. "And you are gorgeous, both inside and out."

"Even with fangs and red eyes?" There it was, my

insecurity. He'd always made me feel beautiful and desirable, but I wasn't the same as when we'd come together.

His face softened as he looked at me adoringly. "You're as beautiful as the day I met you."

I released his hand and touched my teeth, realizing they were back to normal.

"When you saw me vamped out, were you repulsed?" he asked and arched an eyebrow.

That answer was simple. "No." I'd been surprised, but it had never impacted my view of him.

He was perfect—my perfect.

"And I find you damn sexy both ways." His hand slipped underneath my shirt as he smirked. My body warmed despite the coolness continually flowing through me. "I'm willing to show you if you'll let me." He winked and kissed me, pulling me against him.

His words enthralled me, and I felt high. He'd always made my head foggy before, but this was a whole different level, and I never wanted it to stop.

Desperate for him, I spun him around and shoved him toward the bed.

He stumbled back until his calves hit the mattress and he sat. "Damn, you're strong."

I blurred and straddled him, desire overtaking me like never before. *Shut up and kiss me.*

A low growl came from his throat, but he obliged. His tongue swept inside my mouth, and his hands yanked the hem of my shirt upward.

Pulling back, I let him remove it as I yanked his polo shirt from his body and tossed it to the floor.

He unfastened my bra, removed it, and then cupped my breasts. My nipples peaked, and my body heated as need pulsed between us, stronger than ever. I didn't know if it was the near-death experience, being a vampire, or a combination of the two, but something inside me demanded that I make him all mine.

Gods, you feel so good. He gripped my waist and rolled me over, so he was on top. He stood and unfastened my pants, finally dragging them and my panties from my body. *Your supernatural side wants to claim me, and I want it too.*

So that was this powerful urge coursing through me? I loved him, but something physically stronger urged me toward him. Something similar to the feel of the shadow brushing against me, but for once, it didn't scare me. It gave me comfort.

He kicked off his pants, and his fangs descended as he took me in. He'd never done that when I was human, but damn if I didn't find him even sexier.

I'm feeling it too. He positioned himself between my legs.

I scooted down and lifted my hips so he could enter me quicker. *Now!*

Obliging, he thrust inside me, and the fullness felt amazing. As he moved, it was as if every cell in my body could feel him, making the pleasure as strong as an orgasm, even though I was nowhere close yet.

He moved slowly and steadily, but I needed to be in control.

I shoved him onto his back and climbed on top, slipping him back inside me as I seated myself. He scooted up against the headboard, and when we were settled, I ground down hard, gasping at the intense sensation.

As if he needed this just as much, he kissed me, letting his teeth nip my lip. He'd liked it when I'd kissed his neck, so I pulled my mouth away and trailed kisses downward. Once I got to the base of his neck, the urge to bite him took hold again. I hissed as my teeth elongated, and the urge intensified.

Do it, he connected, bending his head to kiss my neck as well. His teeth raked the same spot on me. He opened our bond more, letting me feel his pleasure and desire.

He was as desperate for me to bite him as I was for him to bite me.

Letting my new supernatural instincts take over, I bit him gently as his fangs entered me. Ecstasy rocked through us. His blood filled my mouth, tasting uniquely of him. Even though I didn't want to feed, the act was strangely intimate, and I remembered his words. Only soulmates drank from each other.

Our bodies picked up the pace, moving as one as we lapped each other's blood. The mix of shared taste and scent and emotion blended into exquisite sensation, and we fell over the edge. Pure bliss wafted between us as our bodies quivered, in tune with each other.

Satisfaction and contentment filled me. *That was spectacular.*

I lay beside him, and he wrapped me in his arms.

"You're not exaggerating." He kissed me. *We've marked each other by biting and swapping blood.*

Is that what I was so desperate for? I didn't think I could've held off even if he hadn't given me permission.

He nodded and nestled his face in my hair. *Yes, it was. We were connected, but not fully. Our souls wanted to truly unify. Now, all that's left is presenting you to all the vampires as you take your official place by my side in the royal family.*

What does that mean? Although I knew he was a prince, it was hard to think of him that way. He presented himself regally, and other vampires both respected him and were wary of him, but he was only Alex to me.

The love of my life.

Thinking about being a princess was surreal. I'd grown up with people avoiding me, so the idea of being in the spotlight was brand-new territory.

It means you're mine, and if anyone messes with you, the punishment is death. He chuckled. *It was the same when you were human, but there were more things involved. Now, it's cut and dried.*

And later? I hadn't missed the *now* part of the equation.

He tensed slightly. *I'm the next in line to the throne since Matthew has no heirs. If something were to happen to him before he settles down, we would lead the vampires together.*

Why hasn't he taken a wife or found his soulmate? That seemed like the first thing he would do. He liked power, so I'd have thought he'd want to make sure it stayed within his lineage.

Soulmates are very rare. No one had found theirs in

over three hundred years—until us. Alex kissed the base of my neck and breathed me in. A purr sounded from his chest. *He's been changing for the past fifty years, and I don't think he wants to share the power. There were times when he hated me for being the spare. It's ... been weird. We were already growing apart, but when I found you, it progressed much quicker.*

I hated that they were estranged, but I was relieved it wasn't all because of me. Something mostly evil swirled around Matthew. *I'm sorry, but there is something off with your brother. I'm not sure how to explain it.*

You are acclimating to the transition. Alex kissed my forehead. *And he has been a threat to us. It makes sense you are uncomfortable around him.*

Yeah, maybe that was it. *Family shouldn't take each other for granted, and I know that it's him and not you. I'd love to get to know Gwen better.*

She would love that, too. He grabbed the sheet and covered my shoulders before nestling beside me again. *Especially since you won't smell like a tasty snack to her. She was always nervous that she might hurt you and cause a problem between us.*

My cheeks burned as I remembered that first night I'd seen them. I'd assumed that Gwen was his girlfriend instead of his sister, and I'd made several comments about him pleasuring her. I wished I could forget that forever. *She wasn't friendly to me until after the whole Eilam thing.*

We were taught that humans were food and nothing more. That we are superior in every way. When you tried to help her, despite the risk, she understood what I saw in you ... why fate made us for each other.

I love you. Those three words didn't convey enough, but I wasn't sure what could. I pushed all my love toward him.

He kissed my shoulder and pulled me close to his chest. *I love you, too. Good night. Tomorrow will be a big day.*

Those words rang true, and I waited for anxiety to fill me. But my eyelids grew heavier, and I dozed off, safe in his arms, with everything Alex surrounding me.

———

AFTER TAKING A SHOWER, I put on the outfit Sterlyn had laid out for me for the council meeting this morning. Even though I had my own clothes, I hadn't purchased anything appropriate to wear to the meeting—another thing I needed to rectify.

I adjusted the straps of the white tank top with rhinestones at the neckline, then slipped on the stretchy black skirt that cut off three inches above my knees, along with its matching suit jacket, which fastened in front with one button at my sternum. The outfit was simple, modest, and chic.

The exact message I wanted to convey to the council.

Nude lipstick and thick mascara added to my new style. I left my slightly wavy copper hair cascading down my back.

You are gorgeous, Alex connected as he exited the

bathroom, adjusting his black tie. Like me, he wore a black suit with a white shirt. He'd said we should appear united, and I had to admit I liked that we matched. It was obvious we were together, and that thrilled me.

Who would've thought I'd be that girl?

Not me, that was for sure.

You don't look so bad yourself, and it only took you five minutes, which isn't fair. I winked and sashayed over to him. If we'd had time, I'd have taken him back to bed to repeat last night's performance, but our future hinged on the outcome of this meeting. *Not to mention, I woke up, and you were gone.* I pouted. Something had come up, and he'd had to run an errand. I couldn't be mad—he was the prince, after all—but waking up alone had alarmed me until I'd seen the note on my pillow.

I self-consciously rubbed the black stone pendant Sterlyn had given me this morning. I wasn't used to wearing jewelry.

"That jewelry's nice, but I think you're missing something," he said with nervous laughter.

My heart felt as if it had stopped, but with my supernatural ears, I could hear it beating steadily. "What do you mean?"

"Well ..." He sighed, and the corners of his eyes creased.

CHAPTER SEVEN

I BLINKED, unsure what the next words out of his mouth would be. "Alex, what's wrong?"

Sweat coated my palms, and I fought the urge to wipe them on my skirt.

"I had a specific reason for leaving before you woke up this morning." He pulled at his tie and rolled his shoulders. "I needed to get something from the mansion before Matthew woke."

He must have thought I was pissed. "It's fine. I was startled, but you left me a note."

"Let me explain." Alex studied me, his expression unreadable. "First, I need you to understand something. My entire life, I've been groomed for a role I will likely never take, as well as for what is expected from me."

His unease filtered through me, making me concerned. Maybe his brother had finally convinced him that having me by his side wasn't best for the vampires.

Even though I was a vampire now, I hadn't been born one, so the other vampires probably still wouldn't accept me. But last night, things had felt even stronger between us.

"My parents made it clear that I needed to understand the role of the king in case something happened to Matthew, but also that, as second in line to the throne, I needed to support Matthew through thick and thin." He huffed and shook his head. "A united front is one of the most important things that any royal family, supernatural or human, can have."

"What are you saying?" Dread pooled in my stomach. Was this a breakup speech?

"That I believed them." His eyes lifted to the white ceiling as if he were searching for validation or answers. "And because of the extra work I had to do without the"—he lifted his fingers in quotations—"*glory*, my mother left her engagement and wedding rings to me as a token of everything I've had to sacrifice, not only for our people, but for them as well."

My heart began to fracture, but I held back my emotions, not wanting to influence what he said next. I'd heard the "It's not you; it's me" speech several times from foster parents I'd lived with prior to Eliza. I knew what was coming.

"But there was one thing they taught me that was more important than that." His eyes locked onto mine, and he exhaled. "My parents always put their love and relationship before anything else. They proved that they were stronger together, no matter what challenges lay before them. You see, Mother was born a vampire from a family that wasn't prominent. Her family had neither money nor the right connections, and they almost weren't accepted into Shadow City. Their only saving grace was that, before they were forced to leave, the angels closed the gates to the city. My grandparents were appalled when they realized she and my father were soulmates."

His words confused me. I'd never heard him speak about his parents with anything but love and respect, so to learn that they'd dealt with a situation similar to ours surprised me.

"But they *were* soulmates, so Father went against his parents' wishes and completed their bond." Alex smiled adoringly. "If I hadn't heard their story, I never would have believed my father would go against his parents, seeing as Father enforced in me to always stand by my family. But now that I think back, there were times Mother seemed uneasy when she thought no one was watching."

"What about your grandparents and father? Did they work things out?"

"They did." Alex grinned and adjusted his jacket. "They grew to love Mother. My parents were two of the most beloved leaders in the history of Shadow City."

"Aren't vampires immortal?" I relaxed now that I realized this wasn't a breakup speech. Or I hoped it wasn't. "What happened to your parents?"

"Like all creatures, even angels, we eventually die

from something, whether it's an accident or an attack, which is what happened to my parents." Heartbreak flowed from him, and his irises darkened with pain. "I suspect the attack stemmed from political unrest. From what I've gathered, the rogue vampires were forming even back then."

"Wow." My heart sank. "It sounds violent."

"I hate that they died and hope they didn't feel any pain." He frowned. "Immortals always die violently. That's one reason the thought of you turning scared me. I don't want you to experience a violent death, and statistically, that's the likeliest way you will die."

"Hey, it'll be okay." I touched his shoulders to comfort him. "Who says I wouldn't have gone out like that anyway? Humans die from violence, too."

"You're right." He cleared his throat. "Sorry, this conversation wasn't supposed to take such a tragic turn."

I kissed him. "I want us to talk honestly with each other. Always. I love you for your strengths but also for everything else that comes with you."

"And that's how I know being together is the only thing that makes sense." He dropped to one knee and reached inside his pocket.

My mind raced, and my breath stopped. "Alex?"

"Our relationship started in chaos." He chuckled. "And that's how it's continued. Someone is always trying to come between us, or we're constantly facing a threat, but despite it all, I'm the happiest I've ever been. I've found a peace within myself and a love I'd never thought possible."

Tears of happiness sprang into my eyes, and I rasped, "I feel the same way." I opened myself to our bond, needing him to feel how happy I was and how much I loved him.

"May I continue?" He winked, reminding me of the arrogant, sexy man I'd met in a vampire bar.

Nerves coiled inside my stomach. "Okay."

"Though some of my people might not embrace our relationship, in due time, they'll see things differently, just as my grandparents did with my parents. My brother isn't happy, but that shouldn't dictate or change what we want. We decide our future." He removed his hand from his pocket and held out the most beautiful ring I'd ever seen.

The band was pure gold with three intersecting ovals creating a setting that held a two-carat pentagon ruby surrounded by diamonds.

"Veronica Bonds, will you do me the honor of becoming my wife?" His hands shook slightly as he held the ring out to me.

My mouth moved before my brain could process my answer. "Yes," I said breathlessly. "Yes!" Growing up, I had never thought I'd find a serious boyfriend, and here I was, engaged to the love of my life before the age of twenty. And I wouldn't change it for the world.

He stood and slipped the ring onto my ring finger despite my own quivering hands. Intense happiness radiated both ways through our bond. Surprisingly, the ring fit my finger perfectly.

The stone looked gigantic on my finger. "Wow, that

ruby is huge and beautiful." It meant more to me that he'd given me his mother's ring than if it had been brand new. I'd never had a family heirloom before.

"It's actually a red diamond." He smiled, stepping back to admire me. "It's been in the royal family for centuries, going farther back than I know. And I will never tire of seeing that ring on your finger."

"A red diamond?" I'd never seen one before. "Are you sure?"

"Yes. They are extremely rare and beware—the witches will stare at you with it on. Apparently, it harnesses a lot of power. Our family emblem is engraved on the inside of the band, proving it's ours." He stepped toward me again, pushing a piece of my hair behind my ear. "And I can't wait until everyone sees you wearing it."

"Are you sure I should wear it this morning? Matthew might come after you."

"Let him. I don't care." He brushed his lips against mine. "He needs to realize you and I are in this together, always."

Some of my happiness deflated. "Is that why you did this? Because if so—"

"Stop." He wrapped his arms around my waist, pulling me against him. "This has nothing to do with him. I've waited far too long to find you, and now that I have, I want to make you mine in every way. Tradition is important to vampires. I won't let my brother ruin that because he's an ornery prick."

My lungs filled again. "You want this?" I didn't want

him to feel pressured. I would never want to be that girl or allow him to feel like he had to do that for me.

"More than anything." He laughed. "I waited longer than I wanted to, and after last night, I can't any longer."

"Okay." I smiled so wide my cheeks hurt. "Me, too."

He kissed me and lingered, making my body warm.

A knock on the door interrupted our moment.

"Crap." I pulled back begrudgingly. "We've got to go."

"Yes, we do." He pecked my lips before taking my hand and leading me to the door.

I followed him then paused for a second, glancing at the dagger on the end table. It lay there, still invisible, except for the outline I could see. "Should I put the dagger somewhere safe?"

"Probably." Alex released my hand and opened the door, revealing Sterlyn in a classy charcoal-gray suit. "Do you have a place to put the dagger in case someone searches the condo while we're gone?"

Given the way the council was treating us, it wouldn't surprise me. They were trying to get as much evidence as possible against Sterlyn and Griffin to take them down.

Those two were doing everything they could for the community, but I guessed when corruption was deeply rooted in society, those attracted to power weren't the ones you wanted in leadership roles. It was easier to have people who wanted the same thing as you, or who could be easily manipulated or bought off instead.

"Yeah, that's smart." She rolled her eyes. "But I don't think anywhere in the condo is the best place for it. Bring it in the car—no one else has the keys. We can drive and say we were hoping to get back to Shadow Ridge after the meeting. I need to check in with my brother, and I hate being in the city any longer than we have to."

Not needing further encouragement, I grabbed the dagger off the end table. Sterlyn's eyes widened as I faced her.

"Uh ... is that new?" She pointed to the ring on my hand.

My cheeks warmed, and I clutched the dagger harder. "Yes, uh ... Alex and I are engaged." Even though joy still coursed through me, I came off as awkward.

"Oh my God!" Sterlyn squealed and ran past Alex to hug me. "Congratulations! This is amazing. We need good news in a time like this."

"Thanks." I returned her embrace, making sure the dagger didn't stab her. I was overjoyed to have a friend to celebrate with. "He completely surprised me this morning."

"That's why you snuck out." Sterlyn turned to Alex and laughed. "Griffin was complaining about it this morning, afraid you were bringing Gwen here." She wrapped an arm around me and tugged me down the hall toward the living room. "I told him you wouldn't, but I want to spend more time with Gwen anyway. This gives me the perfect excuse."

"What gives you the perfect excuse to get to know

Gwen?" Griffin was standing in front of the elevator with Ulva. He shook his head and frowned.

Sterlyn grabbed my hand and waved it at them. "Because we have a wedding to plan!"

"That's so great." Ulva beamed. "I've never planned a wedding before. This will be so much fun."

I was glad they were so excited over this. Planning wasn't my forte. Hell, I'd never had a birthday party growing up, and a wedding was too important to plan on my own. "What about your own wedding? Or Sterlyn and Griffin's? Won't you two be getting married?"

"Wolves don't have weddings." Sterlyn wrapped an arm around Griffin. "Claiming each other and becoming each other's pack is our ritual. Since vampires don't have a pack to link with like wolves, weddings are how they celebrate."

"Like witches, our celebrations are more similar to human weddings than any other species." Alex shrugged. "But I am not complaining. I love a good party."

"All vampires do." Griffin snorted. "I'm excited for you guys, but we need to get going. I want to get a feel for what's going on."

It sank in that Ulva was dressed up too. "Are you coming with us?" I was surprised since she hadn't attended the last meeting.

"Of course." The older lady patted my arm and pushed the button to go down. "I don't want you to have to sit there all by yourself."

The loyalty every person here had shown astonished me.

As we traveled to the council meeting, I became ridden with anxiety. I despised that the council was taking away the high of the morning.

The capitol building stood out from the rest of the city, covering an entire block with its white rectangular shape and cathedral on top. The parking lot for the building was across the block and one of the few parking locations in the city since supernaturals preferred to travel on foot, or in the air for angels and bird shifters.

My hand clutched the dagger, and its warmth continued to flow into my body. That reminded me; I needed to stash it somewhere. "Where should I put this?"

"Most people can't see it and the windows are tinted, so maybe under Griffin's seat?" Sterlyn suggested.

That would work, and if I needed it, it would be easy to get to. I bent down and placed it underneath the seat, pointing the handle toward me. When I released my hold, I missed its warmth.

"Shit," Griffin growled.

I peered out the window.

Azbogah, Ezra, and Matthew were huddled together in front of the building, away from the rest of the council where the shifter attack had occurred.

Griffin pulled into the lot and stopped the car. The three of them looked our way.

"Let's see what's going on," Sterlyn said and climbed from the car.

The rest of us followed suit and headed toward the three smirking men. Alex took my right hand, though I wasn't sure if it was to calm me or himself. Now that the sun was out, the colorful lights of the city air surrounded me. I lifted my left hand to shield my eyes and keep my focus on the three of them.

Matthew's eyes honed in on my hand, and his smirk fell as his chest heaved.

CHAPTER EIGHT

YEAH, I didn't have to be smart to determine what had set him off. His irises turned the same shade as the red diamond on my ring finger, and he stalked toward us.

"That better not be what I think it is," Matthew hissed, gesturing at my hand. The two buttons holding his navy-blue suit jacket together struggled not to break apart as his body jerked with anger. "Because a turned vampire shouldn't be part of this family, let alone wearing my mother's jewelry."

I'm sorry, I connected with Alex. *I didn't mean for him to notice the second he saw me.*

You did nothing wrong. Alex squeezed my hand and moved to stand slightly in front of me. *I've always admired my brother's excellent observation skills. He notices and remembers details like no one else. This was inevitable.*

That was a good attribute to note.

Sterlyn flanked me on one side while Griffin stood

next to Alex. They were tense, ready to step in if they needed to even if it was detrimental to them. I loved their loyalty, but this was why Azbogah and a few other council members opposed them. Their determination to do right by the ones they loved, and the supernatural race as a whole, might cost them their places on the council.

One thing was certain—I would do whatever I could to make sure they stayed where they belonged. Those two were the kind of leaders whose decisions made positive impacts and didn't result in personal gain.

"Are you that surprised, Matthew?" Azbogah said with disgust as his wintery-gray eyes scanned the ring on my hand. "She's the root of the problem between you and your brother—she'll do whatever it takes to tear your relationship further apart." His solid black wings spread behind his back, making his caramel hair seem spikier and his stoic face more cutting. The maliciousness wafting off him was suffocating.

Not wanting protection, especially now that I was turned, I pivoted to stand beside Alex. "I've never tried to come between them." The last thing we needed was this angel putting more negative thoughts in Matthew's head. Maybe he was behind the divide between the two royal brothers.

"Yet, you've succeeded." Azbogah chuckled. "Probably your human side shining through."

I released Alex's hand and pointed at the angel. "You think me being a former human is the problem?"

Veronica ... Alex warned. *Please don't put yourself on Azbogah's radar more than you already are.*

Like hell, I wouldn't.

The coolness churning inside me felt eerily close to the shadow's touch. That hadn't been a dream. The shadow *was* in me.

I'm sorry. I meant those two words, but I was done letting people push me around. "That's really funny coming from you."

Azbogah marched over to me and towered over my small five-foot-five frame. "Be careful who you speak to that way. Unlike your friends and fiancé, I don't find you adorable or intriguing."

If he thought insults would work, I'd never leave the condo anymore. Every person here was taller than me, except for Kira and maybe a handful of other fox shifters.

"You don't get—" Alex started, but I cut him off.

"And I don't find you scary or ballsy." The breeze blew, blending all our scents together and again reminding me of a perfume store. The smell was unique. If we bottled it, humans wouldn't be able to get enough. The air was devoid of the sulfuric stench of a lie, making my words more powerful. "So, good talk. Now we both know where we stand."

I patted Azbogah's arm, and his eyes widened before his jaw clenched with rage.

Alex exhaled, his shoulders slightly deflating. *That was the opposite of not getting on his radar.*

Sterlyn snorted and covered her mouth with a hand, but the corners of her eyes crinkled with amusement.

"Now, listen here—" Azbogah hissed.

"We're making a scene," Ezra interjected and

gestured toward the sidewalk where several supernaturals stood, watching us.

Ezra's sea-green eyes seemed darker than normal and his olive skin slightly paler as if he were sick. His sable-brown hair fell naturally against his face as he rubbed his neck.

Griffin tilted his head while arching a brow. "Since when do you care about that?"

The third wolf shifter council member averted his gaze, having the sense to be embarrassed.

"Maybe we should continue the conversation inside." Ulva *tsk*ed and waved for us to follow her. "How will anyone take the council seriously if we argue in the street?"

Her words shamed me. She was right. I should've listened to Alex instead of spouting off and making things worse, especially in front of citizens. *I messed up. How will I earn credibility if I pull stunts like that?* I'd let my emotions get the best of me. It wasn't like standing up to Azbogah right here, right now would change him. He was who-knew-how old and set in his ways.

Do not apologize, Alex assured me. He took my hand again and led me around the grumpy angel and upset vampire king. *Your vampire side wants to make her strength known. If anyone is to blame, it is Matthew for confronting us here.*

He seemed genuinely upset. Alex blaming his brother didn't seem fair in this moment. Obviously, the ring meant something to Matthew too, and he had just reacted.

The others followed us, while the three men remained outside. I'd expected Azbogah to charge to the front, not wanting to be seen as a follower.

Alex stepped closer to me and connected, *He doesn't give a damn about that ring, just that I gave it to you. Regardless, he's approximately three hundred and twenty-five years old and a king. He should be able to maintain composure in the face of something that angers him. Whereas, you'll be twenty in two weeks and just became supernatural. There is a world of difference.*

Maybe. But I wasn't sure I agreed.

We walked through the expansive, wooden, hunter-green doors and entered a huge bare room with another hunter-green doorway across the gigantic entryway from us. The once-white walls were stained a pale yellow from time and wear, reminding me of the capitol building in Lexington, which I'd toured once as a student.

The scent of freshly ground coffee beans hit my nose, and I pointed to the small coffee stand built into a corner of the room. Caffeine sounded good. "Do you mind if we get some coffee?"

"Sure." He glanced at Sterlyn, Griffin, and Ulva. "You guys interested?"

"No, I'm going inside to see what I can hear." Ulva lowered her voice and pointed at Griffin and Sterlyn. "But it might be smart if you two go with them. Since I'm not an actual council member, I'll be sitting along the wall, and sometimes the other members forget that I'm there. I might be able to glean what they're thinking."

Sterlyn hugged her. "I'm never one to turn down

coffee, and I love your stealth. You could give Kira a run for her money."

Kira—the fox shifter who might be an ally.

"If my mate wants a cup of coffee, then she'll get a cup of coffee." Griffin kissed Sterlyn's cheek and grinned.

"All right." Ulva motioned for us to head toward the coffee stand. "Scoot. I'll see you all in a bit and take your time."

The four of us were continuing to our destination when the tall, pale man dressed in loose black clothing, who had attacked me the last time we were here, walked out with a spray bottle and a washcloth. The overwhelming stench of decay slammed into me, churning my stomach. I had thought that smelling him the first time was awful, but it didn't compare to this.

I held my breath, unable to take it. *What did he do again to earn this?*

He spoke out against the royal family sixty years ago, saying Matthew shouldn't lead the vampires. Alex frowned. *Instead of putting him in jail, Matthew punished him by assigning him to take charge of cleaning the capital building so he could see Matthew take part in the council. He threatened anyone who feeds him blood beyond his allotment to survive with imprisonment.*

So not even his family will feed him? I felt bad for the guy. In the human world, people spoke out against their leaders all the time, and as long as they didn't take dangerous actions against them, they had the freedom to say what they wanted. *Did he do anything to Matthew?*

No. His family died a long time ago, so he has no one.

Alex shrugged like it was no big deal. *And Matthew had to put a stop to his insults. If others had backed him, a revolt could have happened.*

Similar to Eilam and the rogue vampires on the outside. It irritated me far more than it probably should have that Alex didn't see anything wrong with this man's situation, but this was my world now. *Yet, Matthew allowed the bar owner—despite us thinking he's part of them—to keep the bar open. Gwen informed me that they closed it in the last few days and didn't punish anyone like this guy.*

Alex paused as my words sank in. *They weren't challenging him like this vampire was.*

Weren't they? I pushed as we reached the coffee stand. *Only with actions instead of words, by living the exact life you say the royal family stands against. And why do you stand against it?*

Because when vampires feed too much on humans, we lose our humanity and begin to think of the world as our own personal feeding grounds, which would eventually expose the supernatural world to humans. His forehead wrinkled. The conversation was making him uncomfortable. *Though we may be stronger than humans, they have a much larger population. Making them aware of our existence would be catastrophic. Once a vampire loses their humanity, they don't care about the consequences, believing instead that they are invincible—similar to a human on drugs.*

A woman walked from the back of the coffee stand and stopped short when she saw the four of us standing there. Her long red-orange hair was pulled back into a ponytail, and she was several inches shorter than me. Her musky cedar scent mixed well with the coffee smell. "What can I get for you all?"

Is she a fox? Her small stature and red hair were the giveaways.

"Two coffees." Alex lifted two fingers as if his words weren't enough. *Yes, she is.*

My eyes focused on an open glass case to the left that held bagels and other breakfast foods. "And a cinnamon raisin bagel, please."

Alex stiffened, and the fox shifter stared at me like I had two heads. "You want a *bagel*?"

I stared back. Why was that so odd? "Yes, please." I could feel Sterlyn's and Griffin's gazes on me, but I was hungry, and I wanted a bagel. *Is that not okay?*

No, it's fine. Just be ready for it to taste bad. Alex snickered. "You heard her. Give the girl a bagel."

"Okay," the fox shifter said slowly and glanced at Sterlyn and Griffin. "Two coffees as well?"

Sterlyn smiled. "Please."

Alex and Griffin paid, and then the fox shifter went to work on our food and drinks.

We huddled over to the side, and Griffin said quietly, "I don't like that those three are still outside. They appear to be arguing, and I want to know what it's about."

"Agreed." Alex nodded. "It's unusual, and somehow, they've convinced Ezra to join their ranks. I don't understand that. He was always on your side."

"There's nothing malicious wafting off him like

Matthew and Azbogah." Sterlyn ran her fingers through her hair. "Ezra is doing what he thinks is right."

Yeah, but being right was subjective. "For the supernatural races, shifter race, wolf shifters, or himself, though?"

Sterlyn's eyes darkened to violet. "Fair point. Nonetheless, if we can show him why his outlook is skewed, it might bring him back on our team."

"Matthew always thought that Ezra was an opportunist." Alex sighed, and his guilt flowed into me. "Also, Ezra met with Dick often while Griffin was finding himself."

"Dude." Griffin glared. "Really?"

"How else would you like me to word it?" Alex challenged. "Hiding? Hurting? Scared?"

Sterlyn lifted her hands. "He has you there."

"Fine, let's stick with finding myself, since it's technically true." He admired Sterlyn adoringly. "After I found you, everything changed."

Their love was sweet and true, and I could only hope people would soon feel the same about Alex and me.

"Here you go," the fox shifter called, and my stomach rumbled at the smell of the toasted bagel.

I blurred and reached for the bagel instead of the coffee from the counter, then took a huge bite. The cinnamon filled my mouth with spicy flavor, and the raisin added the perfect balance of sweetness. I swallowed and took a sip of my coffee reverently. The hunger I'd felt since I'd finished the blood this morning receded.

The three of them stared at me strangely.

Sterlyn's brows furrowed. "I thought vampires didn't like human food."

Alex bit his bottom lip. "They don't."

The doors to the capitol building swung open, giving me a reprieve from their attention. But the three fox shifters who walked in, followed by Ezra, Azbogah, and Matthew, made our situation all too real again.

CHAPTER NINE

"OF COURSE, those three would come in with them," I whispered so only Alex, Sterlyn, and Griffin could hear me.

Kira's emerald eyes cut to us. She stood between an older man with the same poppy-red hair and a fair-gold complexion. He was only a couple of inches taller than her five-foot-four frame and her cousin, Grady, who was part of the police force that had abducted me from Griffin and Sterlyn's condo.

A frown marred Grady's face as his gaze followed Kira's. His short ruby-red hair was disheveled, and he had a black eye.

I smiled, remembering how Kira had attacked him.

Unfazed, Sterlyn took a sip of her coffee. "I have a feeling Grady is here to testify on what went down at the condominium the night they came to take you, which is why Hank—Kira's dad—is here."

Alex shook his head. "They might try to use the

attack as an opportunity to punish Kira and set Grady's succession in place."

"But doesn't Kira only need a majority vote from the shifter representatives—so, Sterlyn and Griffin's backing, not the entire council's?" That still didn't make sense to me.

"Azbogah and Matthew are hoping we've been discredited enough to make the vote a council-wide decision." Griffin clenched his hands into fists. "I'm so sick of all the games."

"This is how things have played out all my life." Alex sipped his coffee and winced. "Gods, this is awful."

Sterlyn chuckled. "Then why do you drink it? You come into the coffee shop at the university regularly, too."

"Because caffeine helps with blood cravings at times." Alex shrugged. "I guess it's the bitterness. It turns my stomach to the point that I become nauseous rather than ravenous."

"You drank three blood bags on the way here." I took another bite of my bagel and nearly moaned at the taste.

He lifted his cup at me. "I figured I'd just get one with you." Concern etched his face as he watched me eat. "That has to be a delay or something from being turned."

"No clue, man." Griffin pursed his lips. "I've never been around a newly-turned vampire, since we aren't allowed in Shadow Terrace."

Griffin had Alex there.

"What are you looking at?"

My head snapped to where Hank had growled at Kira.

He turned to us, rubbing his fingers through his orange goatee. He wore a tan suit that was several inches too long for him and a horribly mismatched button-down brown shirt.

Grady wore the same outfit as Kira's father and appeared even worse. Whoever dressed them had not done them any favors.

Alex and I were dressed similarly, but not identically, like those two. Did they think wearing identical clothes would prove that Grady was the clear heir?

"She's staring at the human we secured from Sterlyn and Griffin's condo—the one the vampire prince has been panting over." Grady sneered as he pulled up his slacks, which were dragging on the floor.

Anger wafted from Alex into me. He went to move, but I caught his hand. I connected with him, *Babe, don't make a scene. We've already given them enough ammunition.*

He exhaled, remaining tense, but didn't move again. *You are right, but one of these days, I will put that fox in his place.*

"Is everything okay?" Matthew asked Hank and glanced over at us, smirking.

The prick was hoping we'd done something unwise or were about to. We had to keep level heads.

"Yes, sir." Hank bowed his head. "Kira got distracted. You know how women are."

"Oh, yes." Azbogah laughed loudly. "We do. They are known to cause a whole lot of trouble." His ebony eyes focused on Sterlyn, and then me.

Coy was not his specialty. Then again, he wasn't trying to be.

Though I didn't want them to influence me, I lost my appetite. These men were not only sexist but also full of themselves.

A toxic combination.

"Let's go." I threw the remainder of my bagel in the garbage and strolled toward them.

What are you doing? Alex asked as he caught up to me. *You were right. We shouldn't do anything rash, or we'll make the situation worse.*

Don't worry, I reassured him. *I'm just going into the council room. If I have to stay out here and listen to this crap, I will lose it.*

Matthew rubbed his hands together in anticipation as we approached.

That was all it took to confirm what I'd thought. He, Hank, Grady, and Azbogah were trying to provoke us. They wanted us to lose our cool so the other members would witness us at our worst for themselves.

What they failed to realize was that we weren't at our worst. *They* were. We rallied together and supported one another; we didn't tear others down. For them, power was everything.

But that was the old way of doing things. The outdated way.

The new way—our way—was to fight them head-on with truth and integrity. They couldn't force me to lower myself to their level. People had been trying to do that my entire life, and that was one reason I'd kept my circle of trusted friends small.

Do not acknowledge Kira, Alex connected. *It will give them the idea that we are on her side. We need to keep them off guard.*

But won't that make Kira nervous that Griffin and Sterlyn won't back her like we promised? I didn't want her to think we'd betrayed her, especially when she had information about the rogue vampires in Shadow Terrace. We needed to take charge of that situation so that what happened to Annie didn't happen to anyone else.

Alex placed a hand on the small of my back as we passed their group. *It doesn't matter, and I have no doubt that Sterlyn and Griffin will follow through on their promise. They're annoyingly good and predictable like that.*

I watched from the corner of my eye, and as expected, Matthew's face fell, and Azbogah tensed.

"Wait." Hank didn't sound pleased. "I thought you said she was human."

"She was human when we took her into custody." Grady crossed his arms and turned to Matthew and Azbogah. "What happened?"

I hid my own smirk. Their plan hadn't gone as they'd hoped.

Good.

It was strange to see the nuances of people's body language so clearly with my new supernatural vision. Now I wondered what people had seen me do that I hadn't been aware of.

Kira's eyes sparkled with interest, but I kept my focus forward, trusting Alex's judgment.

Sterlyn's and Griffin's goodness is not annoying. I couldn't believe he'd say something like that, and I allowed him to feel my disappointment. *They're honorable in a world that has lost its ethics. Do you realize how hard it is to stand up for what's right when it would be so much easier to turn a blind eye?*

He huffed. *Oh, believe me, I know. I used to have it a whole lot easier until a sexy redhead walked into my life and turned my world upside down. I'm now finding myself more aligned with wolf shifters than my own kind.*

Even though he didn't hold any resentment, the impact of his sacrifice hit me hard. *I'm sorry.*

Don't be. He opened the hunter-green door that led to the council chamber and waved me through. *I wouldn't have it any other way. I rather enjoy being annoyingly ethical, so I am worthy of standing beside my amazing mate.*

I cut my eyes to him, but I couldn't help smiling even in this situation.

If you keep looking at me that way, it could get awkward for many people in this room. Alex winked. *Except, maybe, the angels. They are strangely liberated about sexual acts, though they don't normally perform them in front of others.*

The few times Rosemary had scoffed at Sierra for making crude references about our affection replayed in my mind. The angel had surprised me with her stance, but after a while, I began to enjoy their back and forth.

Most of the council was already there. Ulva sat in one of three wooden chairs against the center of the white wall. If I hadn't been searching for her, I might not have noticed the older wolf shifter. She gave me a little wave and gestured to the seat next to her.

It comforted me that I'd be between her and Rosemary. I needed allies, not someone who would stab me in the back ... literally.

I headed over to her with Sterlyn, Griffin, and Alex following me. As I walked, I took a discreet scan around the council room, which I had only been in once before, less than a week ago.

A U-shaped table sat in the center of the room, the open area facing the door. Twelve chairs sat around the outer edge of the table so that each person could see the door. Six wooden chairs sat behind the middle section with three chairs on each side.

Most of the members were already here, except for Yelahiah and Pahaliah. I slid into the seat. *Where are Rosemary and her parents? I figured they would be here already.*

Alex stood in front of me. *They don't need to be. They already know the truth of what happened, and they avoid dealing with Azbogah's games when possible.*

"It's a good thing we got here early," Griffin murmured as he stood in front of his mother. "They had fox shifters arrive early to influence the others before we arrived and give their side of the story without us interfering."

"I still don't understand why Azbogah has so much

influence." Sterlyn glanced over her shoulder at the council table. "He's an asshole."

"Being an asshole is the main reason he has so much influence." Ulva leaned forward. "When the city shut down, Yelahiah took a step back, allowing him to take control while she struggled with the loss of her brother. At the time, the council was being formed, and the angels needed someone who could make decisions quickly. Azbogah is the angel of judgment, and it was easy for the other angels to fall behind him."

All this history I didn't know put me at a disadvantage. Maybe there was a textbook at the university that detailed their history.

Erin, the witch priestess and coven leader, chuckled as she pushed her scarlet-streaked black hair over her shoulders. She leaned back in her seat and said, "How odd that today, of all days, you three get here early. And how odd that Veronica here has already turned." She arched a brow and squinted misty-gray eyes surrounded with thick black eyeliner at us.

The last time I was here, Erin had appeared to be allied with Azbogah and Matthew, meaning we couldn't trust her.

"It's a win for us either way," Diana said, desperate to show her priestess she was on her side. She pulled her long maroon hair into a bun and sat on the table, facing us. "She did it before she was forced into it, obviously."

Breena, another witch, rolled her coffee-colored eyes. They were a few shades lighter than her waist-long, forest-brown hair. "You do realize she might have wanted to turn?" She mashed her signature black-stained lips together.

"Oh, silly girl," Erin mocked. "Sure, she did. It's a coincidence that it happened just before the council was going to force her hand."

"My brother never would have allowed that to happen to his mate if she hadn't wanted it." Gwen stood from her seat on the right corner of the table. Her blonde hair had its usual tousled beach-hair look, and she wore a crimson dress with a cutout that revealed her lean waist. Her long fingernails were painted a matching shade of red. "I wouldn't get too confident if I were you." She blew a kiss at Erin with her cranberry lips.

"You're insinuating he would've defied the council?" Erin sneered and glanced back at Alex.

Alex opened his mouth, but I cut him off. Knowing him, he would say my wants and desires were more important to him than the entire world. That was how much he loved me, but now wasn't the time to say that. We were already on shaky ground. "You can insinuate whatever you want." I batted my eyes sweetly and stood to make sure Erin focused on me. "What matters is that I'm now one hundred percent vampire. Are you really trying to argue what might have happened when I'm standing here in the very form the council desired?"

"Well ..." Erin opened and closed her mouth, speechless.

"I think that's exactly what she was saying." Sterlyn laughed, enjoying the witch's discomposure as much as I was.

The doors opened, and the rest of the council members filed in. Rosemary and her parents led the pack with Matthew, Azbogah, and Ezra trailing them.

Rosemary made a beeline to us and took the seat next to mine. Her twilight eyes lightened to purple. "Are you okay?"

"Yeah, I'm fine." I placed my hand on her arm. "Thanks for your concern."

She glanced at the group around us. "No ravenous cravings?"

"Nope, not a one." Sterlyn beamed. "I'd say she was meant to be supernatural."

Griffin lifted a hand. "Maybe it's because she was mated to a vampire already."

I hadn't considered that, but that could be the reason.

"All right. Everyone take your seats," Azbogah commanded. "It's time for the council to begin its emergency meeting."

Alex stiffened, not wanting to leave my side.

Go. I regarded him. *We have a big enough target on our backs.*

He sighed and headed to the table, with Sterlyn and Griffin following suit.

Alex sat on the left side of the table, between the witch Diana and Yelahiah.

The gorgeous angel leaned toward Alex, her full blood-red lips moving as she whispered something to him. Forest-green eyes, surrounded by long black lashes, glanced at me as a tendril of her auburn hair fell along her face. Her white dress fit her body perfectly and made her gorgeous black feathers stand out. Goodness radiated from her, similar to Sterlyn and Rosemary.

I wanted to rip out her throat at her proximity to my mate.

Calm down. Our bond is making you feel that way. I'm all yours.

"We are on Sterlyn's and your side," Yelahiah told Alex. "Officially."

Some of my concern left me. I'd known we could count on Rosemary, but I hadn't gotten a chance to know her parents yet.

I glanced at Pahaliah, who was sitting next to Gwen, and found his sea-green eyes locked on me. He nodded slightly, and his olive skin took on a faint glow. He wore his usual white suit, which made his white feathers look even more gorgeous.

Ezra obediently followed the angel's orders and took the last seat on the right side, next to Pahaliah. "And what is that emergency?" The asshole was pretending he didn't have a clue when *he'd* led the raid.

The rest of the council took their seats as the chamber filled with tension. This was going to be a war, not a battle, and I hoped we would wind up on even ground.

CHAPTER TEN

AZBOGAH TOOK his spot at the center of the table. "Multiple transgressions by the *silver wolf,* Griffin, Alex, and the prince's mate have been documented."

Of *course*, the jackass had claimed the center seat. My dislike of him grew the more I saw the dark angel, which was saying something. And, of course, he hadn't named Sterlyn and me, unlike the two males.

Pompous prick.

"Oh ..." Erin drew out the word as she leaned over Sterlyn to see Azbogah. "I haven't heard much and would appreciate an account from someone who was there."

"At least four of us on the council can give you a play-by-play," Sterlyn said, leaning forward in her seat next to Azbogah to block Erin's view of the angel and catch her attention.

Nose wrinkling, Azbogah stared down at her. "Your ignorance of council protocol astounds me. Griffin should have taken it upon himself to educate his *mate* about due process."

"I'm sure *you* won't mind enlightening me on the matter," Sterlyn deadpanned.

He shook his head. "Apparently, I will have to be the one to teach you council procedure yet again." His wings fluttered, and I got the sense he was trying to intimidate us. "Council members can't testify, so we invited friends of the council to provide their testimony."

The fox shifters.

The doors opened, and Kira, Hank, and Grady entered.

They must have been listening for their cue to join the meeting.

Grady's eyes bulged, reminding me of a child's, as he took in the council chamber. I guessed it was his first time in the room. Hank and Kira seemed more matter of fact as they moved toward the council with determination. They stopped in front of the table, their backs to Ulva, Rosemary, and me.

"But these people are here to tell us everything." Matthew grinned. "Please, Grady, tell us about the night in question."

"Oh, yes." He cleared his throat. "As ordered, I and several of my fellow officers went to the Shadow City wolf alpha's condominium to pick up the human."

Yelahiah tapped her long, silver-polished nails on the table. "Why did that happen when the council voted on Veronica staying with Sterlyn and Griffin? The orders violated the decision made by the collective."

"There was a reason for the change." Azbogah glowered. "Please continue, Grady."

"After the human's—er, formerly human's presence during the rogue shifter attack on three of its council members resulted in the death of multiple vampires who couldn't control their urges around her, we were ordered to take her into protective custody." He puffed out his chest and stood on his tiptoes as if no one would notice.

Matthew lifted a hand. "The situation had changed. Her presence put Shadow City residents in harm's way. We had to pool an emergency one-third vote to put protective measures into place."

"One-third?" Pahaliah steepled his fingers. "From what I gather, it was Azbogah, Matthew, and Ezra. Who is this fourth person who voted on your side?"

Azbogah frowned as Erin piped up, "Me."

A smile spread across Sterlyn's face. "But you said you hadn't heard much, yet you voted with those three?"

"It sounds as if Erin didn't know the facts, yet still voted for my mate to be taken against her will." Alex cut his eyes at the woman. "Either she rushed to vote on something she didn't know all the facts about, meaning she did not follow the vows we've all made as members of the council, or she was coerced into voting with the other three."

"This isn't why we're here." Azbogah frowned. "We're here to discuss how Sterlyn, Griffin, and Alex reacted once the cops arrived to get the human. Grady, please proceed."

I waited for someone to object, but everyone remained quiet.

Timing is everything, love, Alex assured me. *Let them dig their own grave.*

Ugh. I wanted this meeting to be over. Now.

Grady fidgeted. "When we arrived, and Ezra, as the council representative, informed them of what was to happen, they attacked the cops, who were only following orders. I'd like to add that my cousin used the opportunity to attack *me*." He pointed at Kira, who bared her teeth at him.

"Wait." Matthew ignored their interaction and placed his elbows on the table, his chin on his hands. "Are you saying they disobeyed emergency council orders?"

Both he and Azbogah were orchestrating the situation to keep the focus on us and not on anything they'd done wrong. White-hot anger coiled inside me.

"Yes," Hank interjected. "And to make matters worse, my own daughter was at their condominium, already involved and doing God-knows-what, which brings up another reason the three of us came here."

Kira ground her teeth.

She already knew what her father would say.

"Because of the embarrassment she continues to place on my family and the fox shifter community, I want to eliminate the hope she's clinging to by announcing Grady as my official successor."

"It pains me to say this." Ezra paused and lowered his head. "But not only have Sterlyn and Griffin lost their hold on the shifters, but they've also encouraged others—

like Kira—to act out. They've caused drama within the shifter races and have brought attention to their decisions that no leader should want. Between the attack on their own people and their inability to keep the shifter community at peace, the council should consider the consequences if Griffin remains in the position as alpha within the city."

Yeah, that was all I could take. "That's complete bullshit." I jumped to my feet, and Rosemary glanced at me out of the corner of her eye.

She mouthed, "Stand down."

But that wasn't happening. I was so *sick* of these games. We needed to call things the way they were, and this was becoming far too convoluted. These assholes were painting their own reality.

Alex's irises darkened to cobalt, but he said nothing. The only feeling he had was concern, likely due to me getting involved.

"Excuse me," Matthew hissed, his fangs descending. "You need to sit down. You are not part of the council, and you are only here because of my brother."

And I was female.

Even the coven members weren't as esteemed as the men. The men grouped together to make plans, and the women did their bidding.

"You can manipulate the story to make Sterlyn, Griffin, Alex, and me look bad?" Also Rosemary, but since she wasn't directly involved with the council, they weren't attacking her. "No, I won't sit back and listen to you manipulating words so no one can smell the lies. You acted without an informed one-third vote to have me abducted."

Azbogah stood, lifting his chin. "Are you accusing us of collusion?" He smirked. "An accusation like that could be deadly."

Veronica, I know you're frustrated— Alex started.

I'm sorry, but I can't remain quiet. I'm tired of them controlling everything and everyone allowing it to happen. Everyone backed down to them. That was how bullies got more powerful and amped up their treachery. "It's not an accusation. Everyone sees it, but no one has been brave enough to do anything about it."

For a moment, the entire room went silent in shock.

"Does anyone else feel like this?" Azbogah's dark eyes sparkled with humor. "Or is this newly-turned vampire the only one?"

The sicko was enjoying himself, and that proved how damn arrogant he was. He thought he was untouchable, and he knew my friends would have my back, no matter what. He was banking on it.

"There have been a few occurrences, such as taking Veronica from the condominium, that, when examined all together, seem convenient." Alex climbed to his feet and made his way to me.

You don't have to do this. I hadn't considered that Alex would literally come to stand beside me, but of course, he would. I'd only meant for me to make waves, not him. Not when he'd done so much for me. But I wouldn't keep my mouth shut any longer.

Silence was complicity, and that was worse than weakness.

But Alex standing beside me gave Azbogah another example of how I'd come between the two brothers.

You're right. Enough is enough. Alex took my hand, his eyes locked on Matthew. "Then there was Matthew pressuring Veronica and me to stay in Shadow City, and not even twelve hours later, he tried to force her to change without so much as discussing it with us first."

"And how Dick and Azbogah were so close when Griffin and I became involved with the council just a few months ago," Sterlyn said and stood as well. "They also planned the shifter attacks on the local wolves and set Griffin up to take the fall."

Griffin sighed and ran his hands through his gelled hair, making it stick up in random spikes. I could tell he wasn't happy with what was going on, but like Alex, he wouldn't let his mate go down without him. He straightened his shoulders. "Or how Saga poisoned my father, and their daughter sat by without alerting anyone to her actions."

"All I hear is that you aren't fit to lead the shifters." Erin grinned cruelly. "Even your father lost it all at the end."

"You—" Griffin growled.

Sterlyn cut off her mate. "The more pressing issue is that Erin voted in the emergency decision without being informed."

Thank God she'd intervened before Griffin lost it. He didn't speak of his father often, but the way his face crumpled when passing by his father's office and his sadness when someone spoke of Atticus revealed all I needed to know.

All the pain, regret, and remorse of his father's death still haunted him.

Erin's mouth dropped open in surprise that we'd circled back to that nugget of information. "I—"

"She's not the one on trial here." Azbogah huffed. "So that issue is irrelevant."

"But it isn't." Yelahiah arched one perfect eyebrow. "And this isn't a trial. It is a scheduled council meeting that got moved up because a portion of our members grew power-hungry and took matters into their own hands."

I believed Erin thought that, by siding with Azbogah, she would be welcomed into his inner circle. She wanted to elevate her own status, but also seemed smitten with the dark angel.

I snorted as I scrutinized her. "Do you really think you're integral to the council in Azbogah's, Ezra's, and Matthew's eyes? They're typical male chauvinists who have continually left you out of their discussions and asked you for your vote without bothering to inform you of the circumstances. And what's so sad is that you willingly went along with it."

With one eye twitching, Erin considered my words.

Ezra laughed nervously. "Why are you dragging me into it? I did what I thought was best for the council, and you don't know—"

"We aren't dumb, Ezra." Sterlyn placed her hands on

her hips and stared the third wolf shifter down. "None of us are. We know what's going on. Don't take our kindness as stupidity. Eventually, everything comes out in the open."

"Are we seriously letting a newly-turned vampire and a silver wolf derail this meeting?" Matthew slammed a hand on the table. "This is outrageous and proves that everyone who stands behind them is unfit to lead."

Alex laughed without humor. "*I'm* unfit to lead, dear brother? Me? The very person who did your dirty work for years?" Hurt and anger wafted from him.

"That was your place." Matthew rose from his chair and marched around the table. "And you should still be doing that, but you've let a human turn you into her puppet."

The vileness emanating from Matthew's soul suffocated me. He'd become more immoral than Azbogah. Part of me was repelled, but another part felt drawn to him. These two conflicting instincts churned inside me, grating against each other. This wasn't because he was working against me. This was some sort of premonition.

"Do not speak about her that way," Alex said and edged in front of me. "She's the most important person in my life, and the best thing you can do is accept and respect that so we can return to a somewhat amicable working relationship that won't harm our people."

Hank grabbed Kira's and Grady's arms and tugged them back several feet closer to the wall. I wasn't the only one who'd realized things were unraveling.

The scent of roses hit my nose, and I knew that Rosemary was standing behind us. Not so close that she was part of the conversation but near enough that, if she needed to intervene, she'd be beside us in a second.

"You do not get to tell me what to do." Matthew pounded his chest. "I am your king." He blurred, charging at my mate.

Alex braced himself for impact, and I did the only thing I knew to do. I stepped between them and grimaced, waiting for Matthew to slam into me.

CHAPTER ELEVEN

MATTHEW STOPPED an inch from my face and sneered, "You stupid bitch. You keep getting in the way." He drew his hand back to punch me. Something took control of my body, and I dodged his blow.

I glared at him. "He's done nothing to deserve your malice. You don't like me, and you're taking it out on him. It's not his fault fate made me his other half."

Alex's anger hit me hard. *You don't get to step in front of me and risk yourself like that.*

He'd never been mad at me like this before, but this wasn't his battle.

It was mine.

"You self-centered, arrogant girl." Matthew clicked his tongue. "His loyalty to me should be above all else—even you."

"And you say I'm arrogant." I laughed, letting my breath hit his face.

Alex moved beside me again and hissed, "If you want

any chance of having a relationship with me, you will have to respect her."

"You choose her, always?" Matthew's nostrils flared. "With or without me?"

"Yes. She's my life. And though I'd like for you to be in it, I'll be fine if you aren't."

My head snapped to him. *Are you sure?* Alex had set the boundaries, but I didn't want him to regret it.

"Things are getting out of hand," Yelahiah said. She might as well not have spoken at all because I saw Matthew's fist barreling toward my face again.

Veronica. Alex's eyes widened as he leaned around me to grab his brother's hand, but Matthew was moving faster.

My blood cooled as my supernatural side—no, as the shadow took control. It didn't feel so threatening, and I didn't fight it.

Pivoting on my heel, I grabbed Matthew's wrist with my left hand as something hit the palm of my right. Instinctively, I closed my hand, grasping an object that warmed my blood.

The dagger—visible for everyone to see.

As if the dagger were an extension of me, I swung my right hand around and placed the blade at the base of Matthew's neck.

Several gasps filled the room.

I could feel every pair of eyes on Matthew and me. My chest heaved as I tried to retain some control over my anger. "Are you that much of a fucking coward that you would strike me while I'm distracted?"

"You bit—"

I dug the blade into his neck, nicking the skin, and blood trickled down his chest onto his shirt.

"Careful what you say," I growled as the heat coming off the dagger grated through me. Unease filtered through me.

Alex touched my arm. *Love. Something strange is coming off you. Is he doing something to you?*

Maybe? I didn't know, but the blood in my right wrist began to burn, the sensation similar to when I'd blacked out and met the shadow. My actions had been her ... or me—a separate part of me that wanted to control me but couldn't because of my human side.

What's wrong? Alex connected as he shoved Matthew away.

"Your mate is insane!" Matthew exclaimed. He rubbed his neck, wiping the blood away. "She threatened her kin with a weapon! Where the hell did that dagger come from?"

But the pressure didn't ease with him free from my grasp.

"She didn't have it on her," Sterlyn interjected, watching me with concern. "It just appeared. She didn't bring it in here."

You're in pain. He's not touching you, but you still feel off. Desperation clung to Alex. "What the hell did you do to her?"

"Me!" Matthew exclaimed. "She attacked me, and you're trying to make me the bad guy?"

His tone had always irritated me, but I wanted to snap.

"Veronica." Alex placed his hands on my shoulders. "What's wrong?"

"Are the witches doing something?" Rosemary asked loudly, and her burgundy hair flew by as she approached the council table.

I shook my head, but I couldn't speak. *It's my wrist. My skin feels as if it's burning.* "Ugh," I grunted as I tried to drop the dagger. The damn thing was glued to my palm.

"We aren't doing anything," Erin said with disgust. "Of course, you'd blame us."

"Forgive us if we aren't too trusting of you all." Griffin laughed. "You haven't been the most forthcoming with us either."

"The council turning on itself won't change anything," Pahaliah said, his voice sounding as if he were right next to me.

Alex sounded broken as he said, "I don't know what to do. She said her wrist is burning."

The white angel touched my wrist and jerked back. "Her skin is hot."

The burning pain intensified, and I sucked in a breath, burying all my emotions so I wouldn't lash out.

"We need order," Azbogah commanded, but no one listened to him.

"Mom, what do we do?" Rosemary asked, drawing closer to me.

I could feel bodies circling me, but I couldn't see them. My eyes closed from the pain running through me.

"Nothing." Yelahiah sighed. "There's nothing we can do. No one here is doing anything to her."

Babe, I'm here, Alex connected. *Lean on me.* He opened our connection and tugged some of the pain from me.

Just as quickly as the pain had come, it vanished. I inhaled sharply, filling my lungs, and opened my eyes, blinking away tears. I looked at the underside of my wrist and found the same design that was on the dagger there in black ink.

What the...?

"Whoa." Sterlyn examined my new tattoo and chewed her lip.

I blinked around to find the witches in their seats and Azbogah and Matthew whispering to each other, faces drawn. The foxes seemed uncomfortable, and Kira's forehead was lined with concern.

Great, their attention was on me.

"Uh ..." I wiped a tear away and glanced at the circle of people around me—all the people I trusted: Alex, Sterlyn, Griffin, Ulva, Rosemary, Gwen, Yelahiah, and Pahaliah. "Yeah. I don't understand."

"Where did you get that?" Yelahiah asked, her gaze on the dagger.

I'd left the weapon in the Navigator so no one would know I had it, yet here it was. "I ..." I glanced at Alex, at a loss.

"She didn't take it," Alex said. "The dagger found her."

"Wait ... is that from the artifact building?" Matthew asked, his eyes brightening.

There was no getting out of this. "Yes, but—"

Azbogah said menacingly, "Now we can add theft to her ever-growing list of offenses. This is enough." His wings flapped, lifting him off the floor, and he flew at me.

Before anyone could react, the dark angel had snagged my hand to take the dagger away.

My left hand cooled, and I clutched his arm as coldness flowed from my skin into him.

Alex touched the angel, but Azbogah lifted his other hand and threw Alex backward.

The cold and the hot clashed in my body, but the combination felt like a part of me that should've always been there. The mixture created a warmth that flowed through my body, the temperature I was always meant to be. Despite this being an uneven match, something inside me said that Azbogah couldn't use his brute strength alone on me.

The corners of Azbogah's eyes tensed as he tried to pry the dagger from my hand. His strength had slackened, but his jaw clenched. He refused to give up.

I kicked the jackass in the stomach. He released his hold and stumbled back a few steps.

Someone fisted their hand in my hair and yanked my neck back. My hand cooled as I grabbed the person's forearm and spun around. I found myself face to face with Matthew—again.

He gasped, and I released my hold on him. I wasn't here to beat anyone up, only to stand my ground.

His face turned a shade paler as he pulled his jacket sleeve up, unbuttoned his shirt cuff, and shook his hand. Where my hand had touched him was now black.

I had no clue how this was happening, but I would take any advantage I had over them. "Is everyone willing to hear what I have to say instead of throwing around accusations and attacking me?" My gaze flicked to Alex, who was standing again. *Are you injured?* I asked him, ready to kick ass if he was harmed.

I'm fine. He headed back over to me, and his attention went to his brother's hand. *How did you do that?* The lack of emotion coming off him concerned me.

I ... I don't know. "I didn't steal this." I lifted the dagger. "I didn't even have it on me when I got here. You all would've seen it."

"I agree." Yelahiah nodded and pointed at everyone in the room. "We need to calm down and take a moment. Maybe we need a break."

"No." Sterlyn shook her head and looped her arm through mine. "We keep putting things off, and nothing gets accomplished. Instead, the council gets more fractured."

You two will be the death of Griffin and me, Alex complained, his frustration leaking back between us. *You assert yourselves when we just want to protect you.*

This wasn't about him. This was about Sterlyn and me having each other's back and standing up to the council together. *This is who we are. Take your griev-*

ances out with fate because I'll continue to stand up for myself.

Azbogah looked at Matthew's arm, and his face turned into a mask of indifference. "You can't come here and harm council members, and that dagger doesn't belong to you."

"What are you going to do, Azbogah?" Rosemary smirked. "Pry it from her hands? Oh, wait, you've already attempted that."

"You—" Azbogah rasped.

"What Rosemary is trying to say ..." Pahaliah gave his daughter a stern expression "... is that the dagger has attached itself to Veronica, and even though it needs to go back to the artifact building, first, we have to figure out how to unbind them from each other."

"You're right." Breena leaned across the table. "That's the most powerful kind of magic. Only the strongest of the supernaturals could have performed it."

Oh, great. The last thing I needed was for someone hugely powerful to be upset that their dagger had attached itself to me.

"Given the severity of this situation and that Alex's soulmate has turned, punishing them would make the situation worse, especially when the full council had agreed that she stay with Sterlyn and Griffin." Yelahiah walked into the center of the room where everyone could see her. "I do not think that the vampires' attack on Veronica should be deemed her fault. We dismissed ourselves and agreed to reconvene in a week so we could all deliberate on this rare circumstance. In other words, to consider whether the divine would sanction us forcing someone to change in order to live harmoniously with us. An arrest was not warranted under the emergency clause."

"You weren't there," Matthew's fangs protruded, and his eyes turned crimson. "You can't know—"

"You've insulted several council members and attacked your future sister-in-law." Gwen sashayed over to us, holding her head high. "You've done enough damage. It would be wise to think twice before adding an angel to your ever-growing list of enemies."

"Just because you're my sister doesn't mean you have the right to talk to me like that," Matthew rasped. "I am the eldest and hold the crown."

"And that is why I haven't pointed out that you willingly killed vampires who wouldn't have needed to die if you hadn't forced Veronica to come here." Gwen jabbed her finger in Matthew's chest. "It's like you orchestrated their deaths to justify taking her prisoner."

Matthew narrowed his eyes at his sister. "One more word about my leadership, and you will be punished. And I know how to make it hurt by freezing your income."

"I agree with my wife." Pahaliah clapped his hands. "Because of the very questionable motives behind taking Veronica to the artifact building, we should let this one go, especially since she's turned, resolving the issue."

"What?" Matthew said with shock. "You have to be kidding. This won't pass."

"We are not." Yelahiah lifted her chin at the vampire king. "Everyone in favor, say aye."

Alex, Gwen, Sterlyn, Griffin, Yelahiah, and Pahaliah said "aye" immediately while the other five council members said "nay." We would be split down the middle when Azbogah agreed with the nays, and I didn't know what that would mean. Maybe they'd have to schedule yet another meeting?

The dark angel walked to his chair, reveling in having all eyes on him. I had no clue why he was dragging this out. We all knew how he would vote.

When he reached the chair, he placed his hands on its back, and his hateful eyes locked on me. "Aye."

What? I must have misunderstood. There was no way he was agreeing with us. *Did I imagine that?*

No. Alex touched my shoulder as we faced the council members who had taken their seats. Griffin, Sterlyn, Alex, Gwen, and I stood next to the fox shifters.

"You mean nay." Matthew laughed nervously. "I think you have misspoken."

"I said what I meant." Azbogah's face pursed like he'd bitten a lemon. "Aye. There. It's done. Now let's move on." He pointed at the fox shifters. "Let's focus on the remaining problem of the shifter attacks."

"Given the circumstances and the disruption caused by Veronica's unsanctioned detention, we did not get to focus on who orchestrated the shifter riot, so we need more time." Sterlyn crossed her arms, glaring at the angel. "We can provide the council with an update when we have solid information, and I assure you, we do have a lead."

Azbogah flinched. "Like that will change anything."

"You can't know that." Gwen crossed her arms, making it clear where her loyalties lay. "Didn't you say that assuming was a sign of a bad leader?"

The dark angel's chest heaved, and I was pretty sure he would have breathed fire if he could have.

"Actually, he did." Breena nodded. Something warm radiated from the dark-haired witch, unlike the other two witches in the room. "It was last week—"

"Breena! Enough!" Erin commanded, silencing the poor witch.

"No, she's right," Alex said as he placed his free hand in the pocket of his slacks, the pose effortlessly casual. "Unless Sterlyn and Griffin are unfruitful in their discoveries, there is no reason they should be removed from their current roles."

"Which means Sterlyn, Ezra, and I must decide who should lead the foxes, since any leadership changes must be approved by the race representatives on the council." Griffin scanned the room. "Sterlyn and I agree that Kira is the rightful heir, not Grady. Because of this, she should have a place on the Shadow City Police Team."

"Ezra! Do something," Hank raged and pointed a finger at Sterlyn and Griffin. "You're going to turn more people against you."

Sterlyn shook her head. "It's what's right. A father should want what's best for his child."

"A real leader does what's best for his people," Hank said, gesturing to Ezra. "What do you think?"

Ezra shrugged. "It doesn't matter. I'm already outnumbered by the other two shifter representatives, who happen to be mates."

The insinuation rang throughout the room. Ezra had added fuel to the revolts.

"Then that settles it." Yelahiah nodded to each council member. "There is no reason Veronica can't leave the city. Welcome to Shadow City, dear girl."

No one added anything, indicating the meeting was over.

Let's get the hell out of here, Alex connected, taking my hand. Clearly, Sterlyn, Griffin, Gwen, Rosemary, and Ulva were on the same page as we all turned to the door.

When I fell in step behind Alex to head outside, a hand clutched my arm, forcing me to turn around.

Matthew snarled quietly, "Don't get too comfortable. Your small victory will last minutes. Not hours."

I hated the fact that my blood ran cold.

CHAPTER TWELVE

ALEX APPEARED beside me and stared his brother down. "What did you say to her?"

"Nothing worth repeating." Matthew smirked and rocked back on his heels.

Not wanting to cause another scene, I took Alex's hand. The dagger warmed in my other hand as if it were asking me to use it. "Come on. This isn't worth it."

The urge to attack Matthew overcame me again. We had to get out of there.

Did he threaten you? Alex tensed, becoming a wall, glaring at his brother. He channeled all his betrayal and anger into his look.

I tugged on his hand and pushed calmness through our bond, taking the edge off him. I sighed. *Yes, but don't react. He wants us to do something to make Yelahiah and the others regret taking our side. We can't do anything rash.*

He bared his teeth at his brother and hissed, "You

need to stop obsessing over her and focus on our people. You need to handle those rogue vampires."

"Do not tell me how to lead our people." Matthew tugged on his jacket. "I do what's *best* for *my* people all the time, unlike someone here."

His meaning was clear—Alex had put a measly human before his role as heir. It wasn't true, but there was no altering his perception. The only way to change his opinion was through actions, not words. "Then we should let you get back to it." I squeezed Alex's hand, hoping to pull him back to the present with me. "Sterlyn and the others are already outside."

You're right. Alex had regret flowing through him. *There's no point talking to him.* He turned his back on his brother and stepped toward the doorway.

Matthew frowned. "See. You can't even counter my statement, which proves I'm right."

I glanced over my shoulder to find the remaining council members and the fox shifters watching the scene unfold. It felt as if we were a prime-time television show and our viewers wanted to see the next train wreck go down.

"No." Alex paused but didn't turn around. His voice was loud, ensuring everyone could hear what he had to say. "You're not worth arguing with anymore. You've lost all reason."

I bit the inside of my cheek to prevent a smile from spreading across my face. That was the perfect response to the vampire king.

The two of us had started heading to the door again

when Matthew growled, "You're pathetic and too scared to have this conversation because you know I'm right."

He was doing everything to get a reaction out of Alex, but despite his hurt, my mate didn't respond. I risked a glance over my shoulder to see what Matthew would do.

When he realized he wouldn't get a response, Matthew headed to Azbogah and Ezra, which wasn't surprising. Ezra didn't appear happy as the dark angel stuck a finger in his face.

Trouble in paradise. Maybe that threesome would finally combust.

We walked out the door, leaving the rest of the council behind to scheme or whatever they did.

I didn't care.

Please tell me we're getting the hell out of here. My heart increased in pace.

Shadow City was beautiful. The most gorgeous city I'd ever seen. But that beauty hid corruption and violence.

Yes. I'm sure our friends are ready to leave, Alex connected, leading me to the main door. The stench of decay nearly overwhelmed me as the starved vampire moved methodically past us, mopping the floor near the coffee stand. We needed to help the poor man since he was being unjustly punished. I'd talk to Alex about it when everything calmed down.

Outside, the unique colors surrounding me caught my attention. When I was human, the colors had blended together, but now I could see each shade separately, making the overall effect less overwhelming. As we walked, the colors seemed to brush against my skin, but I felt nothing. They were still disorienting, but I was able to focus and keep my legs steady.

Sterlyn, Griffin, Ulva, and Rosemary stood in deep discussion by the hood of the Navigator. When we reached them, Sterlyn asked me, "Are you ready to go back to the Ridge?"

"Yes," I said without hesitation.

"You guys know how to give a woman a complex." Ulva winked at me and patted Sterlyn's shoulder. "Even though a select few citizens are allowed to come and go, I'm not one of them. And you all seem so desperate to leave—please tell me it's not because of me."

Griffin grimaced. "Of course not, Mom. But there is a whole lot of crap that goes on here that is missing outside these walls."

"One day, I'd love to experience that." Ulva sighed longingly. "Maybe when things calm down, you and Sterlyn can help me get on the list of people who can leave. I know it's still limited, but I'd like to experience the rest of the world."

"The only reason Griffin and I are on that list is because we attend the university and I'm more likely to assimilate into the human world than my parents are, seeing as they've been alive for a millennium." Rosemary's wings sprang from her back, and one brushed my arm.

Familiar warmth surged through me. I gasped in shock. The sensation reminded me of the feeling the dagger had caused.

Rosemary stepped away, her eyes narrowing. "I must talk to my parents." She seemed unsettled as well. "I'm going back in to find Mom and Dad. If you four are heading back to Sterlyn and Griffin's in Shadow Ridge, I'll meet up with you there later."

"Sounds good." Sterlyn's gaze flicked between Rosemary and me. "We'll drop Ulva off at the condominium and grab some things before heading out."

Feeling my worry, Alex pointed at Rosemary. "Should we discuss whatever just happened with them?" *And what exactly did happen?*

I don't know how to explain it, but when her wings touched me, it caused my blood to warm just like the dagger does. It sounded crazy, but there was a connection between my supernatural side and Rosemary. I had no clue what. I wasn't an angel.

Rosemary headed toward the council building and turned back to wave. "I'll see you all soon."

Griffin pursed his lips and motioned to the SUV. "Let's roll before someone we aren't friends with walks out here. And Mom, yes, Sterlyn and I will get you approved. I just don't want to cause more of a ruckus with the council until we finish integrating the entire shifter population into the world."

"Yes, let's go, and I know you two have been working hard on that. No hurry, just something I wanted you to know I desired." Ulva walked to the back door behind Sterlyn. "I used to think the council could never become dramatic, but today proved me wrong. I may have to come to meetings more often just to relieve some of my boredom."

"Let's hope it doesn't continue that way." Sterlyn opened the front passenger door and climbed inside. "We don't need a repeat of what happened today."

The rest of us got into the car, and the dagger hid itself in my hand once Griffin had pulled onto the main road.

Ulva turned around and leaned toward me in the backseat, squinting at my hand. "How did you make the dagger invisible again?"

"I'm not sure." I was as clueless as the rest of them ... maybe more so. "It's as if the dagger knew I was safe and no longer needed it." I wondered if I could set it down now, unlike in the council room.

There was only one way to find out.

Leaning over, I placed it under Griffin's seat again, and the dagger allowed me to release it. The warmth wasn't uncomfortable anymore, and not touching it gave me a weird sense of loss.

Strange.

Alex fidgeted in the backseat.

"Does anyone have any idea what might be going on with Veronica?" Alex rubbed the back of his neck. "She's got daggers appearing in her hands, she wants to eat human food, and she and Rosemary had a moment back there."

"Aw, don't worry, man." Griffin glanced in the rearview mirror, smirking. "If she was going to leave you for anyone, at least it's Rosemary. Maybe you and Rosemary can take turns."

Oh, my God. He went there.

Sterlyn smacked her mate on the shoulder, while Ulva grimaced and closed her eyes.

A low, rattling growl emanated from Alex's chest. "I do not share. She is mine. That was not funny."

"Yeah, don't say anything like that again." Ulva shivered. "There are things I want to pretend my son knows nothing about, and that is one of them. Thank God you found your fated mate because that ..."

"That's something I'd expect Sierra or Killian to say." Griffin was usually too tense and uptight, so his comment had surprised me. "Are you missing them that badly?"

"That's all Griffin, all right." Sterlyn kissed his cheek. "Normally, he only says things like that to me."

Alex pinched the bridge of his nose. "This conversation needs to go in a different direction now. I can't be held accountable for my actions if he makes another comment like that."

"I'm all about changing the conversation," Ulva agreed. "So ... what did happen with Rosemary?"

"I don't know. It's like part of me knows her. I always felt like that with her and Sterlyn, but the feeling was so much stronger today." That was the best way I could describe it.

Sterlyn turned around and looked at me. Her forehead creased. "That night Alex brought you to our doorstep, I sensed something in you too—it helped me decide to let you stay. I wonder ..." Instead of finishing her words, she reached over and grabbed my hand.

Similar to Rosemary, my blood warmed at her touch, but not as much as with the angel. It gave me a little rev, but nothing overwhelming. "It's not as strong, but I feel it too."

"There's one thing you and Rosemary have in common." Griffin turned onto the side road that led to the underground garage of the condo.

My brain tried to catch up.

Alex groaned. "Angel."

That was right. I often forgot Sterlyn was part angel because I always thought of her as a wolf. But they both were angels.

"That's why Yelahiah and Palahiah sided with us." Alex lifted his hands. "They felt a connection with Veronica as soon as they walked into the room. I wondered why they finally agreed to be our allies and why she told me and not Sterlyn. But how can Veronica be part angel? Is that shadow some sort of angel?"

"She does have a sweet jasmine scent," Sterlyn said, examining me. "And she held her own against Azbogah."

"I thought angels couldn't turn into vampires." Griffin coasted down the garage toward his spot. "Or rather, that no supernatural can."

They were talking about me as if I wasn't in the room, but I didn't have much to contribute. They knew more than I did about what was and wasn't possible, and I couldn't shake the feeling that they were on to something.

"It doesn't matter," Ulva declared. "Veronica is a

vampire—her sweet scent confirms it. There's enough going on without adding to your mess. You all need to focus on the shifter revolution and, unfortunately, Matthew. Once that's resolved, you can figure out what this means."

"You're right." Sterlyn nodded. "It doesn't matter what Veronica is. She's our friend and Alex's soulmate. Nothing will ever change that."

Her words relieved me. It wasn't like I had any living family to ask why I felt drawn to angels. I wanted to figure it out eventually, but first, I needed to learn how to be a vampire. Things were still intense, and I'd learned that, sometimes, ignorance was a blessing. The truth could cause more problems and prevent you from enjoying what you already had.

Griffin pulled into his spot, and we all climbed out. I didn't have too many things to pack. I'd planned on going back to Eliza's to get the rest of my things, but I wasn't sure I wanted to go home like this. I didn't want to put Annie or Eliza in danger. Granted, bloodlust hadn't caused problems for me ... yet.

We rode up the elevator and dispersed into our individual rooms to get our things.

Once we were in our room, Alex pulled me into his arms. "If you want to investigate what's happening with you, we can. All you have to do is say the word."

His support meant so much to me. I kissed his lips and laid my head against his chest, enjoying the rhythm of his heartbeat. "I do, but we have more than enough on our plates."

"I don't care." His arms tightened around me. "If you want to know, then that's the most important thing. We will put all our time and energy into it. I don't want you to put off learning about yourself."

"Honestly, I'm not in any hurry." I leaned back to stare into his eyes. "As long as you're with me, everything else doesn't seem as important. Let's figure out what's going on with *our* people, and when that's done and we've enjoyed some time as husband and wife, we can start digging."

"Husband and wife?" His soft eyes twinkled. "I *really* like the sound of that."

"Me, too." I wanted to push him down on the bed and have my way with him, but we could have sexual adventures back in Shadow Ridge. "Let's pack. I'm ready to get the hell out of here."

We packed our few belongings and hurried out the door. The scent of musky cedar filtered down the hall.

Kira was here.

The two of us hurried into the living room. Ulva, Griffin, and Sterlyn were already with the fox shifter. They were staring at each other in disbelief.

Something was wrong.

"What's the problem?" I asked.

"I came here to fulfill the last part of my deal." Kira homed in on Alex. "I know one person involved with the rogue vampires that you'll want to know about."

Alex tensed, preparing for the worse. "Who?"

CHAPTER THIRTEEN

KIRA PAUSED as if to build the tension. Or maybe she was nervous.

After a few seconds, she exhaled and licked her lips, then started bouncing on the balls of her feet.

Shit. She *was* anxious, which put me on edge.

As if I hadn't been tense enough lately.

"The vampire situation goes high up the hierarchy." She glanced at her watch and tugged at her dress. "It's going to be hard to believe."

The confident fox shifter I'd met just days ago had been hijacked by someone insecure and self-conscious. I blamed it on her father, who disregarded her and treated her like crap.

"Okay." Alex hissed out a breath. "Out with it."

Go easy on her, I connected with him. *She's not comfortable telling you who it is.*

"Easy, bloodsucker," Kira snapped, her face turning

stern. "Lucky for you, I need to leave before Dad realizes I'm gone."

Alex trembled with tension, and I cut my eyes to him.

Whatever he saw in my expression was enough for him to keep his mouth shut.

Kira rolled her eyes. "I slipped out while he was yelling at Ezra. He wasn't happy that Griffin and Sterlyn's named me as the fox leader, and I need to rush back because your brother and Azbogah were getting involved, siding with my father against Ezra." She grimaced and looked at the two wolf shifters. "Supporting me will make things worse for you. I'm sorry."

"Even if you hadn't tried to bribe us, we would've backed you." Sterlyn smiled. "There is no reason you shouldn't lead the fox shifters, regardless, unless Grady challenged you and won."

"That coward doesn't have the balls." Kira snorted. "You saw what happened. He was the one with the black eye." Her cockiness slipped back on like a glove.

Annoyance flashed through Alex.

I intervened before he did something to upset her further. "Kira, you said you need to head out. Do you want to tell us who Matthew and Alex should keep an eye on?" I wanted to include myself in that statement, but I didn't want to overstep.

"Yeah, you're right." She nodded and squared her shoulders. "Someone in your trusted circle is involved."

"Our trusted circle?" Alex tapped a finger on his chin and studied the ceiling. "Color me intrigued. Please, do share. The sooner the better." A vein between his eyes bulged as he clamped down his frustration with her. *You better realize how much I love you because I want to strangle the information out of her.*

For a three-hundred-year-old, he sure wasn't patient. They said age gave you that quality, and if his patience had improved, I'd hate to have seen him two hundred years ago. *You catch more bees with honey.*

I'm not interested in her honey. Alex winked at me. *Only yours.*

My body warmed.

"Okay, that was all the encouragement I needed." Kira waved her hand in front of her nose. "It's Blade. He's involved."

Alex's head snapped around, and he stared at her in disbelief. "No way. Where did you hear this?"

Blade.

Why did that name sound so familiar? "Who is that?"

"The vampire who manages Shadow Terrace." Alex's right eyelid twitched, and his sense of betrayal washed over me. "Since we were locked in Shadow City for practically one thousand years, we had to assign someone outside to help rule over the Terrace and be responsible for managing the guards. Blade is the second person to have that role, one he inherited from his father about a hundred years ago." He stared at Kira. "How certain are you?"

It still blew my mind how long vampires could live.

"I told you; I hear things." Kira tapped her fingers on her legs. "Some vampires were talking about him at the vampire side of the city gate when they were receiving a blood shipment. They were laughing about how stupid you and Matthew were for not realizing Blade's been playing both sides."

Alex crossed his arms and lowered his head. "Why were you there that late at night? Those shipments come around midnight."

"Because I've had to learn things to get anything for myself here." Kira spread her arms out. "If I want to know anything, I have to discover it on my own, so I learned how to sneak around without being caught."

Damn. I felt bad for the girl. Hank wouldn't win any father of the year awards. I bet she'd grown up feeling unwanted like I had for most of my life in foster care.

Alex sighed and pulled at his ear. "If people are hearing about it here, you'd think they would've told Matthew."

"A vampire guard on the city side said that Matthew is aware." Kira lifted a hand. "Maybe he does know."

"Not possible." Alex shook his head. Then hope spread through his chest. "Unless that's why he closed down Thirsty's. Maybe that was why he was there the day we confronted Eilam. He was checking out the source since Blade hangs out at the bar. But that still seems far-fetched. He never said anything to me."

If she was lying, we'd know. I understood that he didn't want to think more poorly of his brother. *Maybe you're right about why Matthew was there. Did he say anything the week after when I was hanging out with Sterlyn?*

He tensed. After a moment, he replied, *No. Dammit.*

"I heard about it three weeks ago." Kira crossed her arms defiantly. "At least, I can sleep well knowing I held up my end of the deal. You can do whatever you want with the information."

But ... if he knew, why didn't he tell me? Alex frowned, hurt clear on his face.

That was the crux of the problem. I turned to Kira. "Thank you. We appreciate you keeping your promise."

"You seem to be the only one." Kira headed toward the door but stopped beside the couch. She turned to Griffin and Sterlyn. "I do have a favor to ask."

Griffin arched a brow. "Yes?"

"I'd like to attend the university." Kira rubbed her hands together. "Maybe take more modern classes so that, as the city borders open, my people won't have as many problems acclimating."

"That's a good idea. We already decided we need a shifter from each race in Shadow City to attend. It makes sense for her to be the first fox since she'll be the next fox leader." Sterlyn glimpsed at Griffin and Alex. "How do we go about getting her permission to attend?"

"A council member has to approve it and give her name to the guards at the wall." Griffin examined the fox. "Is there any other reason you want to leave the city?"

"And they say you aren't smart." Kira chuckled. "Yeah, I want to help with the shifter and vampire issues. I'm smart and fast on my feet. It would be a win for all of us." She lifted a finger. "And I was sincere about the main reason. I want to help bridge the gap between the way supernaturals live here and how they live in the outside world. Maybe new people will move here, and others will move out."

"That was Griffin's father's goal." Ulva smiled sadly. "He dreamed that Shadow City could help the races that are struggling outside our strong city, and he wanted to bring fresh blood and ideas here. Things are moving slower than we'd anticipated."

"It was smart to start out with a limited number coming and going." Griffin rubbed a hand down his face. "Think of all the chaos there's been already between Sterlyn's pack, the shifter attacks, and the rogue vampires. We need to take care of these problems before we add to them."

"I agree, but there will always be something not ideal going on." Sterlyn placed a hand on her mate's shoulder. "This might be as good as it's going to get."

"But not without taking care of the vampires first." Alex shook his head. "You saw how they reacted to Veronica. If they can't control their urges, they'll become part of the rogue vampires in Shadow Terrace. I had a hard time with my cravings too when I first started spending time in the Terrace."

I remembered Sterlyn telling me that Alex had attacked a human on campus. He had obviously struggled, and the thought made me sick. If all the vampires became free to leave the city at once, there could be a killing spree.

"Yes, we need a strategy for when we lift the borders." Griffin exhaled. "But I think that's something the council could get behind."

Sterlyn turned to Griffin, and the two of them had a conversation using their mate connection. Sterlyn rubbed her hands together. "Kira, we'll get you on the list to attend the university and give you access to leave. Griffin will let the city guards know, but we'll need to work on the university part. Maybe you could meet us at the campus tomorrow?"

"Yeah, that would be great." Kira beamed, and her hands shook with excitement. "Thank you. I better go. You have my number, right? Just text me what time, and I'll be ready."

"Okay." Sterlyn laughed and grabbed her duffel bag from the floor. "We can pick you up at the gate."

When the door shut behind Kira, Griffin dangled the keys from his hand. "You two ready?"

"God, yes." I wouldn't even pretend to hide my eagerness. "Maybe once things settle down, being in the city won't be so bad, but this week has been a doozy. I'm ready to focus on something other than the council."

Alex intertwined our fingers and smiled at me adoringly. "Like our wedding."

That wasn't what I'd been thinking, but he was right. We definitely had a wedding to plan, and I needed to call Annie and Eliza to tell them the good news.

My stomach soured. They were human, and I was a vampire. I wasn't sure how that would work concerning them attending the wedding, but the thought of excluding them was equally heartbreaking. Either way, Alex and I shouldn't put our future on hold over my fears. I'd already missed out on several experiences like prom and college due to my fear of branching out.

I pushed away my unease, not wanting him to think that our wedding had caused that feeling and smiled. "Yes, I can't imagine a better distraction." I kissed his cheek.

"Well, this old lady is going to change into sweat-pants and a shirt and lounge around since I'll be all alone again." Ulva hugged Griffin and Sterlyn then made her way to Alex and me.

When she threw her arms around the two of us, Alex's jaw almost hit the floor. His reaction was pretty funny.

She squeezed my shoulder. "You all be good and make sure my son and Sterlyn stay out of trouble."

"I don't know, Mrs. Bodle." Alex's arrogant demeanor fell right back into place. "They are quite a handful. I'd hate to make promises I can't keep."

"And to think you only became part of this family recently." Ulva laughed and headed down the hallway. "I'm glad you are now."

Griffin pointed at Alex and growled, "Don't get any ideas. *Family* is pushing it, but I'll settle for a friend."

"Aw." Sterlyn pretended to wipe a tear from her eye. "Our boys are growing up."

"Time really does go by way too quickly," I said, joining in to give them shit.

Alex pulled me against him and licked my nose. "You keep it up, and there'll be more of that."

I laughed at the random threat, and for a split second, things felt normal.

"Come on." Griffin chuckled as he pushed the button to head down to the garage. "Killian just linked with us. He's begging us to get over there. Sierra is driving him crazy."

The four of us walked down to the garage, and Alex and I climbed into his luxury Mercedes SUV and followed Griffin and Sterlyn out of the garage. When they turned right, heading toward the bridge to the Shadow Ridge side of the river, Alex stopped the car to look at me. "Do you mind if we take a detour?"

"Uh … no, but should we tell the others?" I didn't want to leave Sterlyn and Griffin hanging. They'd expect us to arrive at their house at the same time they did.

"Can you call them?" Alex turned left, heading toward the vampire side of the city. "I need to follow up on the Blade situation before I can go over there and deal with Sierra's mouth … er… humor."

I laughed. He sometimes had a hard time handling Sierra's snarky personality. He was older and more reserved than my favorite mouthy shifter.

My hands brushed the cool, black leather of his car as I pulled the phone from my pocket. I dialed Sterlyn's number and watched the bustling city pass by.

She answered on the first ring. "I was about to call you. I take it Alex wants to check out Blade."

"Yeah, so we'll be there a little after you." I wasn't excited about us going alone, but I couldn't ask Sterlyn and Griffin to come. That would cause more issues.

"Okay." She didn't sound happy. "If you need us, don't hesitate to call. We'll come there, no matter what."

"I know, and I will."

When I ended the call, I took Alex's hand, needing his comfort. "Do you really think you'll find out anything?"

"We won't know until we try." He squeezed my hand.

We drove past the four-story Neo-Renaissance-style mansion that Alex had called home for three hundred years.

When we reached the gate to the Shadow Terrace side of the river, several vampires rushed to lower the drawbridge. While they worked the lever, Alex grabbed his phone and typed out a message. "I'm asking a man named Joshua to meet us at Thirsty's to keep an eye on you while I'm inside. He owes me several favors. I know the bar is closed, but I want to do some snooping. We can't risk you coming across any humans while I'm distracted."

"Okay, I trust you." The whole royal family was all about favors. They didn't realize that people could simply be your friend. Granted, I thought Alex was finally seeing that friendships could form, even across races.

We were soon driving through the gate and over a bridge identical to the one on the other side of the city. The design reminded me of pictures I'd seen of the Golden Gate Bridge in San Francisco. Shadow Terrace appeared in front of us with its buildings of varying sizes in shades of white with red rooftops. All the structures in the town had been built during the same period, and the look was uniform throughout, except for one gray stone building with a dome on top in the center of town. For me, that was the landmark near Thirsty's Bar.

We pulled off the cement bridge and onto the cobblestone road that led into the town. Humans were out and about, some with families, others laughing without a care in the world. My stomach turned. These people would be drained of some of their blood tonight and then brainwashed to forget the ordeal and think they were having an amazing vacation. But the vampires had to feed somehow, and this was the lesser of the evils.

We pulled up to Thirsty's, and a vampire—Joshua, I assumed—was standing out front. His espresso hair was disheveled, and his mocha eyes watched us. He leaned against the brick wall near the door as a few people exited the bar.

"This place is supposed to be closed." Alex parked out front. His neck was tight as he glared. "It must have reopened while we were in Shadow City. Please stay here. I'll be right back. Lock the doors behind me. Don't let anyone in, including Joshua."

I nodded. "Just ... please be careful and let me know if you need me."

"I will." He kissed my forehead then climbed out of the car and went to the door. He said something to Joshua, who nodded and stayed outside.

As Alex rushed inside, my worry increased. Something seemed ... off. I didn't know how to explain it.

I glanced around, expecting the shadow to appear. A tingle at the base of my neck made me even more uneasy.

Are you okay? I hoped and prayed the sensation had nothing to do with Alex.

Alex connected back immediately, *Yes. Blade is here. I'll be out in a moment. Are* you *okay?*

No, but I knew he had to do this. Otherwise, he'd be on edge the entire time at Sterlyn's. He wasn't close, so he wouldn't smell my lie. *Yep, just worried.*

I gagged at the horrible smell that filled the car. It reminded me of rotten eggs. Ugh, no wonder supernaturals hated it when people lied.

From the corner of my eye, I saw something flying at me. I jerked my head around and locked on it—it looked like something out of a war movie ... a grenade.

My breath caught, and my body plunged into coolness as I realized the damn thing was aimed at the car. There was no way I could get out in time.

My vision warped like heat wafting from hot asphalt in the summer, and I lost sense of my fingers and toes just as the car exploded.

CHAPTER FOURTEEN

THE HEAT SLICED THROUGH ME, and I waited for pain or darkness to overtake me. Instead, I felt as if I were floating skyward, and it disoriented me. My vision wavered, yet I could still make out everything clearly. The entire process was strange.

Maybe Heaven existed, and I was heading toward the light. In all the movies I'd seen, the light hadn't been the sun, but maybe that was one of the great unknowns.

I could see everything, but I had no human form. I literally was smoke flowing upward with the smoke from the explosion. I wanted to get away from the stench of gasoline, but I didn't know how this was possible, let alone how to escape it.

My heart sank as fear took hold.

Joshua ran toward the rubble, his eyes wide and frantic. His medium-brown skin tone appeared quite pale.

He seemed concerned. If Matthew had been here,

he'd be dancing around the car, overjoyed that I'd died or disappeared.

Whatever this was.

Joshua yelled, "Help! I need water!" Despite the flames, he went to the passenger door and tried to move the wreckage, searching for me. His white shirt turned gray from the smoke.

Grief and terror swept through me as the door to the bar swung open and Alex blurred to the pile of rubble. The black smoke billowing from the car and surrounding me began to disperse, and I flowed over the rooftop of Thirsty's Bar.

Like a shadow.

No. It couldn't be. I'd turned into the very thing I'd feared for most of my life. This had to be a sick joke.

But what if I was the shadow and there was no after-life? Would I slink around, existing and watching the ones I loved continue on with their lives?

That thought was more petrifying than death. In death, I would eventually find peace, but not in this form.

Not like this.

The thought of watching Alex move on with his life and find someone else to love gutted me. Even though I would never want him to be miserable, the very idea of seeing him with someone else broke my heart.

"I'll call Blade to get some men here to help, but, man, you need to prepare for the worst." Joshua stepped back, pulling his phone from his pocket while deep worry lines etched into his forehead.

Alex didn't hesitate in pulling part of the door away from the wreckage. "Call them, but I feel her. She's scared, and I have to find her!"

If he felt me, that meant I was alive, right? I was banking on yes, but the warm spot in my chest was missing, so I hadn't considered I could still talk to him. I tried to use our soulmate connection. *Alex?*

Something popped as if our connection had needed a little push.

Thank the gods. Alex's fear waned, but not by much. *Where are you? I can feel your terror, but I don't feel any pain. I thought maybe you'd blacked out.*

I'm not in any pain. I hovered over Thirsty's Bar and glanced at the slanted red rooftop. A decomposed body littered the slats, and it looked oddly human. The skin was flaking off, and it was so bad I couldn't tell whether the body was male or female. There was no smell.

My stomach revolted. Luckily, I wasn't in human form, or I'd have been puking.

What's wrong? Alex yanked at the last piece of debris blocking the passenger seat. Flames licked the sides of the car, getting too close to him. *I'm almost there.*

No, you're not. I had to focus on my mate and not on the horrible scene below me. *I'm not in the SUV.* If I told him I could see a dead body, he would go into overdrive. I needed to concentrate on getting out of this form. Hopefully, there was a way to do that since I was still connected with Alex.

I couldn't consider any other options.

Alex glanced around as if he expected me to be standing near him. *Then where are you?*

In the air. Yeah, that sounded crazier than I'd expected.

His head snapped up, and he squinted to find me in the smoke. *I'm so confused. Did Rosemary save you? I don't see you.*

That would have been a whole lot easier to explain. *I'm hovering over the bar's roof.*

He blurred as he spun on his heel, searching for me. *Veronica, this is not funny.*

I'm not laughing. Believe me. Every other emotion ran through me *except* humor. *I'm like a shadow.*

The wind blew, pushing me farther over the rooftop, and I almost cried. Staring at that dead body wasn't doing me any favors.

We need to get you down. Alex shielded his eyes from the sun. *I still don't see you.*

That was so strange, although no one else could see the shadow whenever it appeared to me. Maybe I was like the dagger and only a handful of people could see my outline, but the shadow had been me, so I figured whatever was happening was connected to my supernatural side.

Who knew anymore?

Let me figure out how to land, and I'll let you know where I am. I had to lock down all the emotions whirling inside me. Otherwise, I might be stuck in this state forever. If turning into a shadow was one of my abilities, it was the only reason I was still alive.

Nobody could have survived that explosion.

Veronica. Alex's shoulders sagged. *Just be careful.* He appeared so broken, standing there, unable to help me.

Joshua ran to him again, and I closed off our connection so he wouldn't distract me.

I looked around, not wanting to float farther and farther away from Alex. There had to be a way to control my motion.

Tension ran through me, and the farther I drifted from Alex, the more my anxiety rose. Maybe if I calmed myself, I could change back into my human form.

Being stuck in this form forever was not an option.

I closed my ... eyes? I guessed they would still be called that since I could see despite not being in a solid body.

Hysteria clawed inside me.

Focus, Ronnie, I chanted to myself.

All I could see was darkness. I took control of my breathing and listened to the sound of my heartbeat.

Wait.

My heartbeat.

Hot damn. That meant I was alive. It *had* to.

With renewed determination, I inhaled deeply and exhaled. Multiple times. Sterlyn had told me whenever I felt stressed, overwhelmed, anxious, or scared, to take three deep breaths to level out my emotions.

Filling my lungs, I was relieved to find I could breathe. I drew in fresh air with hints of caprese and cedar instead of the thick, suffocating smoke from the explosion.

Though I wasn't a full-blown nature girl, I enjoyed the outdoors. The trees, rivers, and wind had a way of calming me when nothing else could.

After taking three deep breaths, I went to the next part of the coping mechanism: thinking of three happy things.

Dear God, I had to be channeling Peter Pan.

But in *Peter Pan*, you thought about those things to fly, whereas I wanted to get back to the ground.

First, I focused on Alex's face. His soft blue eyes filled with adoration, gazing at me, and his sexy lips set in that arrogant smirk I secretly loved. He made me feel safe and cared for, more so than anyone in my life, and I wouldn't be standing here today if it weren't for him.

He'd saved me from Klyn, a rogue vampire, the first night I arrived in Shadow Terrace in search of Annie, my sister by all rights. She'd disappeared from our home in Lexington and snuck down here to be with Eilam, another rogue who had been messing with her mind. Klyn had found me a couple of minutes after I'd arrived in Shadow Terrace when I'd been searching for Annie at this very bar. He'd planned to feast on me. Thankfully, Alex had been there that night, or I would've been drained of blood.

After Alex, Sterlyn and Rosemary appeared in my mind. Those two women had become family just as much as Eliza and Annie were. They'd made sacrifices for me even before they'd really known me, proving that whatever flowed through me linked me to them.

Finally, I thought about Annie and Eliza. Even with

this new love and family I'd found, my heart held so much love for them. They'd taken me in and accepted me before anyone else; we'd forged an unbreakable bond that would last, no matter if I were human or vampire.

Those five people made up my three happiest memories. It wasn't material things or my accomplishments. My happiest thoughts were of the people who'd touched my very soul.

People for whom I would die without a moment's hesitation.

My body tingled, but I kept my eyes shut. Laughter trickled into my ears, but I held on to the images in my mind, needing them to ground me.

Literally.

My feet felt as if they'd touched something; then they grew heavy with my weight.

Had I accomplished it?

I opened my eyes ... and almost cried with relief. My gaze darted to my hands and my feet, finding them in solid form. I was still wearing the black suit and white tank top I'd borrowed from Sterlyn, and there was no damage to the clothing.

No one would believe I'd almost exploded in a car.

I took in my surroundings and realized I was around humans. *Alex, I'm behind the bar.*

Their scent filled my nose, and my stomach gurgled. They smelled appealing, and I froze in terror.

But it was a different kind of fear.

One I'd never experienced before.

I felt like a predator, and all these people around me were prey.

Don't move, Alex connected. *I'm on my way with Joshua.*

Thankfully, he had backup. If I became unhinged and attacked, he might need it.

I waited for the urge to drink blood to overtake me. That was how the vampires had reacted to me at Alex's family mansion and how my friends had expected me to act after being turned.

I figured the bloodlust hadn't hit me because I hadn't been around any humans. Sterlyn and my other friends smelled nice, but not the "I want to bite you" type of good.

In other words, they didn't smell like cinnamon rolls.

Come to think of it, these people didn't either.

I relaxed marginally but kept my guard up and inspected a family of four only a few feet away. They were gazing into the window of a bakery offering fudge, cakes, and crimson-colored pudding.

I had a feeling I knew what the pudding was made of. A little something for the residents of Shadow Terrace. No one reacted to my presence, as if they hadn't seen me materialize out of thin air.

Strange.

A couple walked past me, hand in hand, and my gaze instinctively went to their necks. I could see each beat of their pulse, and I braced myself for my fangs to descend, but they never came.

I cut my eyes to the corner that led to the bar just as Alex and Joshua came into view. Joshua's brows furrowed as he examined me, and his almond skin appeared even paler than it had been when I'd seen him running toward the car.

He seemed scared and confused.

I was, too.

They moved at human-like speeds—a little faster than most, but nothing remarkable.

Alex hugged me and kissed my forehead. *Don't ever do that to me again!*

I thought I was a goner. My body quivered, and I allowed some fear to bleed through. *When I saw that grenade heading toward me, I knew it was over.*

Joshua cleared his throat. "I hate to interrupt, but we should get back to the bar. There will be a lot of questions."

No, I didn't want to go back to that place. Not now. *Alex, there's a dead body on the bar's roof.* Now that I was back in solid form, I felt like I could tell him that.

His arms tensed around me. *Just one?*

I sighed. *That I noticed, but I didn't really examine the area. It was disgusting. There was powder on it, like baking soda—maybe to hide the smell.* I should've forced myself to look harder, but the sight had been ghastly.

"I've heard enough." Alex released me and took my hand. He turned to Joshua. "I want to bring Veronica somewhere safe, and I need your help."

Joshua's eyebrows lifted, and the corners of his lips turned upward. "Why should I help you? That was the last favor I owed you, and that *is* how you and your brother operate."

"Listen to me," Alex hissed too softly for human ears. "You *will* help me, or I will make you. I am your prince." He clenched his hand, and I grimaced, waiting to see what happened next.

CHAPTER FIFTEEN

WHOA, that had escalated quickly. I touched Alex's hand to calm him down. The family of four glanced at us.

Hey. I pushed calm toward him and wrapped my arms around him, not wanting to add to his tension. *Maybe just talk to him like a person? He seems like a nice guy.*

A nice guy? Alex huffed. *He's a vampire. I've spent my entire life around this race, so believe me when I say I don't trust him.*

Ugh. I had to get him to listen to me, or we'd be heading back to the bar, and whoever had tried to kill me would see I was still alive. *Remember when I told you I could feel something off with your brother? I don't think it's just because I'm getting acclimated to being supernatural. I get a reading from everyone. Your brother and Azbogah have this negativity rolling off them. This guy doesn't. He has a warmth to him like you, Gwen, Sterlyn, and all our friends.*

Alex glimpsed at me. *You can sense intent? That's not possible.*

That view did have merit. *Since becoming a vampire, I can feel it like a tidal wave trying to overtake me.*

Only angels can do that. Alex turned and pulled me against him, needing me as close as possible. *It's the only supernatural race with that ability.*

Interesting. But now that I'd distracted Alex, I needed to use that to my advantage. I looked at Joshua and tried to smile, but I couldn't get my lips to move accordingly. "I understand what Alex is asking is a huge inconvenience, but after almost dying, I want to get home." I licked my lips. "I would really appreciate it if you took us to our friends' house if you have time."

Joshua's face smoothed, and he tilted his head, examining me. "Okay. Fine. Someone did try to hurt you." His eyes narrowed, and he pressed his lips together. "Stay here. I'll get my car."

Shock wafted from Alex to me, but I tried not to react. If we made a funny move, Joshua could change his mind. For some reason, he wasn't comfortable around Alex. "Thank you."

He nodded and hurried off toward the front of the bar.

"Now we owe him." Alex ran his hands down my arms. "But as long as it gets you to safety, it's well worth it."

My mind was still stuck on what he'd said earlier. "How could I possibly be an angel? I was human.

Wouldn't you know if something was different about me?"

"You smelled and tasted human." His gaze landed on my neck. "When I drank from you that one time, my blood seemed extra charged, but I figured it was due to our soulmate connection."

He hadn't said anything about feeling extra charged, but I understood why he hadn't and assumed the feeling had come from our connection. His parents were the last vampire soulmates anyone had heard of until us. "Maybe it wasn't."

"I don't know." He surveyed the area. "But we need to get you back to Shadow Ridge before something else happens." *I don't want your bloodlust kicking in and risk you losing your humanity.*

I agreed with that. *I don't have any overwhelming urges. Don't get me wrong, humans smell good, but I could just as well go for another cinnamon raisin bagel.* My stomach growled at that thought.

We need to determine what else is influencing you. He kissed me. *I'm glad you aren't struggling, but this is rather peculiar. You haven't acted like a normal vampire once since you've turned.*

But that's good, right? The thought of bloodlust controlling me didn't sound appealing. I'd much rather be like this than drinking from one of the children focused on the bakery.

Yes, but we have to get to the bottom of what is going on.

For all I knew, my change into a vampire wouldn't take, and I could be slowly dying.

A silver Jeep Renegade pulled up to the curb, and the tinted driver's side window rolled down, revealing Joshua. He waved us over. "Hurry up before I change my mind."

I rushed to the driver's side backdoor and climbed in. I didn't want to sit up front with Joshua.

He wasn't hitting on me, but I felt like a puzzle he was trying to piece together.

Alex motioned for me to scoot over.

I shook my head. *No, you need to ride up front with him. If you sit back here, he'll think we view him as a chauffeur.* Joshua seemed unsure about helping us, and I wanted to ensure he felt like an equal partner in crime.

"We don't have all day," Joshua snapped while he rolled up his window. "Someone will see us."

"Fine." Alex blurred to the front passenger seat and climbed in.

As soon as he shut the door, Joshua punched the gas, narrowly missing a family of four crossing the street.

I glanced behind in time to catch the dad throwing a fist in the air as he yelled, "Asshole."

He had some balls. If he had remembered that vampires surrounded him, I bet he would've hightailed it out of town.

"Do the workers at the blood bank drain the kids too?" I asked before I could stop myself. The thought of kids being hooked up to tubes made my stomach roll.

Alex shook his head. "Absolutely not. Only adults.

The kids are put into a deep sleep, so they don't wake up while the parents are gone."

Joshua glanced at Alex and frowned. "You really think that?" He sounded surprised.

Alex sneered at the vampire. "I've seen it myself."

"Yeah, because they knew you were coming. At one point, it *was* that way." Joshua scoffed and glanced at the rearview mirror. Sweat beaded on his forehead. "Until your brother took control."

"What are you talking about?" Alex's voice was loud with frustration. "Matthew hasn't changed the,law. Every vampire would know if he had."

Something sketchy was going on. With the vileness wafting off Matthew, I'd bet he'd changed the law without telling Alex, or he'd decided not to enforce it.

"Where am I taking you?" Joshua stopped at the main cobblestone road that ran through the center of the Terrace. He wiped the perspiration from his brow.

"Shadow Ridge." Alex exhaled. "We're staying with the Shadow City alpha and his mate. It's crazy, but that's the safest place for Veronica and me."

Joshua gaped at Alex. "Are you serious?"

"Yeah. That way." Alex pointed toward the low-traffic, two-way road that led to Shadow Ridge. "I get that we owe you."

He turned right, following Alex's instructions, then glanced at me in the rearview mirror. "If that's the case, I want to know how you escaped that vehicle and materialized behind the bar."

Yeah, that question had been long overdue. I didn't know the answer, so I remained quiet.

"That's none—" Alex started.

Joshua held a hand up to him. "I was talking to your girl."

"Fiancée," Alex hissed. "She's my fiancée, and I'm the one who owes you, not her."

"That's my call." Joshua lifted his chin, daring Alex. "Or I can let you out here. I'm sure the vampires who tried to kill your fiancée would love to know she survived."

Anger flashed through our connection. Alex hated being threatened, and this would go sideways if I didn't intervene.

"I can't decide if you're dumb or you want to piss me off." Alex clutched the door handle, ready to open it. *Get ready to jump out. This asshole is using our situation to his advantage.*

How is it to his advantage? The guy seemed nervous, and if Alex would stop needling him, we could find out why. "I don't know how I did what I did." There was no harm in being honest. *It isn't as if we need to hold back information. He was there. He saw what happened.*

Joshua glanced at me again. "I find that rather hard to believe."

"Yet the rotten stench of a lie isn't filling the car," I retorted. The best way to combat someone who wasn't wanting to help you was with facts, not coming off like an asshole.

A grin peeked from his face as he focused back on the road.

My stomach dropped as we entered the maple and cedar woods. I was reminded of the night, about a week ago, when Zaro and his friend had taken me into the woods and through an underground tunnel to the hidden room below the blood bank. Eilam had been waiting with Annie and Gwen. On Eilam's order, Annie had almost taken my life, but she had overcome the rogue vampire's mind control.

"Rumor is you were human the night of the attack." Joshua was referring to the event I'd just been thinking about. "I helped clean up the blood bank and heard all about how the vampire prince had fallen for a mere mortal. And now you're a vampire with these strange abilities. It seems rather ... suspicious."

Yeah, I couldn't blame him for being curious. "I was human, and I don't understand it, either."

"Are you accusing my mate of something?" Alex asked, anger lacing his words.

"No." Joshua shook his head and rubbed his neck. "But I'm helping you, so there's a chance whoever tried to kill her could have his sights on me now. I deserve to know why she's a target."

I hadn't thought of it that way. No wonder the poor guy was nervous.

"We haven't done anything." Alex crossed his arms. He didn't like being questioned, even if it was good for him. He was used to others cowering in fear or trying to stab him in the back. He was acting like the cagey and arrogant ass I'd met not long ago.

As we passed through the last section of woods before the bridge that marked the boundary of Shadow Terrace, Joshua pointed out of the windshield. "Yet you have me taking you to Shadow Ridge where no vampires live."

"Yes, because a certain *silver wolf*, her mate, and an angel have a vested interest in protecting my mate." Alex arched his brow. "An interest that started while she was human."

"Her abilities are neither wolf nor angel, so I'm not sure why you would even say that." Joshua chuckled. "And to think the prince of the vampires is seeking asylum outside his kingdom. I bet Matthew is ecstatic."

Alex tensed. "That is none of your concern." *This guy is asking way too many questions.*

It's fine. I was reassured as we crossed over the bridge. We'd be in Shadow Ridge in minutes. *We need to figure out who attacked us and didn't need to chance someone seeing us.*

"You can pull over here. We can run the rest of the way." Alex gestured to a small cut out on the side of the road. "I appreciate you taking us this far."

"I can't, in good conscience, drop you off here." Joshua frowned. "What if someone is following us and catches up to you? I'll take you to your friends' house and head out from there."

"Fine." Alex settled back into his seat, and an uncomfortable silence descended on us.

After a short while, we drove into Shadow Ridge. I

felt most at home here, though I wasn't sure why. Like Shadow Terrace, most of the buildings in downtown Shadow Ridge were brick, but that was where the similarities ended. The colors were all different, and the structures came in multiple architectural styles.

Alex directed Joshua toward a wooded area with thick cypress trees on both sides of the road. As we turned into the neighborhood of craftsman-style houses where most of Killian's pack lived, I noticed a wolf standing among the trees, watching our approach. It had to be one of the guards that were always on duty. As a human, I'd always missed seeing any guards, but with my better vision, I could see each strand of this one's toffee fur.

Tearing my gaze away, I took in the comforting neighborhood that I'd grown to appreciate. The houses were painted in various shades of whites, blues, greens, and yellows.

"Griffin and Sterlyn's house is right there," Alex said, gesturing to a sizable white house with a wide front porch.

They lived next door to Killian, whose hunter-green house appeared almost identical, except Griffin's was slightly larger.

As Joshua slowed in front of the house, the front door swung open, and Griffin and Killian exited, their eyes locked on the vehicle. I smiled and started to wave at the friend I hadn't seen in too long.

Killian's warm, dark chocolate eyes turned ebony. His hands fisted, making his imposing biceps bulge. He was almost as tall as Griffin, and his chiseled face was lined with worry as he ran a hand through his short cappuccino hair.

A few wolves appeared from behind the house and ran toward the car, their teeth bared, ready to attack.

"I thought you said they were friendly!" Joshua slammed on the gas, and the tires squealed as he turned the vehicle hard and headed back toward the front of the neighborhood.

Dammit, if they'd been suspicious before, now they really would think we were doing something shady. "Stop the car."

Joshua hissed, "Are you crazy? They were about to attack us."

I tried to unlock the door, but it wouldn't budge.

Son of a bitch. The prick had put the child safety locks on. Oh, *hell* no.

CHAPTER SIXTEEN

"STOP THE CAR," Alex commanded. "Now."

Get out or call them. My phone had blown up in Alex's vehicle, so I had no way to connect with them. We didn't need to start a battle over a misunderstanding. *We should've called them to let them know about the change of car.*

A tri-colored wolf ran in front of the vehicle. Joshua slammed on his brakes.

Alex rushed out of the car and lifted both hands. "He's with us. There's nothing going on."

Griffin appeared in front of the car and growled, his eyes glowing brightly, "A little warning would've been nice. We heard something happened in the Terrace, and then an unknown car comes rolling in. You can't blame us for being on edge."

I glanced out my window just as Killian appeared beside Griffin. He held his hand up to the gray wolf with a darker face. The cream wolf stopped a few feet behind the car.

Good. Killian was holding his pack back.

I had to get out there to diffuse the situation. Whether Alex wanted to admit it or not, we needed more vampires on our side, and Joshua seemed different from the others I'd met, including Gwen, at first. "If you don't let me out of this vehicle, I will climb over the center console and get out Alex's side."

Joshua turned in his seat to lock eyes with me. "I've never seen vampires get along among themselves, let alone with other races. This is strange."

He didn't feel safe, so seeing people getting along didn't make sense to him. "Yeah, I know. But this is a good thing. We need to learn how to live together."

Joshua ran a hand down his face and smiled. "You see the bigger picture. Must be because you were human. You've mellowed out at least one member of the royal family."

"I didn't change him." I couldn't—no, I *wouldn't* take credit for that. "Alex was always a kind and protective man. Don't give me credit for something he already had within him."

He snorted. "That's what I'm getting at. Most vampires would take the credit."

"You might not be saying that much longer if I don't get out of this fucking car." I was losing my cool, and I didn't like it. All my life, I'd tried to contain my emotions without letting anything slip through. Losing my temper let other people see they had control over me, and I hated giving anyone control over me.

Maybe it was my orphanage upbringing, but I wasn't a fan of authority figures, especially if they were unreasonable.

"They're going to eat me alive." Joshua shivered. "If I get out, they'll attack."

No, they wouldn't, but I didn't want to waste any more time dealing with him, so I climbed over the console.

"Dammit, you're going to mess up my interior," he grumbled.

He should've thought of that before he'd activated the fucking child locks on the back doors.

"Why are you climbing out of the car like that?" Killian asked and arched an eyebrow just as Sterlyn, Sierra, and Rosemary rushed out the door.

"Because I couldn't get out the back door, and he wasn't in a hurry to let me out." I stood and slammed the door, letting some of my anger bleed through.

Sterlyn ran to me and hugged me. "Thank the gods you're all right. We heard Alex's car exploded, and we've been worried sick about you two."

"We've asked the guards to stand down," Griffin rasped. "But why didn't you call us?"

Yeah, that would've been the smart thing to do, and I was kicking myself that it hadn't crossed my mind. "A lot happened, and the car ride was tense. But you're right. We should've called you. Of course, you'd be on high alert." I twirled a lock of my copper hair around my finger.

"Holy shit!" Sierra squealed, pushing past Killian as she raced toward me. Her usual dirty blond ponytail bounced with each step. Her gray eyes homed in on my engagement ring, and she grabbed my hand. "What is that?"

Laughter bubbled from me. I could always count on her to ease a tense situation. I looked up at her since she had several inches on me. "Uh ... surprise." Everything that had happened in the past twenty-four hours seemed surreal. Not only had I become a vampire, but I'd also gotten engaged, stood up to the council, and turned into a shadow. And I'd thought my first few weeks here had rocked my world.

I stood corrected.

Joshua opened his door and cleared his throat. "Uh ... can I get out, or can one of you get the wolf to move away from the front of my car?"

"Excuse you." Sierra placed a hand on her hip and turned to the new vampire. "We're discussing something very important here. No interrupting, okay?"

"You're safe to get out," Sterlyn assured him.

He climbed from the car. His body was tense, and he continually surveyed the area, expecting someone to attack him.

This was one of the biggest problems the supernatural community faced. They were all nervous around other races. I'd learned they couldn't even trust their own race—Ezra had turned on Griffin and Sterlyn, and

Matthew went out of his way to undermine Alex's and my relationship. "We all like each other, so feel free to go."

"Yeah, right," he grumbled. His eyes darkened to ebony, surprising me. Most vampire's eyes became laced with red when they got upset, but his did not.

"Oh, my gods." Sierra stomped her foot. "Do I need to yell?" Each word grew exponentially louder than the last until I wanted to cover my ears.

"No." Rosemary marched over, her wings folded behind her. "You're plenty loud enough for everyone."

Sierra pounded her chest. "Seeing as no one's addressing the most important topic, you can see how I'd be confused."

"It's a ring." Killian scoffed. "So what?"

"I get it. Shifters do things differently, but you've watched a ton of chick flicks with us." She lifted my hand and pointed at the huge red diamond. "This, my dear, clueless alpha, is an engagement ring."

"No, engagement rings are diamonds." Killian pointed at the ring. "That stone is red, so it has to be a gift from Alex."

"Dude, there are plenty of different types of engagement rings." Sierra jeered. "And that *is* a diamond."

Griffin scowled. "Here I thought the most important topic was—I don't know—that this is the first time you've seen Ronnie as a vampire... or that a random vampire I've never seen before drove them here and tried to take off when we came out of the house."

Sierra rubbed a hand down her face. "And this proves

how completely hopeless these two are. I feel sorry for you, Sterlyn. There can't be much romance in your life with Griffin thinking that way, and I pity Killian's fated mate if he ever finds her."

"Griffin is romantic, and he takes care of my every need." Sterlyn winked at her mate. "But I agree with him. Their engagement is huge news, but our safety is more important, so they can live to have a wedding."

"Oh!" Sierra dropped my hand and nodded like she was on the same page. "We have to ensure there is a wedding." She glared at Joshua. "Why did you try to drive away?"

"This is the weirdest conversation I've ever been part of in my life." Joshua scratched his head, staring at Sierra. "You guys really are friends?"

"Of course, we are," Alex hissed. "Did you think I would admit to something like that if it wasn't true? As more vampires learn of my new alliances, Matthew's stance that I'm no longer fit to be the spare gains strength."

Joshua opened his mouth and closed it. He'd thought better of whatever he wanted to say.

"There's no reason to make him stay. He wasn't involved in the explosion." If we treated him like a person and not a suspect, I hoped he would be more transparent with us. "Before Alex's car blew up, Joshua tried to save me. Then he helped us get out of Shadow Terrace."

"What?" Sierra gasped. "We almost didn't have a wedding!"

"Because that was the most important component of

that entire conversation." Rosemary sighed in defeat. "Not Veronica almost dying."

"You said *tried*." Sterlyn, as usual, focused on the important points, ignoring the banter. "You got out on your own?"

Her intuition always astounded me, even though she'd been trained to think strategically since she was a baby. She always focused on the right questions.

"No." I wasn't sure how to explain it. I hadn't told them about the shadow because I thought it sounded crazy, but I didn't now.

Not anymore.

The shadow was me and maybe had been all along. It had my face for a reason, and it had always felt familiar to me. "No, I—"

"She disappeared," Joshua interjected. "It was the damnedest thing I've ever seen."

That was when it hit me. He talked more like me and the wolves than Alex, his siblings, and the other vampires I'd been around. He still seemed more mature than most of us, but not by centuries.

"What do you mean, disappeared?" Rosemary zeroed in on the conversation.

"She was there one second," Joshua deadpanned, "then she wasn't just before the car went boom."

I pressed my lips together, trying not to laugh. I liked him more and more each second he was around us.

"I'm glad my fiancée's near-death is a joke to you," Alex growled.

Joshua cut his eyes at Alex. "No, I'm relieved."

I had to get us back on track. "My body tingled, and my vision grew hazy. Then when the explosion hit, I was hurled from the car and into the air." I didn't want to say too much with Joshua there. I liked him, and he'd helped us escape, but he hadn't earned my trust yet. I would tell them about hovering above the bar and the body I'd seen when we were alone.

Be careful, Alex connected, thinking the same thing I was.

I won't say anything he doesn't already know. "And then I wound up behind the bar, surrounded by humans who weren't surprised to see me magically appear."

"When humans have blood taken, they're compelled not to remember anything strange that happens in town," Alex explained for the entire group. "And humans are apt to forget or explain away things they don't understand."

"Donate?" Joshua's laughter was devoid of humor. "That's an interesting way of putting it."

"And how would you put it?" Alex asked, stepping toward him.

I grabbed my mate's arm to calm him down. *Please, don't intimidate him. He already feels threatened enough, and he just helped us.*

Alex sighed but relented. *This just proves how much I love you.*

"More like forced to donate and made to think that they volunteered of their own free will." Joshua wrapped his arms around his body. "Which is worse than the blood being taken against their will."

My blood turned colder.

Annie had gone through the same thing.

Not only had she been drunk from like a fountain, but the guy had used her as a plaything.

At least, she couldn't remember that. Alex had made sure of it for me.

Alex must have thought the same thing because he stilled. *I'm so sorry. I didn't—*

Yup. He had. *No, it's fine. You didn't cause anything.*

Rosemary turned to Sterlyn. "If we're done with the new addition to the group, I'd like to go inside and talk through something that my parents and I may have figured out." Her gaze flicked to me, and I thought their idea might have something to do with my heritage, given how the council meeting had gone down.

"Uh, yeah." Sterlyn faced Joshua. "You're free to go if you want."

"More than ready." Joshua blurred and was back in his car within seconds.

The wolf standing in front of the car trotted off as Rosemary gestured to me. "We may have an idea of what you are, but it doesn't make sense."

My heart picked up its pace. I'd always wanted answers, but I wasn't sure I was ready.

CHAPTER SEVENTEEN

ALEX BRUSHED his arm against mine and connected, *If you don't want to hear what she has to say, we can tell her you're not up for it.*

That suggestion was so damn tempting, but we needed answers. Unfortunately, I was learning that ignorance put me at the mercy of others. I needed to find a way to grab Matthew by the balls and twist, and if that was figuring out why I was different, then so be it. *No. We need to hear her out.*

I had no clue what she would say, but one thing was sure—I wasn't reacting like a typical vampire, and I had a feeling the shadow was the reason.

"Okay, let's hear it." The sooner she got it out, the quicker I could handle the fallout.

Rosemary's mouth tightened. "Once we're inside."

No one moved, waiting for my reaction.

Not wanting to be under the microscope, I marched

toward Sterlyn and Griffin's front door with Alex following me like a guard.

With all the turmoil churning inside me, I didn't doubt he could feel my hesitation, fear, and unease—everything the shadow had made me feel while growing up with no one to turn to.

The others followed silently as we entered Griffin and Sterlyn's house.

The familiar blue-gray walls were a sight for sore eyes. This place had come to feel like home. I strolled into the living room with its pearl-gray couch, which complemented the color scheme, sitting against the room's longest wall, and a flat-screen television mounted on the opposite wall. I sat on the matching loveseat perpendicular to the couch and across from the windows, which were accented with white blinds.

Whatever Rosemary was about to say, I needed to be sitting down to hear it. As expected, Alex sat next to me and took my hand as Griffin, Sterlyn, and Sierra sat on the couch next to us. Killian paused next to the television, deep in thought.

Sierra sat on the end closest to me and grabbed my left hand, inspecting the ring again. She exhaled. "That's so pretty. I need to hear every single detail of how he proposed." She glanced at Sterlyn beside her, and her smile fell. "Wait! Were you there when it happened?" She gestured accusingly at Alex. "How dare you exclude the friends who aren't allowed in Shadow City from the occasion!"

Okay, this wasn't where I'd expected the conversation

to go, but Sierra seemed genuinely upset. "No. He didn't ask me in front of anyone. We were alone in our room."

Rosemary marched into the center of the room and scowled at us. "Before we go further into this topic, can we please discuss Ronnie's heritage?"

"I agree." Killian strolled to the windows that overlooked the backyard. "Here, lately, shit has been happening at random. We need to talk before anyone else makes an appearance."

He was so right about that. Between the Shadow City police showing up at the condominium and all the attacks, we were always rushing from one disaster to the next. Talking about our engagement was a whole lot more fun, except when I realized I couldn't inform Annie and Eliza. We wanted the wedding to happen soon, and if I told them, they'd want to be there. I couldn't put them at risk around me.

"First, is there anything you omitted in your story about how you survived the car bombing?" Rosemary stood almost as still as a statue, waiting.

The hussy knew. "Yeah." I filled them in on how I'd drifted over the building.

"Can you explain that a little more clearly?" Rosemary placed her hands behind her back and leaned forward.

Yeah, I wasn't sure I understood it. "I was like smoke, or a shadow, hanging in the air. I moved slowly, and the wind kind of led me, but I think if I'd known how, I could've gone in any direction I wanted." The vision of the shadow inching toward me as a child flashed through my mind. Now that I'd experienced being the shadow, I wondered if it had been trying to figure out how to get to me.

Griffin pinched the bridge of his nose. "How is that possible?"

"Could anyone see you floating?" Sterlyn pursed her lips. "I'm assuming not, since Joshua said you disappeared."

"I ... I don't know." I didn't think so, but it wasn't like I'd been on the ground, looking for myself.

Shaking his head, Alex said, "I couldn't see her. I was losing it, but our connection wasn't dead. Rather, it felt like it was missing. Enough to freak me out, but then something happened, and it formed again. She told me where she was, but even then, I couldn't see her, like when the dagger disappears."

The dagger, but right now, it wasn't important. I assumed it was still in Griffin's car and I could get it later. Or it would just appear in my hand again.

Something foreboding flashed through Rosemary's eyes. I waited for her to say something, but she remained quiet.

Since she was processing, I went ahead and told them about the dead body I'd seen on the roof. The thought still made me want to vomit.

"Bastards," Killian growled. "I'm assuming it was human and not an animal."

"I'm not sure." My stomach gurgled uncomfortably. "I think so."

"Are you sure just one?" Griffin studied me, his eyes taking on the alpha glow.

Yeah, I should've sucked up my discomfort and taken a closer look, but I was still new to the whole blood-and-gore situation, unlike everyone else here. "I couldn't keep examining it. I'm sorry."

Rosemary rubbed her hands together. "Anything else?"

"The strangest thing, other than her not craving blood and eating a cinnamon bagel this morning, was that when she became ..." Alex trailed off, and his gaze flicked to the ceiling. "When I could see her again, there were humans all around her, and her vampire side didn't come out even a little."

"I swear, things keep getting weirder around here. Between silver wolves existing, dead brothers reappearing, a dagger that magically appears, and a newly-turned vampire not attacking anything with a pulse, I'm not sure if I should be comforted or scared shitless." Sierra leaned back in her seat and crossed her legs. "I always wanted our little place to stop being dull, but boy, I didn't know what I was wishing for. The chaos has to stop eventually."

She'd said what I hoped for myself. I was so tired of all these mysterious things being hurled at us.

"This world is huge with so many occurrences we don't understand." Sterlyn mashed her lips together. "I doubt this will be the last odd thing that pops up. With the borders slowly opening at Shadow City, more turmoil is sure to happen."

"We need to teach vampires how to control their urges." I scooted closer to Alex. "We all saw what happened when I was in the city and still human."

Alex grimaced. "That's true, and Matthew keeps putting it off, saying we have more pressing things to address. I still can't believe Thirsty's is open again. Blade must have opened it while we were distracted, thinking we wouldn't notice."

Of course, we'd have noticed something like that.

"All this is adding fuel to Azbogah's desire to shut down the city again." Rosemary rolled her eyes. "He never wanted it open, to begin with, and that's another reason only a handful of people are allowed to leave the city. He and his buddies weren't happy when they learned Kira was granted permission to come and go as she pleases."

Griffin groaned. "That was the whole point of having the university. To open the city, educate its residents, and welcome new people, so we can slowly assimilate again."

"We're digressing." Alex's voice held an edge. "I want to know what the angels have realized about Veronica. Something was up with Azbogah at the end, and I don't like it."

Rosemary cleared her throat, showing some discomfort. She had a good poker face, so for her not to want to talk about it made me uncomfortable. "Just give it to me straight."

"Fine." Rosemary nodded, glad I had that attitude. "I deal best with bluntness."

I fidgeted in my seat.

I'm right here, Alex connected, brushing his finger along my skin. *Forever and always.*

I held on to those words like a lifeline. Everything inside me told me I'd need him to get through it.

"Oh, my *God*," Sierra gasped. "It's not even about me, and I'm about to strangle you if you don't spit it out."

Used to her, Rosemary ignored Sierra. Her eyes lightened to a lavender, almost the same shade as Sterlyn's. The angel inhaled. "The dagger that bonded to you is demonic."

I blinked. She couldn't have said what I thought she had. "I'm a demon? That's impossible. I was human."

"We think you were mostly human." Rosemary licked her lips. "Too human for your demon side to take hold. Growing up, did odd things ever happen to you?"

The shadow.

"Yes, but I thought I was crazy." All this time, there'd been an explanation.

I told them everything about seeing the shadow as a child. "And when I turned fourteen, the shadow appeared more distinctly. It inched toward me with reddish eyes and whispered promises of pain and revenge. It scared me. That night, I had a near breakdown, and Eliza saved me. She heard about the foster kid who was being sent to a mental hospital and offered to take me in. They almost didn't let her, but she insisted. Once I moved in with her, the shadow disappeared. Until I came here searching for Annie. It was around me when Klyn attacked me, then at the blood bank, and even at the artifact building."

"I never saw anything, and I've never heard of a shadow like that. Besides, I can see the dagger, so shouldn't I have been able to see the shadow, too?" Sterlyn glanced around the room. "Did anyone else see it?"

"No." Griffin tugged his ear. "That's new to me."

Rosemary paced. "We believe the shadow is her supernatural side, and she was projecting it. The two hadn't merged. Have you seen it since you've become a vampire?"

Now *that* was an interesting theory. "No, I haven't. Not since the dagger cut me in the artifact building and Alex turned me." Three months ago, if anyone had told me something like this would happen to me, I'd have laughed and called them insane. But this was all real. "And the rest you know."

"Did the dagger strengthen her demon side?" Killian leaned against the wall next to the window. His orange shirt contrasted starkly with the cool, gray-toned room. "Could it override her human side?"

"Possibly. When she turned completely supernatural, the power finally merged into her, the way it should have all along," Rosemary said with awe.

Alex placed his arm around my shoulders. "This all makes sense. She wasn't susceptible to mind control. She likes blood but doesn't crave it because she's part whatever created us, and she can still eat human food. Her demon side keeps her grounded, and she still has her humanity, because she was also human."

"But for the shadow to disappear once she went to

live with Eliza means Eliza must have done something to suppress it." Sterlyn regarded me. "Is there anything about Eliza that might indicate she's supernatural?"

"No—" I shook my head, but my words stopped. Sterlyn was right. For the shadow to have vanished until I'd left Eliza's house and come here was a little too convenient.

Alex sighed and connected with me, *Not to mention, Eilam didn't have complete control over Annie. Maybe Eliza does have some sort of magic.*

Ugh, he was right, but that thought stung. One thing Eliza cherished most was open and honest communication. How could she have pride in that if she hadn't been completely honest with Annie and me?

Not wanting to think about the potential fallout, I changed the topic. "How many demons live on Earth?" Maybe someone could teach me about my shadow and how to use it. "And what is a demon?" The demons I'd seen in movies never materialized.

"I'm not sure, but it can't be too many for the sake of balance." Rosemary closed her eyes. "And demons are truly fallen angels."

"Why aren't there any in Shadow City?" Out of all the supernatural races, that one just so happened not to be there? That probably meant someone or something didn't want them there.

Rosemary's shoulders sagged. "It's not common knowledge, but that was one of the main reasons the city's borders were closed almost one thousand years ago. The angels made a deal with the fallen."

"No." Griffin's brows furrowed. "It was because of the civil war that started with the angels taking control of the city and making it what they wanted it to be. Shadow City was meant to be a haven for all supernaturals, but when the angels came to Earth and learned about the city, they stepped in and changed its intended purpose. They got away with it because they were stronger than all of us. The city went from being created as a place of safety to a place where only the strongest people from every race could live." He grimaced. "The families invited to live there were flattered, and most moved there, but they didn't realize the angels planned on ruling over everyone. The city was built with angelic materials, and it was so gorgeous that no one wanted to leave. When the silver wolves were created and named as the protectors of the city, they united the races and took down the angels."

"That's partly true." Rosemary lifted a hand. "Yes, there was a civil war, and the silver wolves were the leaders, but demons also wanted to live in such a grand place, too. Angels don't respect demons because they gave up their souls and humanity and the desire to do good. Demons hate angels because we remind them of what they used to be. Living together would have resulted in disastrous wars. The angels in charge at the time wanted a safe place to live like kings, so they made an agreement with the demons. The demons could have the rest of Earth if they left this area alone. The angels closed the gates, and that's one reason angels aren't happy about the city opening up again."

"But people have the right to be free and live where they want," Sterlyn said with conviction.

Rosemary shrugged. "Many angels fear it. That's why very few leave Shadow City."

All this convoluted history, and not one person knew it all.

Sierra sat upright, on high alert. "Does that mean Ronnie will develop wings? That would really make you stand out on your wedding day."

Yeah, that wasn't the look I was going for at all. "I was more interested in learning about my potential abilities and training to use them."

"Training." Sierra raised both hands, pretending they were balance scales. "Wedding. Equally important."

"When an angel truly falls, they lose their wings." Rosemary gestured to her back. "They turn into a shadow-like creature that can suspend in the air and not be seen, like you did and like your dagger does. No one in Shadow City can help you with your abilities. I'm sorry, but your vampire side is descended from the Princes of Hell. Vampires aren't as strong, since they were human before they changed, but you weren't completely human, since one of your parents was a demon. So as a complete supernatural, you're not as strong as a demon but stronger than a vampire. Demons fathered the vampires, wanting to make sure their terror on Earth could always be felt."

That was why vampires were so susceptible to temptation—they didn't have an angel side to keep their minds centered. Demons gave up the center, wanting to terrorize the world, which was what the vampires struggled with. At least, I wouldn't be a threat to Eliza and Annie.

Griffin stiffened, pulled out his phone, and read the text message. "Dammit."

"What's wrong?" Sterlyn asked with concern. "Did something happen?"

"Kira just texted me," Griffin growled. "And she could cause us some serious trouble."

CHAPTER EIGHTEEN

THE LAST THING we needed was Kira causing problems, but because she was a shifter, the issue ultimately fell on Sterlyn and Griffin to resolve, so I couldn't say much. I wanted to be selfish and focus on what being part demon meant and how that was even possible, but every single person in this house had been there for me when I'd needed help. I couldn't act like a child, even though I was having an identity crisis and feeling betrayed by Eliza.

One thing about my foster mom I knew, without a doubt, was that she was a good person and did everything for the right reason. Sometimes, it irritated me, but I admired that about her. She'd taught me what was right and wrong when I was almost too old to learn the difference.

"Who is Kira?" Killian's jaw clenched as unease flitted through him.

Sierra scoffed. "Right? We need to figure out a way

we can go into the city with them, so we aren't left out of so many things."

"Don't be too eager." The words tumbled from my lips. "I was trapped in there, and let's just say it's much better out here." The long days the council members were deliberating the divine, their doctrine that they viewed as their constitution, trying to figure out if they could force me to turn or not because the vampires in the city didn't know how to control their urges around me, truly wore on me.

Unhappiness floated into me from Alex as he connected, *It's sad because I grew up in the city, but that is so true. After being out here and finding you, I'd never want to raise our children there.*

My heart skipped a beat at the thought of us having children. *Can I even have children? And Shadow Terrace isn't much safer.* In some ways, Shadow Terrace was turning more ruthless than the city we'd left behind.

You're a vampire now, and though you may not age, your body isn't frozen. Alex ran his fingertips along my shoulder. *Whether you're turned or born, you can have children as long as your humanity stays intact.*

Interesting. *Vampires who lose their humanity can't?*

All magic has a balance, and that is one of them.

"Kira is a fox shifter who's taking over her father's role because Griffin and I supported her." Sterlyn twirled a piece of silver hair around her finger. "She told Alex who might be part of the rogue vampires on Shadow Terrace's side."

"She's sneaky as hell and has a knack for overhearing

things." Rosemary arched her brow. "But she can cause trouble. Let me guess, she left Shadow City, not even a couple hours after you gave her access?"

"Yeah." Griffin frowned. "She said she needs our help."

Alex's face was lined with confusion. "What the hell is she doing? You guys have already stuck your neck out for her."

"She said your brother is about to leave Shadow Terrace." Griffin tossed his phone onto the armrest. "Apparently, she heard him and Azbogah chatting. The vampire king is heading to Atlanta to find someone there. Azbogah refuses to leave the city, so Matthew is going alone. Kira wants to follow him but needs transportation."

My stomach dropped. "How often does your brother leave this area?" During the month I'd been here, Matthew had stayed mainly at their homes in Shadow City and Shadow Terrace. He rarely came to Shadow Ridge, unless he had business to take care of, like threatening me and Alex.

"He's only left this area a handful of times when we were first allowed out of Shadow City. He hasn't gone anywhere in over forty-five years." Alex's body coiled as if he was prepared to fight. "Something's not right."

"Let's go pick her up." Sierra stood and gestured to the door. "We need to get out there before we lose him."

"We'll have to pick her up at the gate since she doesn't have a car, so it's best if you stay here. Azbogah and Matthew will have people watching us, so none of our core group should go with her. It would raise questions and might force them to do something hasty. But she shouldn't go alone." Sterlyn rubbed her hands down her pant legs. "I'll link with Cyrus and see if he and a few silver wolves can go with her. Matthew hasn't met them in human form and won't know what they look like."

I'd heard her talk about her twin brother a few times, but I'd never met him. She'd grown up not knowing he existed. A witch had attended the birth of the silver wolf alpha heirs and spelled Sterlyn's brother, stopping his heart long enough for the family to believe he was dead, before whisking him far enough away that their pack bond and his and Sterlyn's twin bond couldn't develop. He was raised by bad people who had intended to use him, thinking he was the next rightful alpha heir of the silver wolves because he was male. Long story short, Sterlyn was the rightful heir, and because they'd taken her brother away, he was never able to shift and find his family. When they finally met, things had been tense, but he was changing and stepping up as the beta and commanding alpha while Sterlyn claimed her place on the Shadow City council.

"Can they get here in time to follow Matthew? If he's on a mission, he won't be hanging around long." Rosemary headed toward the kitchen, her wings exploding from her back as she walked.

"Yeah, I've linked with them. Cyrus and Darrell are driving over now." Sterlyn stood and rubbed her hands together. "They should be on the outskirts of Shadow Ridge in ten minutes, but we need to get Kira and take her there. It would be weird if we didn't meet up with her, since we're the ones who gave her permission to leave Shadow City."

"I'm going back to Shadow City to see if my parents know what Matthew and Azbogah are up to." Rosemary stepped outside and slammed the door shut. Her black wings flashed past the window as she flew away.

"Sterlyn, let's go get Kira." Griffin removed his keys from his pocket and grabbed his phone. "We should introduce her to Cyrus and Darrell. We'll be back shortly, guys. Just keep the place in one piece."

Sierra pouted. "Where's the fun in that?"

"Are you sure you don't need my help?" Killian asked.

Sterlyn smiled. "Yes, we're sure. Just keep an eye on everything here. Something is going on, and we can't let our guard down."

She wasn't lying. The group was charged with tension.

Once they left, the house filled with silence. No one knew what to say.

I'm going to call Gwen and fill her in. Alex unraveled himself from me and walked around the loveseat to the room we stayed in here.

What do you mean? Gwen had seemed to be on our side.

Alex lifted the phone to his ear as he entered the bedroom. *She might have overheard something without realizing what's going on.*

If Azbogah and Matthew were trying to pull something, I had a sinking suspicion it might involve me. I wasn't usually narcissistic, but I felt like my existence had bonded those two idiots together.

Sierra plopped down beside me, taking Alex's spot, and batted her eyes. "When's the big day?"

"The big day?" Killian squinted. "What are you talking about?"

"Oh, my God." Sierra exhaled nosily. "I swear, for him to be so handsome and smart, he can be really dense."

Her words piqued my interest. "Handsome and smart?" Their relationship had always seemed more like brother and sister, but maybe something was going on between them.

"Yeah, in a brotherly way." Sierra placed a hand on her chest. "Olive was like my sister, which makes Killian my brother. So ... ew. Don't think like that."

Sadness darkened Killian's eyes at the mention of his late sister, and he remained speechless. He appeared broken.

Sierra cleared her throat and clapped her hands. "Wedding! When is this shindig?"

"Uh ..." Alex and I hadn't talked about it. "We just got engaged this morning."

"And the planning commences immediately." Sierra grabbed my hand again and gazed longingly at the ring. "The beginning of August is the perfect time of year."

"Oh." A summer wedding. I liked the sound of that. "We'd have a little over a year to plan that." We'd probably need the time with all the drama constantly swirling around us.

"Girl." Sierra laughed and bumped her shoulder with mine. "You're funny. But yeah, we can totally pull this off in two weeks."

"Two *weeks*?" She was insane. "I'm not pregnant. No need for a shotgun wedding."

Killian ran a hand through his hair. "Thank God."

"Shut it." Sierra stuck her tongue out at him. Then her laser vision landed on me. "This is the supernatural world, and Alex is a prince. The sooner you two get married, the more secure and respected your relationship will be."

My heart picked up speed. So much had changed, and even though what she'd said made sense, I was surprised at the timeline. "But is planning something that fast possible?"

"Girl, yeah." Sierra smacked my arm. "Alex *is royalty.* Anything is possible."

Annoyance flashed along the connection between Alex and me. I connected with him, *What's wrong?*

Matthew hasn't told Gwen anything specific, nor has she overheard anything, but he informed her ten minutes ago that he's leaving Shadow City for a few days for business, and he wants her to stay in the city to keep an eye on things.

He made it sound like he was heading to Shadow Terrace?

That's what he implied, but I won't know for sure

unless I look for him myself. But Gwen is excited that he asked her to handle things in his absence.

His sister rarely seemed happy, so hearing that bit of news made me smile. *That's good?*

Not really. Alex opened the bedroom door and stepped into the hallway. *He usually asks me to watch over things. This is the first time he's ever asked her.*

The insinuation was clear, along with the hurt that floated from him. *It could be because you're in Shadow Ridge.*

We both know that's not why. He rejoined us in the living room and stopped in front of Sierra.

She blinked and smiled. "Yes?"

"Move." He pointed to the bigger couch then crossed his arms. "You're in my spot."

"You're the one who got up." She tilted her head to the side, almost like a dare.

In a blur, his arms slid around my waist, and he hoisted me against his body. He pulled me onto his lap on the bulky couch and kissed me deeply. My body warmed.

"Fine," she growled. "You've made your point."

Alex ignored her, kissing me until my head spun. My fingers threaded into his hair, pressing his mouth more firmly to mine. Since becoming a vampire, or whatever I was, my emotions and senses were so heightened that it was easy to get caught up in the moment.

"All right." Sierra huffed. "I'm sorry I took your spot. I was just talking to her about the wedding."

Warmth exploded between us as Alex pulled away, smiling. "Really?"

"Yes." I tried to clear my head from the hormones and focus on the topic at hand. *We're continuing that in a few minutes after we've humored her.*

His eyes twinkled. *I'm all for that.*

Then why wait? I teased ... sort of. The thought of him naked made me flame even hotter.

"Okay, I'm gonna get some cold water if you two don't take it down a notch," Killian rasped. "Sterlyn and Griffin were never this bad."

"Oh, yeah, right." Sierra snorted. "They were, too. I swear, finding your mate must be a lifetime pass to hornyville."

"Hornyville?" Killian sounded disgusted. "How old are you?"

"Hey, I'm working with my audience here," Sierra shot back. "I'm only as good as the stuff they give me."

Can't they just shut up? Alex growled, but the damage had been done because he pulled away, instead of continuing to kiss me.

In other words, Killian and Sierra had won. They'd annoyed Alex into retreating.

Wanting to change the topic, I jumped back into the one I knew Sierra would have no issue with. "She wants us to get married in two weeks."

Alex's soft blue eyes lightened to crystal blue. "That sounds perfect."

I hadn't expected that. "What? Are you serious? That's not enough time!"

"It's plenty." Alex laughed. "We can get married wherever you want, and our people will be more than willing to help us prepare for it. But there is one thing we have to do before we officially begin planning."

"Uh ... no." Sierra shook her head and pointed at the ring. "You did the one thing you have to do before planning."

"No." Alex groaned. "We need to visit Eliza and Annie so I can do this right."

"Do what right?" I was still lost. I understood if he wanted to find out what Eliza was, but I wasn't sure what that had to do with our future.

"They're your family," Alex murmured and cupped my cheek. "I need to ask for their blessing. We can't officially begin planning something until then."

My heart grew larger. This man wanted to do things the proper way for me, and I never in a million years would've thought that it would thrill me. But he knew how important they were in my life; he wanted to include them. *I love you.*

I love you, too. He kissed me sweetly. *I really would like to get married sooner rather than later, so do you want to call Eliza and see when we can visit?*

The thought of calling her after our last conversation turned my stomach, but he was right. Not only did I love Annie and Eliza and want them to be part of our special day, but I also needed to find out whether Eliza had done something to me. If she'd protected me, maybe she knew about my heritage.

When I didn't respond, Alex's irises darkened, and disappointment flashed between us before he could hide it.

I was being a coward and hurting the man who had given up so much for me. I nodded and stood up. "Let me make that call so we can get the planning underway."

"Hell yeah." Sierra fisted her hands in the air. "That's what I'm talking about."

"Do you mind if I borrow your phone?" I held out my hand to Alex. "Mine got blown up in your car."

"Oh, yeah." He placed it in my hand, but concern was etched on his face. "There you go. Do you want me to be with you when you speak to her?"

I wasn't nearly as good at controlling my emotions as him, but this was something I needed to do alone. I had a feeling I wouldn't want him to overhear the conversation. "No, I'm good. I'll let you know if I need you."

Before I could have second thoughts, I hurried into the bedroom and dialed the number. As the phone rang, I closed my eyes in silent prayer that she wouldn't answer.

But on the first ring, Eliza's strong voice filled the line. "Hello? Who is this?"

CHAPTER NINETEEN

I INHALED, taking a second to work up the nerve to talk to her. I felt fifteen again.

"Who is this?" Eliza's voice turned hard in a way I hadn't heard before. "Answer me."

"It's me," I said, nearly stumbling over my words. "It's Ronnie. I lost my phone."

"Ronnie?" Eliza sighed, her voice returning to normal. "You scared the living poop out of me. Do you know how worried Annie and I are about you?"

I laughed, not able to bite my cheek in time. She refused to curse around Annie and me, even to this day, and I found it hilarious to hear her fudge her words as if we were still children. "I'm sorry. We talked yesterday, and I sent Annie a text."

"But so much has changed," she said so softly I was sure she hadn't meant for me to hear her.

She knew something, which alarmed me. I wanted to demand answers, but it didn't feel right. This was a conversation meant to be had in person. I needed to look into her eyes when we had it. I wanted to see her reaction. It would tell me so much more than just getting the answers I desperately wanted over the phone.

She cleared her throat. "Are you doing okay?"

That was a loaded question, but I respected her too much to lie. "You know what, I am."

"You sure?" She clicked her tongue. "You've never been away from home this long before. Maybe it's time you came back and left all that nonsense behind."

"That's why I'm calling." I chose to ignore the second half of her statement so we wouldn't get into an argument. She and Annie argued like mother and daughter often, probably because Annie hadn't known any other parental figures besides Eliza.

But not me.

I respected the sacrifices she'd made, and I did everything in my power to reciprocate. This was the first time I'd ever gone against her wishes, and even then, I was trying to keep my mouth in check.

"You're coming home?" So much hope filled her voice it was heartbreaking.

Okay, maybe I should've phrased it differently. "No, not exactly."

"Then what are you saying?" Disappointment laced her words, cutting me.

But she was the one who'd been pushing me since my high school graduation two years ago to figure out my future, not hers or Annie's, telling me I was sacrificing too much of myself for them, and I needed to find balance so I could stay happy.

Now I wondered if she'd meant health-wise or supernatural-wise.

"I told you I met someone." I had to keep reminding myself that I wasn't doing anything wrong. I was becoming who I was meant to be. "And I want to bring him home."

"What?" she gasped. "You want to bring him here?"

"Why? Is that a problem? I thought you wanted me to so you could meet him."

"Oh, I do," she said quickly and paused. "I just ... I didn't expect ..."

"That's fine." Some hurt broke through my words. She was acting odd, and I wasn't sure how to proceed. Maybe things had changed between us after all. "We don't have to come. I just thought it'd be nice—"

"Oh, baby girl." Her words cut off. "Of course, you can bring him home. I just never expected this ... so soon. But this is your home, and you will always be welcome here."

A fractured piece of my heart mended back into place. That was the Eliza I'd always known. "I don't want to make anyone uncomfortable."

"I'm being difficult." She huffed. "Even though I found you when you were older, you were still a little girl in so many ways. And suddenly, you seem so different, so mature, and it caught me by surprise. Sometimes, fate has a way of making things work out. I just wasn't prepared for it."

She wasn't kidding. Destiny had determined a long time ago—over three hundred years, to be exact—that Alex and I would be together one day. Well, I assumed because he was created with only half a soul that fate knew when to bring me along.

Since Annie had gone back to Lexington after the hell she'd been through, I still hadn't talked to her, though we'd shot texts back and forth. From the sounds of it, she'd thrown herself into her work and was barely home. Every time I called, her phone went straight to voicemail, and I got a simple text back. "How's Annie?"

"Struggling." Eliza must have moved because I heard the phone brush against her skin. "She hasn't been the same since coming back."

My throat tightened. "Has she said anything?"

"No. And in appearance, she's the same ol' Annie, but there's something different inside her. Maybe when you come home, we can have a family discussion."

"Okay." There was no point in putting off going home any longer. Things with Alex and me were settled, and I wasn't a risk to Eliza and Annie. Plus, Alex might be able to help Annie, since he was the one who'd erased and adjusted her memories after Eilam had brainwashed her. Maybe fate was once again weaving its influencing hand. "It's been a long day, so we'll head up tomorrow. Annie mentioned that she's off tomorrow. Monday. Right?"

"Yeah, Mondays are her days off. She was at the home all weekend with a troubled kid, so tomorrow sounds perfect," Eliza replied. "All right. Call me if you need me before then." The line clicked dead.

Her flustering habit had a grin breaking across my face. I sat on the queen-sized bed centered against the far wall and ran my hand over the smooth charcoal comforter. Lying back on two stacked white fluffy pillows, I turned my head toward the gigantic walk-in closet that held some of my clothes.

A soft knock on the door and the *yank*ing inside informed me who was on the other side.

Come on in, I connected with Alex. Despite being a strong supernatural, I was exhausted. At some point, things had to calm down. Surely.

The door opened, and Alex entered, and his syrupy smell filled the room. He shut the door and locked it as I took in a deep breath and held it in my lungs until they burned. His scent was my very favorite in the world.

He walked around the bed, passing by the mounted television, and crawled up next to me. "How'd it go?"

I inched over to him, and he wrapped his arms around my body, holding me tight.

"I hope you don't mind, but I told her we'd go visit them tomorrow." When he didn't respond, I tensed. "I thought you wanted ..." I trailed off as my face turned hot. "... to ask—"

"Of course, I do." He placed his fingers under my chin, tilting my head upward so I stared into his eyes. A breathtaking smile crossed his face, and my body warmed. "You surprised me."

"What do you mean?" I asked breathlessly, staring at

his full lips and sculpted face. He was the definition of handsome and my perfect other half.

He lowered his head and kissed my cheek, his sweet breath skimming my face. "Considering how you were reacting in the living room before you took the call, I thought you might put off going back there for a while, so to hear we're going tomorrow ... well, let's just say that makes me very ..." He kissed my lips. "very..." He brushed his mouth against mine, and I moaned. "... happy."

My head grew fuzzy as the *yank*ing of our physical connection urged us together. I pressed my lips to his, deepening the kiss, not wanting any more teasing. His hands clutched my sides, and I rolled onto my back. He scooted next to me, leaning on one arm as his free hand slipped under my shirt.

Every time he touched me was better than the last. The buzzing of his skin against mine added fuel to the growing inferno inside. His taste, touch, and smell were an overwhelmingly sexy combination.

I stroked his tongue with mine and unfastened his jeans, slipping my hands inside his boxers. As I touched him, his fingers teased my nipples, making me move faster.

Veronica, he connected, reminding me of a song, driving my urges more.

When I'd been human, I'd wanted him desperately, but our connection was so much stronger now that we were both full supernaturals. I had no clue where I began, and he ended. The fact should have scared me, but it did the complete opposite.

He pulled his mouth from mine and kissed his way down my neck toward my breasts. He unbuttoned my suit jacket and lifted me enough to remove it, followed by my tank top and bra. He looked adoringly at me before lowering his head and drawing one of my nipples into his mouth.

My body bucked underneath him, the pleasure growing so intense. "Oh, Alex."

He groaned as his fingers worked the zipper of my skirt, and before I even realized what he'd done, I was naked on the bed.

"God, you're beautiful," he whispered as his fingers slipped between my legs and stroked me.

I grabbed his hand, not wanting to climax without him. The pleasure was so damn intense, and I wanted to experience it with him.

"Get naked," I commanded and yanked both sides of his button-up shirt, ripping it apart. The buttons exploded everywhere, adding to the sexual tension in the room.

He removed his jacket and ruined shirt then lifted his hips and pulled the pants from his body. He was ready for me, and I took a moment to take all of him in.

Climbing between my legs, he cupped my cheek. *I love you.*

I love you, too, I replied as he slipped inside me.

We moved slowly at first, our lips meeting and

moving in rhythm with our bodies. Each touch felt like a promise, and he took his time worshipping my body.

We began moving faster, relishing the pleasure cascading between us as our connection opened, pushing us closer. My back arched, my body begging for an increased pace, and he responded.

I tore my mouth from his and kissed my way down his neck until I felt his heartbeat against my lips. My teeth extended, and I nibbled.

"That feels good," he groaned and followed my lead.

When his teeth sank into me, the connection intensified. The most intense orgasm of my entire life ripped through my body, and he thrust inside me hard. His body quivered with his own release as we rode out the pleasure together.

I didn't know how long it lasted, but when we collapsed, I was covered in sweat. I licked my lips, tasting a bit of his blood, making the moment even better.

"That was amazing," he whispered and tucked me back in beside him.

Before I could process what had happened, I slipped blissfully into a peaceful rest.

I woke up alone in bed with a blanket over me. I blinked and reached for Alex but came up empty-handed. *Where are you?*

Sterlyn and Griffin got back a few minutes ago, he connected.

Everything flooded back to me. They'd taken Kira to meet up with Sterlyn's brother and another silver wolf pack member. Crap, something must have happened.

For a moment, I'd forgotten about the craziness that had become our life. *Why didn't you wake me up?*

Because you were resting so beautifully.

Yeah, that didn't make me happy with him. I jumped out of bed and dressed quickly. *Not a good excuse.*

I marched out of the room and joined them in the living room. Sterlyn, Sierra, and Griffin sat on the couch with Killian on the love seat. Alex was leaning against the wall beside the television, his face grim.

Obviously, I'd missed something. "What's up?" I glanced outside, noting the rising moon.

How long had I been napping?

"If you hadn't done such *strenuous* exercise," Sierra started and waggled her eyebrows, "then you'd be up to date."

I stopped in my tracks and covered my face with my hands. I couldn't believe she'd said that. Alex and I hadn't been quiet.

"We said we wouldn't speak of it," Killian growled, not enthused with our friend. "Next time, I'll make sure you can't bring it up."

"Oh, stop." Sierra laughed. "They just got engaged. Of course, they're going to get it on. Look at her. If I were him—"

"For the love of the gods," Alex hissed. "Do not talk about her that way. She is my mate."

"Whoa." Sierra held up a hand. "Someone is a tad sensitive."

"Okay," Sterlyn said sternly and pushed Sierra's hands into her lap. "We get the point." The corner of her lips ticked upward, but she hid the smile that wanted to spread across them. "We were just telling the others that Kira is with Cyrus and Darrell. We have another pack member stationed in the woods a mile away from the road that Matthew will be taking to head to Atlanta. When the wolf hears the Porsche, our group will be ready to follow him."

I must have misunderstood her. "You think he'll take his Porsche?"

She rubbed her bottom lip. "If he doesn't follow his normal routine, it'll raise questions, so he'll likely take his Porsche for the first stretch then maybe switch cars. But I doubt it. He's pretty arrogant."

When she put it that way, I could see her reasoning. If he took anything less flashy, people would notice. He and Azbogah had a plan. "What do we do now?"

"We wait for Matthew to make his move." Griffin sighed. "We know he's heading to Atlanta. We just don't know why."

Alex's phone dinged. He pulled it from his pocket, and his face tensed. The amount of unease wafting from him was overbearing. "Matthew must be on the move since he just created a distraction."

"Why do you say that?" I asked.

"Joshua just texted me. He's being attacked." Alex fisted his hand. "He needs our help."

CHAPTER TWENTY

THE WORDS SETTLED OVER ME, eliminating the last bit of peace from my nap. We had to do something … anything. Joshua had helped us; we had to return the favor.

As I snatched my car keys from the end table, Alex grabbed my arm and pulled me toward him.

Frustration rooted inside me, and I yanked my arm away. "We have to help him." I spun around, ready to leave.

He stopped me again and held up his hands. "I know. But all it should take is me or Matthew showing up and telling the vampires to stop."

Shit, he was right. I was ready to run headlong into a situation I knew little about like I had with Annie, and we'd seen how well that had gone. "But how do we *know* that will work?"

"Because I'm the vampire prince, and from what

Joshua said, only vampires are attacking." Alex smiled cockily. "They have to listen to me."

Sterlyn coughed. "Not to be an ass, but if it's rogue vampires, they might not. There's no way to know that you can stop them. You need backup." She stood and walked to the window, staring at the moon. It was half full, and her olive skin glowed faintly, but not like it did on a full moon or what the silver wolves called a silver moon.

"You don't have to come with me," Alex said gently. "I don't want to cause you and Griffin any more problems."

"Of course, we do." Griffin climbed to his feet and squared his shoulders. "We're family, and we fight for each other. Joshua protected Ronnie, and that means we owe him. We'll need your support with the council if shit gets real and we have to get involved."

Alex emitted gratitude and guilt. "Okay. You have it. But it shouldn't come to that."

Despite his insistence, doubt wafted through our bond. He was completely unconvinced.

"What's the plan?" Sierra rubbed her hands together. "We go in all wolf-like and rip out some throats?"

Killian groaned. "Says the girl with the least amount of combat training out of everyone here."

"Not true." Her gray eyes sparkled. "Ronnie is here now."

I wanted to smack her. Alex was already protective of me; I didn't need her to remind him that I didn't have any battle skills.

As expected, Alex jumped at the opportunity. "Maybe you two should stay here. Like I said—"

"Nope." I shook my head. I didn't care if all it took to save Joshua was the vampires seeing him—I wouldn't be left behind. "Remember what happened last time we were apart? Klyn attacked me here."

Alex's irises turned navy. "That bastard. If I could bring him back to life and kill him again, I would."

"But she's right," Killian said. "This could be a diversion so someone can attack her."

A low hiss emanated from Alex's chest. "I'd kill my brother if he tried that. I don't care if he is my king."

Okay, I hadn't meant for him to go super dark, and though I believed each word he vowed, I hoped he never had to make that decision. "Do we know where Joshua is? We need to get there before the vampires hurt him or worse."

"She's right." Sterlyn gestured to the door. "We need to move. We can shift into our wolves and follow you in your car. I'll link with the silver wolves to be on standby in case we need more backup. We don't want to risk people seeing Griffin and Killian's pack mobilizing if Matthew is behind this. We'll meet you at the woods in front of the bridge to Shadow Terrace."

The bridge was the border between Shadow Ridge and Shadow Terrace. No wolf was supposed to travel beyond the bridge into the vampire town, but this wouldn't be the first time Griffin and the others had gone beyond the border.

"Fine." Alex typed something on his phone and

headed to the door. "They're attacking his house. It's on the edge of the city anyway, so that works out. Hopefully, all it will take is me getting there and informing everyone that Joshua is under my protection. But let me drive, please." He held out his hand for my keys.

I didn't want to ruin his hope, but I seriously doubted it would be that easy.

We were stuck taking my small Mazda 3 since his Lexus had exploded, but it didn't matter as long as we got there. Within seconds, Alex and I were in the Mazda, and he turned on the ignition.

My blood ran cool as if the shadow inside me were warning me, which seemed impossible. My shadow couldn't know something without us being at Joshua's, but a sense of danger buzzed under my skin.

Everything is going to be okay. Alex took my hand and squeezed it lovingly, sensing the emotions swirling inside me.

The tires squealed as he backed out of the driveway and turned the wheel hard then hurtled toward the neighborhood exit. He was as anxious as I was.

I glanced in the mirror and saw a flash of silver fur in the woods. The wolves were already shifted and heading to meet us.

After a few minutes, I asked, "Do you think it's the same people who tried to kill me?" I had a feeling that was why Alex was so on edge.

"I don't know," Alex hissed. "But if it is, I'll handle it. That's why I hoped you would stay at Sterlyn's, but you're right. This could be a ploy to lure me away and strike while I was preoccupied."

Yeah, whoever was attacking Joshua didn't care where I was. They had a plan either way. "I hate that this keeps happening. I don't understand why your brother hates me so much."

"He doesn't hate you." Alex sighed, his eyes tightening. "He hates that I found my soulmate. It puts more pressure on him, and he resents the fact that you were human. This has nothing to do with you but rather his own issues that he needs to deal with."

"How does us finding each other put pressure on him?" There was still so much of the supernatural and royal world I didn't understand.

Alex glanced in the rearview mirror, searching for Sterlyn and the others. "Because we're soulmates, many vampires will see us as a stronger unit than Matthew."

"Then why doesn't he just find someone?" I didn't realize that our bond would put Matthew's leadership and power into question.

Alex turned left onto the road that led to Shadow Terrace and pressed the gas. "If he commits to anyone less than his soulmate, the union won't be as strong."

"That's stupid." Just because we'd found each other didn't mean Matthew was any less capable. "It's not his fault."

Alex frowned. "That's how things work and why vampire royals tend to hold out for their soulmates. Your soulmate is supposed to make you a whole person and a better leader. If you don't find your perfect half, you're weaker than someone who has found theirs."

The reasoning discouraged me. Unless we could find Matthew's soulmate, the drama between us would never end. "Even if I'd been vampire born, it wouldn't matter?"

"No." Alex slowed as the bridge appeared in front of us. "Calling you out for being human is just a way to diminish your importance—which it might, to some ancient vampires—but everyone knows it doesn't matter. Fate blessed us, and no supernatural creature can deny that. No matter how badly they want to."

The warning tingled down my spine. Matthew more than hated me; he loathed me, and he would do anything to stay in power.

We stopped several feet from the bridge, and I glanced at the WELCOME TO SHADOW TERRACE sign mocking us. Owls hooted in the distance as a warm summer breeze blew through the cypress and red cedar trees. Raccoons scurried in search of food, while flying squirrels leaped from branch to branch.

On any other night, the sounds would have been peaceful, but tonight, the peacefulness seemed eerie, given that an attack was happening not far from here.

My blood warmed as we crossed the bridge, and I glanced across the road to find glowing lavender eyes peeking out from behind a branch. I squinted and saw sandy-blond fur on one side of Sterlyn and honey-brown fur on the other. The next tree over revealed dark, rich chocolate eyes staring right at me. All four wolves were here.

I nodded my head in their direction. "We're ready to go."

Not hesitating, Alex pressed the gas and took off through the woods that signaled we were on the vampire side. The drive to Shadow Terrace took forever. My heart pounded as my anxiety heightened.

I glanced to my left to make sure the wolves were keeping pace with us. They were and still keeping mostly out of sight.

We drove past the place where Zaro had made me stop and taken me into the underground tunnel.

About a mile past the sign, the trees thinned, and the cute town that hid so much evil appeared before me. The Tennessee River ran behind it, giving it a picturesque feel that lured people to visit. Now I understood why they'd made the town appear so appealing, painting the buildings white and the rooftops red. In the center of town was a gray stone building with a dome on top. It stood out from the other buildings and had a different architectural style. I realized the design had been on purpose, a way to draw tourists to the center of town and into the bar where vampires liked to feed directly from humans.

Alex turned onto the cobblestone road that led through town. We didn't get very far before we took another left and headed to the outskirts of the Terrace. The buildings grew farther apart and jetted away from the river where the woods abutted a section of houses. The two-story house at the end of the road with its roof nearly caved in was surrounded by at least twenty vampires, all covered in dark clothing from head to toe.

The house had no front yard, its entrance letting out right onto the street, but there was grass on both sides.

Two vampires were banging on the door as twelve others circled the place with swords. The remaining six were running torches along the base of the house to burn it down.

"Get out here, Joshua!" one vampire yelled as he banged on the door. "You're running out of time, and we're about to kill you the hard way."

Alex stopped the car and unlocked his door. "Stay here." He jumped out before I could say anything.

I wanted to protest and get out of the car, but I stayed put. I'd give him a chance to resolve this on his own, but if something went wrong, my ass would be standing beside him. At least, I could hear everything from here.

"What are you doing?" Alex demanded as he approached the group.

The one that had been banging on the door turned. His skin was the color of the moon, so ghastly pale he appeared dead. His eyes were solid black with no whites around the irises. He sneered at Alex with thin, cruel lips and rasped, "We're taking care of a problem." Though I hadn't been part of this world for long, not even Eilam had looked as menacing as this guy. He must have lost every ounce of his humanity.

"What problem is that?" Alex laughed, but his alarm flowed into me through our connection. "I haven't heard of an issue that would merit such a display, especially when we have *guests* in our town."

Guests, meaning humans. The purpose of the town was to have tourists stay and donate blood before leaving, but the rogue vampires were getting ballsy. They didn't give a damn if they gave humans a show; they'd just erase their memories. They were spiraling out of control with their blatant disregard for humans.

"A meddling turned-vampire got involved in something he should've stayed out of." The man didn't even pretend to be nervous. "Why don't you leave and let us handle things as we see fit."

"I would, Godfrey, but I'm the prince." Alex clenched his hands. "And you all need to stand down. Blade normally tells us when someone has done something wrong, and I haven't heard a word. Until I can talk with him, this is over."

"We have his permission." The man gestured to the tallest figure, who tossed a torch at the front door of the house. "And you aren't our prince."

Flames licked at the wood door, crackling with fire. Considering how quickly the flames shot up, the vampires must have doused the house with fuel. An orange flame reached skyward as the vampire who'd dropped the torch stumbled back. His hood fell off, revealing short ash-blond hair, but despite the man's grimace, he stared Alex in the eye. The man's skin was just about as pale as Godfrey's, and there was a slightly gray color where the whites around his irises had been.

In other words, he was almost as evil.

Who is that? I asked, but I knew before he answered.

Alex's shoulders sagged. *Blade.*

"Capture the prince, and kill the girl," Blade yelled as the fire overtook the house.

CHAPTER TWENTY-ONE

CHAOS EXPLODED as the twelve vampires with swords descended on Alex. The six with torches continued to set fire to the house while the other two watched the windows, anticipating Joshua to leap from above.

Alex spun around and raced for the car, but the vampire closest to him swung his sword.

Watch out, I connected desperately. I threw open the door, needing to get to him.

He ducked, and the sword sailed over his head. The sound of the sword slicing through the air turned my stomach. Had it hit its mark, Alex would be dead.

I thought Blade had said to capture him, but they didn't mind killing him. Did that mean they didn't fear Matthew's retribution?

My stomach soured even more.

A loud howl broke out from behind the tree line, and the vampires with swords stilled.

"Of course, they brought their pets," Blade hissed, face twisting in disgust. "Go attend to them. Show them no mercy. They're trespassing."

Seven of the sword-armed vampires blurred as they charged our friends, leaving five behind with the two leaders and the six with torches.

Stay in the car, Alex connected as if I would obey him.

I jumped out of the car just as three vampires reached me. One in a ski mask held back while two wearing dark hoodies attacked me. The thinner of the two was a woman, her narrow face set in determination as she lifted her sword overhead, ready to swing the blade through my neck.

Never having fought before, I had no clue what to do, so I opened myself up to my supernatural side. I hoped the shadow would take control like it had those few times I'd been in grave danger.

A girl could only pray.

My blood cooled as the air around me bent, like when the car had exploded. The cold glint of metal barreled closer to me, and I twisted away as something appeared in my palm. I clutched the dagger, and I lifted my arm, clashing my blade against her sword.

"What?" the girl gasped and blinked at my weapon. "But you didn't have a weapon. How is that possible?"

Yeah, I wasn't giving away my secrets. I kicked her in the stomach, and she flew back several feet.

The man hissed, allowing his fangs to spring from his mouth as he blurred. He jumped, extending his arms to wrap them around my body. He moved nearly as fast as Alex, but with my new senses, he might as well have been moving at normal speed.

He opened his mouth wide to bite me. I held the dagger tight in my hand and struck, aiming the blade at his neck. It cut through his body like butter, severing his head in one swoop.

Warm blood splattered my clothes and trickled down the handle over my hand. I lowered my arm and wiped the blood on my jeans, ensuring I retained a good grip on the weapon. This was the second time the dagger had come in handy. I wasn't sure I would've survived the girl's attack otherwise.

"No!" the girl screamed in rage and pain. "You bitch!"

She sounded heartbroken. Maybe they had been romantically involved.

With a low growl, the girl charged me, her face contorted in intense pain. Her ebony eyes locked on me as she swung her sword at my side.

Time paused for a split second as I watched Alex pivot around another vampire to get to me. His attention was on me and not on his surroundings. A vampire lunged at Alex's back. He wrapped his arms around Alex's waist, shoving him forward and onto the ground.

Alex! I'm coming. Devastation racked me. He wasn't paying attention to his own battle because he was trying to help me.

No, Alex connected. *Focus on your own fight. I'll get to you in a second.*

I'm fine, I assured him. *The dagger came to me, and my shadow is helping me. Please concentrate on yourself, and don't get hurt.*

The vampire girl swung her sword like a softball bat. Coolness filled my body, and my arms moved of their own accord. My dagger hit her blade, the momentum causing her sword to lift over her head. She countered the movement of her sword, then used all her strength to push against my hold. I expected to struggle against her weight, but with both hands wrapped around the dagger's handle, I shoved and knocked the sword from her hands.

She stumbled back as her black eyes turned crimson. Her fangs extended from her mouth, and she cupped her hands, using her long, blood-red nails like claws.

I had crouched, ready to react, when someone approached me from behind. The vampire in the ski mask? Though I couldn't see him, I felt his energy coming toward me. The two of them would reach me at the same time.

Panic rooted deep within me, but I breathed through it the way Sterlyn had taught me. I was glad I had the shadow on my side.

I watched the vampire in front of me approach as the energy of the vampire behind me grew closer. My body tingled, and my vision wavered. I felt incredibly light. I jumped sideways, and the two vampires collided. The guy toppled over the girl as she brutally sank her fangs into his neck. She jerked her head back, ripping out his throat. He fell dead at her feet.

Her eyes widened in horror. "Jack! Dammit! Why'd you do that?"

Of course, she'd blame the dead guy for ... well, dying.

She jumped to her feet, searching for me. "Where the hell did she go?" She'd already recovered from Jack's death and was ready to attack me again.

At her confusion, I glimpsed down to find only a faint outline of my body. Holy shit, I'd disappeared again, but I still felt the dagger's handle in my palm.

A sharp pain stung inside me, and I spun, searching for my attacker. After one horrifying second, the truth dawned on me. I wasn't the injured one.

Everything in my body quivered with rage as my gaze locked on Alex. Two of the vampires that had been lighting the house on fire held Alex, forcing him to kneel. A tall vampire held a sword to his neck as a fourth—the largest of all—watched with a huge smirk, his vicious gaze locked on my soulmate.

The largest vampire laughed. "Oh, how the mighty have fallen. What do you have to say for yourself?"

Alex didn't flinch, and it scared me that I couldn't feel his fear. Blood trickled down his neck where the sword cut into his skin. His blue eyes turned navy as he stared at the vampires with so much hate.

The girl pivoted, preparing to do something, but I didn't need her to distract them or cause a panic. I didn't know how to move, but I had to do something. At the mercy of the situation, I opened myself again to my supernatural side.

The coolness running through my blood grew colder. I didn't want to be separated from my two sides but rather be one. I had to connect with my shadow side, even if it made me uncomfortable, to truly embrace what I'd become.

And Alex was the perfect reason. I needed to save him.

My blood turned painfully icy as it churned within me. Each heartbeat hurt worse than the last until the organ picked up its pace and the iciness flowed throughout my entire body.

I wanted to recoil but held firm, hoping the change would help protect everyone I loved. Time stood still as turmoil gathered inside me. I'd expected the girl to have reached Alex by now, but no one had moved an inch. I took in the flames climbing the house and the six vampires surrounding it, waiting for Joshua to jump out.

The world froze.

I flicked my gaze upward to find Joshua and three other people at the window, their horrified faces indicating they hadn't found a way out. I turned to see Sterlyn, Griffin, Killian, and Sierra battling seven vampires with swords. Blood coated Sierra's fur; she was injured.

This was not how our story ended.

Something snapped inside me, and warmth shot through my body. The heat chased the iciness, and the two sensations merged.

As quickly as they'd come together, they disappeared, and my body lurched forward. I expected to stumble and fall since I couldn't feel my legs underneath me, but I glided toward the girl, who was moving now that time had started ticking again.

The way I moved reminded me of the shadow I'd seen as a little girl. I pushed my body harder toward her, and it felt as if I was skating across the cobblestone. Focusing on the pressure of the dagger in my hand, I shoved it toward the girl, stabbing her in the heart.

Her mouth dropped open, and her eyes searched frantically for me. I was only six inches from her face, but I might as well have been thousands of miles away.

Needing to get to Alex, I jerked the dagger from her chest, and she fell forward on her face. She groaned as she hit the ground, still alive, but her heartbeat was fading. Her death wouldn't take long.

"I said, what do you have to say for yourself?" the huge vampire demanded. "You are our prince, yet you value human life above our needs and allow shifters to roam our land. We tried to kill your soulmate to rid ourselves of the problem, but that only turned others against us. You are weak, and we can't have anyone thinking you are stronger than the true king."

Alex lifted his chin, allowing the sword to cut into his neck slightly deeper. "Say whatever you must to make yourself feel better."

"You are disgusting," the vampire snarled. "But it doesn't matter. Matthew sees it now. We are the predators, and humans are our prey. We should be feasting on them, instead of hiding and barely getting by."

"My brother would never agree with that," Alex spat.

The guy laughed evilly as he crouched in front of Alex. "Are you so sure about that?"

"Our parents—" Alex started.

"—are dead," the vampire interrupted.

From the first time I'd seen him, something in the energy flowing from Matthew was off, but this morning in Shadow City, I'd sensed a malicious evil to him. I admired Alex for thinking the best of his brother despite him being an asshole, but part of me believed what the vampire was saying.

"Just like you will be for not doing what's best for your people." The vampire motioned for the one holding the sword to kill Alex.

No! In a flash, I appeared next to the vampire with the sword. I stabbed the guy in the shoulder, and the sword fell from his hands.

"What are you doing?" the huge vampire growled, turning to glare at the one I'd stabbed, who was now on the ground. "Get up and kill him!"

Stay still, I connected with Alex, needing him to know I was near. *But get ready to move.*

Veronica. Alex exhaled. *Thank the gods.* His fear slammed into me when our bond reconnected. I didn't know how he'd hidden his terror, but that was a conversation for another time. I had to save the man I loved.

I jumped on top of the man on the ground, and he screamed, "Help! There's someone on me!"

"No, there isn't," the tall vampire growled. "Get up and kill him."

I used the butt of the dagger to knock the vampire

under me out cold. His eyes rolled into the back of his head as he slumped to the side.

"What the—" One of the vampires holding Alex's arms let him go and stumbled back. "That's not possible."

That was all Alex needed. With his free hand, he grabbed his captor's head and pushed the guy down. The guy's hold slackened on Alex's other arm, and Alex ripped the vampire's head from his body.

Vomit inched up my throat at the brutality, but it wasn't like these people didn't deserve it. They'd come here to slaughter Joshua and everyone inside that house, along with Alex and me.

"Get him!" the taller vampire yelled at the one who had released Alex. "*Now*."

Alex spun, grabbed the sword from the ground, and stabbed the other guy through the neck. The sword jutted out the other side as Alex's fangs descended. He growled, "You don't get to make those decisions."

"Oh, yes, we do," the taller vampire hissed as he charged at my mate.

Alex released the sword, but the taller vampire was upon him. If I didn't do something quick, my mate wouldn't survive.

CHAPTER TWENTY-TWO

MY BODY LEAPED into the air and flew the distance to the taller vampire as he thrust the sword at my mate's back. I slammed into the vampire, knocking him down just before the blade could stab him.

As the vampire hit the cobblestones, the sword clattered to the ground.

Alex whirled around. Blood was splattered across his white shirt, and I watched his fangs protruding while his eyes turned crimson. He leaped at the vampire and bent down to grab the sword.

"No!" the vampire cried and put his hands in front of his face as if that would make his plea more sincere. "Please."

"It's too late for mercy," Alex hissed, his words near inaudible. He stabbed the vampire in the heart.

The crackling of wood forced my attention away from Alex and toward the house. Now that Alex was no longer at risk, I had to help Joshua and the others out of the house. The flames had reached the second floor, and the house groaned as its supports weakened.

Are you okay? I asked Alex.

Yes, he connected, his anger palpable. *Thanks to you.*

I'm going to take out the ones surrounding the house so Joshua and the others can get out. In my shadow state, I rushed the six vampires circling the house. Each one stayed focused on Joshua and the others, waiting for them to grow desperate enough to jump.

I'm right behind you, Alex promised. *Just be careful.*

Right now, we had a slight advantage. I would attack the man who'd spoken to us when we'd arrived. He was the ringleader, so maybe taking him out would instill fear in the others.

I appeared beside him, noting the red flames reflected in his dark eyes. My blood hummed in anticipation of the fight, which didn't sit well with me, but it was better than being petrified.

Fighting was merely a means to an end.

I raised my arm but paused, unable to strike the bastard. It seemed wrong because he was unsuspecting.

I might not feel right about killing him, but that didn't mean I couldn't kick his ass. The best way to defeat a bully was by giving him a taste of his own medicine.

Able to move better now, I glided to the side and kicked the asshole in the mouth. With a sickening crack, his head jerked to the side, and blood trickled from his nose. He staggered toward me, his eyes frantically searching for his attacker. "Who's there?" he shouted.

"What are you yelling about, Godfrey?" Blade hissed from two people over.

Godfrey wiped the blood from his nose. "Someone punched me." He glared at the vampire on his right, the one I was hovering beside. "What the hell, Amdis?"

Amdis tore his gaze from the second-floor window and said, "Have you lost your mind?"

"You fucking punched me." Godfrey spat blood on the ground.

"I did not." Amdis snorted. "Don't be an idiot."

"So now I'm imagining things?" Godfrey asked with malice.

Amdis rolled his eyes and focused back on the window. "You said it. Not me."

Silence descended as each person refocused on the house. After a few seconds, I punched Godfrey in the face.

"You son of a bitch," he rasped and blurred the five feet to pummel Amdis.

He punched Amdis over and over, and the sound of breaking bones filled the air. I hadn't expected to cause chaos among the rogues, but the other four rushed to Godfrey and Amdis to break up the fight.

I wouldn't have to do much to make them fall apart completely. I spun around and saw Alex stab the guy I'd knocked out. Consternation filled me, and I averted my eyes from the ghastly sight of the blood and tissue. *He was passed out.*

I know, but babe, he's lost all his humanity, Alex said

as his remorse wafted through our bond. *He would have hurt one of us or someone else the next chance he had.*

His words resonated with me, and I sighed, realizing the truth. *You're right. I just ...*

No, I love you for it. Alex noticed the six vampires fighting just a few steps away from me. *What's going on?*

They can't see me hitting them, so they're fighting among themselves. My eyes went to the forest where the four vampires were still fighting the wolves, but they seemed evenly matched. Sterlyn ripped out the throat of the biggest one there, and his body crumpled to the ground.

The wolves were fine. The only sign of injury was the blood coating Sierra's fur, but it didn't seem worse than when I'd noticed it earlier, meaning Alex and I could tag-team the six vampires here.

I'm going for Blade. Alex ran toward his target with rage etched on his face.

The betrayal he felt was so strong, and I wished I could take all his pain away. That sentiment would grow stronger and stronger over the next few days, especially if what they'd said about Matthew was true, and I feared it was. His brother had changed in the short amount of time I'd known him.

Something crashed inside the house, and I glanced up to find Joshua raising the window. Part of the second story had crumbled, and Joshua stuck his head out to breathe in fresh air.

We were running out of time.

"Look!" Blade cried. "They're coming."

The fighting between the six stopped, and they all turned toward Joshua.

Alex slammed into Blade, and the man fell forward onto his knees. Alex kicked the vampire in the back, forcing him to the ground.

Not wasting a second, Godfrey elbowed Alex in the side, and my mate stumbled over Blade. Blade grabbed Alex's ankle and jerked. Alex crashed down beside him, and the evil vampire crawled on top of him.

My dagger warmed in my palm as I hurried to Alex. I was not losing him today. Reaching Godfrey, I didn't think twice before stabbing him through the heart. He desperately tried to fight me, but each time he grew close, it was like his hands hit a wall, like when Alex and the others had tried to touch the dagger, as if a force field surrounded me.

The remaining four vampires descended on Alex, and I forced myself to move on to my next kill. My stomach roiled, but I remembered what Alex had said. These people would kill or hurt others at every opportunity they had. I repeated those words like a mantra.

I reached the closest vampire to me and shoved the dagger into his stomach before moving to the next and stabbing him in the heart. Amdis had his hand fisted in Alex's hair, holding his head back as Blade stood over him.

Oh, hell no. They kept putting my mate in the execution position.

This ended now.

Rage filled me, fueling me to move faster. Deciding to

give Amdis a taste of his own medicine, I reached inside his hoodie and fisted his hair, twisting the strands between my fingers and jerking his head back. The hoodie fell from his face, and he looked skyward, directly at the half-moon. He groaned and released Alex.

"What are you doing?" Blade growled. "Have you lost your mind?"

"Something h-has me." Amdis's voice broke with his fear.

Alex leaped up and attacked Blade, and the two of them tumbled to the ground.

Wanting Amdis to realize who he was fighting, I closed my eyes and visualized my body. I always disappeared when I didn't want to be seen. Maybe becoming visible was essentially pretending I was back in solid form.

"Oh, my gods," the third man rasped. "It's *her*."

My fingers and legs tingled, and I felt as if I weighed something again, instead of being as light as air.

I placed the dagger against Amdis's neck and leaned into his face. The fear filling his murky eyes confirmed I was back in physical form. His bottom lip quivered as he whispered, "I'm sorry."

Too little, too late. He wanted to kill the people I loved. "Not good enough." I sliced through his neck, ignoring the heartbreak inside me. I would never get used to taking someone's life. There was a darkness to it that made me feel raw and full of guilt. I wished I could help them find redemption, but if their humanity was lost, what salvation could they ever find? I had to hold tight to that last thought and consider how I'd feel if I let him go and he killed others. All those deaths would be on my hands.

The vampire who had seen me first ran for the woods.

Chicken.

I watched Alex climb on top of Blade and punch him in the jaw.

Good, he had him. I needed to chase down the second vampire before he got away. I raced after him right as he hit the tree line. I dug my heels into the grass, pushing as hard as I could to reach him. The dagger handle warmed in my hand, and the urge to toss it overcame me.

Figuring I had nothing to lose, I gave in to the desire. My eyes locked on the center of the vampire's back, and I threw the dagger. It spiraled toward him like a bullet. The blade sliced into the vampire's back right on target, and he flailed and fell, dead on impact.

I stopped, completely stunned. I'd never done any sports before, so hitting a moving target seemed crazy. There had to be more than luck on my side.

My demon and vampire parts had to be helping me.

Shaking off the shock, I hurried to the vampire and removed the dagger from his back. The metallic stench of blood, along with the sound of squelching flesh, had bile churning in my stomach. I wiped the blade on the grass then turned to the house.

Padding paws sounded behind me, and soon, four wolves flanked me, two on each side.

I examined my friends, scanning for signs of serious injuries, but each moved as if they were in good health. Sierra moved without issue, confirming her injury wasn't serious.

When we reached the house, Joshua and his friends had surrounded Blade and Alex. The girl closest to me was maybe five feet tall—someone shorter than me for once. Her vanilla skin glowed under the moonlight and set off her dark eyes. Dark brown hair cascaded down her back over a hunter-green shirt.

The second girl wrapped chestnut-toned arms around another guy's muscular chest and laid her head against his shoulder. Her jet-black hair was pulled into a bun. The guy narrowed his ice-green eyes at Blade, watching as Alex pressed the sword against his neck.

"Why were you attacking Joshua?" Alex asked, his nostrils flaring with rage.

Blade's eyes seemed even more dead, and he remained silent.

"Tell me," Alex commanded as he stood over Blade and pressed the sword deeper into his neck, creating a slice that had blood trickling from the wound.

"You know why," Blade said through gritted teeth. "Or are you really that dumb?"

Yeah, this prick was going to die. He didn't get to insult the man I loved like that. I somehow kept myself still. We needed to get as much information from him as possible before Alex killed him.

Alex's jaw clenched. "Humor me."

"You've always been misguided." Blade's nose wrinkled with disgust. "But Matthew swore you had potential. You just needed time to see things differently."

"Misguided?" Alex's brows furrowed. "Because I don't want to make humans into blood slaves?"

"Yes," Blade sneered. "You don't deserve to help lead this town, especially since you've gotten worse with your mutt allies and impure soulmate." His irises took on a whitish glow as they locked on Joshua.

Joshua and his friends grabbed their heads and cried out in pain.

Something strange was happening.

"Do not talk about my family like that," Alex said, echoing Griffin's words. "I'm not the one who doesn't understand. You have lost your way. So, I'm going to ask one more time. Why were you attacking Joshua?"

Sweat beaded on Joshua's lip, and his voice was hoarse as he answered, "This faction is the one forcing vampires to lose their humanity. They tried to kill Veronica today. Blade is also the vampire who turned me five years ago when my friends and I came to check out this cool town we'd heard about and go hiking."

Alex's shoulders tensed. "You *turned* him? You're not supposed to turn humans who come here."

"We aren't supposed to do many things, but it's time for those rules to change," Blade scoffed.

The four of them groaned and flinched, fighting against some sort of hold.

Sterlyn growled beside me, and her fur stood on her back.

Now would have been a great time for me to be able to talk with the wolves. *Alex.*

"There's only one thing that will change." Alex's chest heaved with each breath. "And it's you having any sort of control over Shadow Terrace."

Blade's unhinged laughter surrounded us just as Joshua and his friends tackled Alex.

CHAPTER TWENTY-THREE

"GET OFF ME," Alex growled as he fought wildly, but the fight was futile against the four of them. The wolves sprang to Alex's aid, but something inside me said this had everything to do with Blade.

"I'm sorry," Joshua growled, his face strained. "I can't help it."

What the hell did that mean? I glared at his red face, and my eyes landed on Blade, whose eyes were glowing.

Blade climbed to his feet, and a smirk stretched across his face.

The smug asshole.

His eyes glowed brighter, almost as bright as the shifters' eyes when they connected with their wolves.

My natural instincts took over, and I rushed at Blade. The vampire's dead eyes focused on me, and he bared his teeth. I had to end him before Joshua, or his friends, got hurt. Somehow, Blade was compelling them to attack Alex.

Blade charged at me, lowering his head to steamroll me. My right palm warmed as the dagger made my blood sizzle. I was going to kill this prick before he could hurt someone I cared about.

I spun out of the way, but he anticipated my counter-move. He pivoted, following my movement, and sank his teeth into my left wrist.

Pain shot into my arm. I groaned and pushed through the ache as I swung my right arm around, sinking my dagger into the asshole's eye. His bite released, and he stumbled back, his mouth open. "What? How?"

He couldn't see the dagger. No wonder he'd attacked without concern.

His hands flew toward the dagger sticking out of his face, but just like with Alex, he couldn't touch it like something was blocking him.

This entire situation was surreal.

I kicked him in the stomach. He stumbled and fell on his back, desperately trying to pull the dagger from his eye. Blood poured down his face and puddled underneath him.

My hands slipped around the handle easily, and I yanked the dagger from the socket. I avoided looking at the tip, not wanting to see what had stayed on it, and sliced deep into his neck.

He gurgled as the life drained from him, and the fighting next to me waned. I turned to find Joshua releasing Alex. His three friends were fighting the wolves, but I could tell Sterlyn and the others were trying not to hurt them, just hold them back.

The petite girl paused, and her face relaxed. She held up her hands to Sierra and said, "I'm so sorry. Please don't kill me."

"He was making us do it," the guy said as he stepped in front of the darker-haired girl. "I don't know how to explain it other than I heard his voice in my head and had to do what he said."

Alex sighed. "That should be impossible. The sire bond is rare."

Joshua shook his head. "He did that to me once before, right after I turned. He commanded me to turn my friends. That's why I refused to gaze out of the house. If I'd seen his eyes, he could have commanded us to come out."

"Sire bond?" I repeated, thinking about all the books and movies I'd seen. Something told me to imagine the dagger disappearing, and I closed my eyes, following my gut. When I opened them, the dagger was gone. I cradled my injured wrist. "And if you turned your friends, wouldn't that have made you lose some of your humanity?"

"Do you mean, do I feel things as deeply as I used to?" Joshua arched a brow and rubbed his arms. "No, I don't. I've lost a piece of myself, and I'm grasping to maintain what I have left. We've purposely stayed off the radar and only ventured out when we knew Blade was occupied. We kept things stocked here and went through the woods when we wanted to leave."

"Then why did you want to get close to Matthew?" Alex asked as he walked to me and placed his hand on my lower back. He led me away from Blade and the house, now engulfed in flames. He gently examined my wrist and frowned at the injury.

It's fine. Even though it hurt like hell, the fight was over. This would heal.

His irises lightened as he stared into my eyes. *You need my blood.*

At the thought, warmth flashed through me. *Not with everyone around. I'm fine.*

"Because I thought he didn't know about Blade and his vampires." Joshua shivered. "The night Eilam captured Ronnie and I helped to clean up, I wanted to alert Matthew to what was going on, but I learned that he already knew, and that was confirmed when Blade showed up, pissed that Eilam had given away the secret room."

Betrayal coursed through Alex. "He knows about the rogue vampires' plans?"

"Oh, he knows all right," Joshua said sternly. "I assumed you were involved too, but I don't believe that anymore." He gestured to the dead people around him.

"If you thought we were working with them, why did you message me for help?" Alex squinted at Joshua, expecting to catch him in a lie.

"I didn't have much to lose." He lifted his arms. "If you were working with them, we wouldn't be in a worse situation."

This attack had worked out to our advantage. "Were you afraid Blade was going to make you do something?"

The darker-haired girl nodded. "They were going to force us to become like them tonight, or kill us, because Joshua helped you two this morning."

I hadn't considered the consequences of his actions until now. I hated that we'd put them all at risk. "I'm so sorry. Had I known—"

"No, this is a good thing." The petite girl smiled sadly. "You took out the twenty most corrupt vampires here—well, excluding ..." She grimaced and cleared her throat. "The king."

Sterlyn whimpered and pawed at the ground. Her purple eyes shone, and she used her head to gesture toward the woods.

They wanted to leave, and I couldn't blame them. If Matthew found out they were here, it would cause more problems. I nodded at her. "Go ahead."

She nodded back and took off for the woods, the three other wolves following her. They stopped a few feet into the tree line and turned back, keeping an eye on us.

They didn't want to leave us without backup, but they also didn't want to be out in the open. With each horrible event, they proved how loyal they were to me and Alex.

"What do we do?" I wasn't sure what our game plan was, but we had to clean up this mess before others found us.

Alex sighed and pulled his phone from his pocket. "I'm calling the Shadow Terrace guards. I'll be right back." He walked off, heading toward the tree line, not wanting Joshua and his friends to overhear the conversation.

We didn't need to stand here in awkward silence, so I held my hand out to the petite girl. "I'm Ronnie."

"Lucy." The girl shook my hand and pointed to the other girl. "That's Peyton, and the muscular guy is Carson."

Carson placed an arm around Peyton's shoulders and nodded. "Thanks for helping us. We would be dead if it weren't for you."

The house collapsed on itself, and smoke billowed from the ruins. Ash swirled in the breeze, and I realized my throat was dry. The house was far enough away from its neighbors that the flames hadn't spread.

"Where are your neighbors?" I turned, searching for signs of people next door.

"We moved out here to get away from everyone. All the houses near us are vacant." Joshua shrugged. "With Blade as our sire, many other vampires want nothing to do with us."

That was interesting. "Are you the only turned vampires in Shadow Terrace?" I'd been turned, so maybe people wouldn't want to interact with me, either.

"Yes. I don't know why." Joshua took Lucy's hand. "Blade initially targeted Lucy, but when I saw him attack her, I lost it. As a result, he turned me and forced me to turn them as punishment. It was the worst night of my life, and I hate that I succumbed to the pressure."

Lucy shuddered. "I'm glad it was you. If it hadn't been you, he would've done it himself."

Something wasn't adding up. "But why only you? Not that I want there to be more vampires, I just don't understand."

"Matthew lost it when he heard what happened. Blade forced us to stay with him the first night after we'd turned, and Matthew called him that morning, telling him he couldn't pull anything like that again. That vampires couldn't turn humans." Peyton's dark chocolate eyes grew cold at the memory.

"That's why we thought Matthew might not realize the severity of the situation." Joshua ran a hand through his hair. "And why I wanted to get close to him that night Eilam died."

Alex walked over to us, chewing on his bottom lip. "The guards are on their way, but I'm afraid this fire may have to burn out on its own."

I turned to find that the smoke was thinning. It wouldn't take too much longer for the fire to die out. "They'll need a place to stay."

"There are plenty of houses they can pick from." Alex took my hand. He looked around at Joshua and his friends. "Who else is part of the rogue group? We need to take care of everyone involved, including my brother."

My heart hurt at his words, but determination coursed through him.

"Honestly, these vampires were the instigators. We can name a few others, but most of the townspeople avoid the rogues as best they can." Carson pointed toward the town. "The people you need to watch out for still hang out at Thirsty's. That's where the rogues congregate and lure the humans they feed from."

"Is that why the bar reopened?" Alex asked, and I realized the extent of how deep this went was finally hitting him.

"Yes. The bar owner is the only one of the core team who wasn't here tonight," Peyton said as she leaned into Carson's side. "Probably because all the flunkies are there with humans."

Four black sedans pulled up to the house, and two vampires got out of each car. They hurried over to us.

A man with feathered, deep brown hair took the lead, striding to Alex. He scratched the scruff on his chin. "Your Highness."

"Frank." Alex got straight to the point. "We need your men to clean up all the dead bodies here and then go to Thirsty's. Arrest every patron and anyone you can track down who frequents the place."

Frank's charcoal eyes bulged. "What? The bar?"

I wasn't sure what his surprise meant. Maybe Joshua was wrong, and more people were involved than he knew?

"Yes," Alex said with a level voice. The only sign of his tension was the vein bulging slightly in his neck. "Is that a problem?"

Frank shook his head. "Not at all. But may I ask what brought this on?"

"Anyone who feeds directly from a human and has lost their humanity must be imprisoned or killed if no other option is viable." Alex stared hard at Frank and every other guard who'd shown up. "This town protects Shadow City, which means keeping our cravings in check. To ensure the supernatural races' secret is our utmost priority. We do not turn humans. We do not drink directly from them or put ourselves at risk of losing our humanity. Our existence is to remain secret, and the blood banks are only used to get the amount of blood needed for survival. The humans who visit our town should get to enjoy their time here, not be drained. If any of you have a problem with those terms or find it difficult to imprison anyone who doesn't follow these fundamental rules, I need to know now."

"We don't, sir." Frank placed a hand on his chest. "We're glad that the royal family is finally taking this stance again."

The sad thing is I don't even need to ask why they didn't inform my brother, Alex connected, revealing his sorrow only to me. "Then get them back in control."

"Yes, sir," Frank said, and all eight guards bowed.

We need to get the wolves back to the house. They wouldn't leave us here after an attack, even if they risked the vampires discovering them.

"Gwen will arrive soon. Is there anything else you need from me or my fiancée?" Alex asked as he wrapped an arm around my waist. *That's fine. Gwen will oversee the cleanup so I can get you back to Sterlyn's and tend to your wounds.*

Frank lowered his head. "No, sir."

"Good." Alex led me toward my Mazda. "Make sure Joshua and his friends find a comfortable place to stay. We'll be back in the morning to check on things."

"Yes, sir," they said in unison.

A small hand touched my arm, and I stopped. Lucy stood there with a timid smile. She whispered, "Thank you, and please let your friends know we appreciate their help. We'd be dead, or even worse off, if it weren't for you."

I squeezed her hand with my good one. "Alex and I will do everything in our power to protect you."

Something unreadable crossed Frank's face as if my words had affected him, too.

We climbed into the car and headed home.

THE NEXT WEEK flew by with messages from Kira, Cyrus, and Darrell as they chased Matthew around. Apparently, Matthew was struggling to find whoever he was seeking in Atlanta, and they'd been there for a few days.

We put off going to Eliza's while we tended to matters in Shadow Terrace. Alex and I met with everyone we could to determine who the rogue vampires were now that we knew who the leaders had been. During our conversations with our people, many of them stated their desire to have Alex as their king and me as their queen. A few even asked when we'd get married to make everything truly official.

Gwen did an amazing job, helping Alex and me get things squared away. The guards had jailed everyone involved in drinking blood directly from humans, and more and more people had come forward to express their gratitude that the rogue vampires had been exposed and taken care of. No one had felt safe, afraid that someone would force them to lose their humanity, and fewer people had been willing to work at the blood banks because of it.

Thirsty's had closed, and the bartender had been jailed for questioning, though he hadn't let anything slip yet. The blood banks were running at capacity again as workers returned.

One of our biggest accomplishments was that we'd helped the man who worked at the capitol building. We'd ended his punishment, and he was back at home, not starving.

Just as I'd suspected, Sterlyn was the only angel descendant present in the group at the time and could see my hazy outline of me in shadow form. That confirmed what we all suspected; any angel descendant could see a demon in their shadow form.

Hey. I woke to the wonderful sensation of Alex pulling me against his bare chest. *Are you awake?*

I moaned, enjoying the feel of his hands on me. *Yes, I am.*

Good. He loosened his hold, the opposite of what I'd expected. *Then we should get moving.*

What? The haze lifted from my mind. I'd hoped he

wanted to have his way with me. Getting up was not what I had in mind. *You're supposed to be seducing me.*

As tempting as that is ... He kissed my cheek. *I have something more pressing to accomplish.*

What could be more pressing than that? I rolled over so I could see him. *I mean ...* I kissed his lips, but he moved away.

Let's go see Eliza and Annie. He beamed at me, excitement clear on his face.

The thought of seeing them had me excited, too, but part of me didn't want to go. Going there meant I'd have to deal with things I didn't want to. *But Shadow Terrace ...*

Is fine. Alex climbed out of bed and winked. *We stayed. Matthew is still gone, and things are better. People are actually happy. Gwen will continue putting the city to rights, and we can spend the day going to see Annie and Eliza, so I can ask her for your hand properly. When Matthew returns, we might not be able to get away. Besides, do you not realize what today is?*

It was Monday, July twenty-fifth.

My birthday.

Eliza and Annie will be excited to see you. Alex waggled his eyebrows, knowing he'd won.

He was right. No wonder Eliza had called me twice yesterday. I hadn't answered because we'd been at the prison, but now I felt like an ass. "Okay, let me call her and let her know."

I grabbed my phone and dialed her number. On the fifth ring, she answered, "Ronnie?"

"Eliza, hi. Sorry I didn't answer the phone yesterday." I should've called her back, but we'd gotten home so late that I'd been drained. I hadn't had the energy to have a conversation.

"Ronnie, thank God." Eliza's voice broke. "We need your help."

CHAPTER TWENTY-FOUR

MY CHEST TIGHTENED. Eliza never asked for help. She was too proud... as if she was trying to make up for something, even though she had sacrificed so much for us.

"What's wrong?"

"Someone's been watching us." Eliza's normally strong voice cracked, and my throat tightened. "We stayed a night in Nashville to lose them, but it's not working. I'm hoping we can come to you."

"Of course, you can." They'd probably be safest here with my friends and me. "I'll text you the address." She must have felt really threatened to want to come here. She'd been dead set against Annie visiting again when we'd thought Eilam was her boyfriend.

"We need to discuss some things when I get there." Eliza cleared her throat uncomfortably. "Things I should've told you a long time ago, but I'd hoped it would never impact your life, never come to this."

In the background, I heard Annie ask, "Who are you talking to? Is that Ronnie?"

"Yeah." Eliza sounded more like her normal self, but it was forced. "She called me back."

"It's about damn time. Let me talk to her." I heard shuffling, and Annie got on the phone. "Ronnie, you'll never believe it. Eliza asked me to go to Nashville with her. My entire life, she's never left Lexington. I don't know what came over her."

The tightening in my throat eased. Annie didn't sound like the distant girl who'd barely texted me back these past few weeks. I didn't know how to respond to her, though, seeing as Eliza hadn't informed her about why they'd left home. "Are you having fun?"

"It's been nice to get away." Sadness crept into her voice. "I needed a distraction."

This confirmed my suspicion. Her memories of her time in Shadow Terrace hadn't been completely erased. I remembered Alex telling me that, when he'd watched over her after Eilam had messed with her mind, Annie had whimpered and talked about me in her sleep. He'd said it was odd because when a vampire modified someone's memories, it always took, even in their sleep. "Bad dreams?" I asked.

"Yeah." She giggled, the laughter high-pitched. That was her tell when she was downplaying something. "But no biggie. I'm sure they'll stop soon."

"Tell her we're heading out," Eliza said. "We should be there in two and half hours."

"Oh, yay! I can't believe it," Annie said happily, then

repeated Eliza's words. "We're coming to see you and that sexy man of yours."

I smiled despite her talking lustfully about Alex. "Then get your ass down here."

"On it." She hung up the phone, obviously having taken on Eliza's trait of hanging up without saying goodbye.

Alex touched my arm, bringing me back to the present. "What's going on?"

"Eliza said someone is following them. They drove all the way to Nashville to lose them, and now they're coming here." My mind raced. Had someone followed Killian and Annie when she'd gone home, then waited until Killian had left so no one was watching her, planning to ... what? Hurt her? Kidnap her? But that seemed far-fetched. "Who do you think it could be?"

"I don't know." Alex opened the bedroom door. "Let's get Sterlyn to link with Cyrus to see if he and Darrell and Kira have any insight. Last I heard, they'd followed Matthew to Louisville, Kentucky."

My breath caught in my chest. "How many days ago?"

"Two." Alex's brows furrowed. "Why?"

I pushed past Alex and hurried into the kitchen where Sterlyn and Griffin were sitting at the round cherrywood table. Three serving plates sat in the center, filled with pancakes, eggs, and bacon. They'd laid a plate, a cup of coffee, and silverware in a place for me.

Sterlyn's eyes darkened as she took in my state. "What's wrong?"

"I need you to find out where Cyrus, Darrell, and Kira are." If they were in Nashville, that would tell me everything I needed to know. Matthew was hunting Eliza and Annie down.

"Okay. He's too far away for me to link with him, so I'll call." She pulled out her phone. After a second, I heard it ring on the other end.

Griffin took a bite of his pancakes. "What's going on?"

"Eliza said someone's watching them. They left town to hide." I couldn't hide the worry that laced my words. "If Matthew is in Nashville, it has to be him."

"Hello?" a male voice said on the other line.

That had to be her brother. I hadn't met him yet, but I would very soon.

"Hey." Sterlyn placed a hand on the table to steady herself. "Where are you?"

"Nashville." Cyrus sighed. "I swear, I have no clue what this guy is up to. He went to Atlanta and picked up a man, who's been with him ever since. It's like we're circling back toward Shadow Ridge, but they're acting really strange, sticking to the shadows."

Probably because they were following my foster mom and sister. If Alex didn't kill his brother, I would, especially if he intended to hurt the people I loved.

"Will you let us know if you head this way?" Sterlyn tapped her fingers on the table. "We're pretty sure they're following Ronnie's mother and sister, and they're coming here."

"Yeah." Cyrus breathed. "I can do that."

"What kind of supernatural is the man Matthew picked up?" Sterlyn asked.

"I don't know. I haven't seen anything like him before, but he's not human. There's something so vile around him that my wolf surges forward. It's strange. Darrell feels it too."

Sterlyn frowned. "Okay. Call us when you leave Nashville."

"Will do," Cyrus replied. "The silver wolves are only fifteen minutes away if you need them."

A tender smile spread across Sterlyn's face. "I know. Talk soon."

Alex touched my shoulder, and intense guilt floated between us. "I'm sorry, babe. I wish I could do something. How did you guess it was Matthew?"

I placed my hand on top of his, trying to ease his guilt. He hadn't done a damn thing wrong. "Because Louisville isn't even two hours away from Lexington, and Eliza and Annie ran yesterday. That was why she called me so much. It seemed too coincidental." I hated that I'd put them at risk. Matthew would stop at nothing to hurt me. He wanted me out of his brother's life, but I'd never imagined he'd go after my family.

"Your brother is a piece of shit." Griffin shoveled eggs into his mouth. "He's right on par with Dick."

Dick Harding, the guy who'd tried to take Griffin's spot as Shadow City alpha and had killed Sterlyn's entire pack. He'd planned on using her as a breeder to create his own, personal silver-wolf army and hadn't wanted Sterlyn's pack to rescue the alpha heir. Dick and his wife had found a wolf shifter willing to breed with her, although Griffin and Sterlyn had yet to determine his identity. Another thing they'd put on hold since I'd walked into their world.

For Griffin to say that Matthew and Dick were on par spoke volumes. Sterlyn was his mate.

"No offense," Griffin added as an afterthought.

Alex waved off the comment. "At one time, that would have angered me, but not after all the shit he's pulled. I don't know what happened to him."

"The truth is, he hasn't changed," Sterlyn said as she regarded Alex. "*You* have. When I met you, you were teetering on the edge between good and bad, like you hadn't made your decision. When Ronnie arrived, she brought out your good side."

"After they stopped fighting their connection." Griffin chuckled. "But it was fun to watch you struggle, after all the hell you put Sterlyn and me through. You know, like when you voted against us a few times in the council."

Alex shrugged. "We were hedging our bets." Then he winced. "Yes, okay. Maybe I am the one who changed."

If Matthew was chasing after Eliza and Annie, then a fight was inevitable, which meant I needed to eat breakfast, even if I didn't feel like it. I'd need all my strength. "Let's wait to hear from Cyrus. Maybe this is all a coincidence." Despite my wishful thinking, the words fell flat.

"Okay." Alex walked over to the silver refrigerator and pulled out two bags of blood. "We should eat."

He placed a bag in front of me while I scooped food

onto my plate. The four of us ate in silence, and the tension continued thickening as we waited for the inevitable call from Cyrus.

I chewed slowly, unable to enjoy the taste of the food or the blood.

At least, no one was watching me eat today. It had taken a few days, since I was the first person anyone had heard of who needed both blood and food to survive. I was pretty much a hybrid, but not quite since demons had created vampires.

In other words, I was an anomaly, which I was ready to embrace.

About ten minutes later, Sterlyn's text alert went off. She picked up her phone and frowned. "Cyrus says they're on the move."

SIERRA PLOPPED down on the couch and shook her head as she watched me. "Girl, you need to sit your ass down before you wear a track into the floor."

That was easier said than done. After cleaning up from breakfast, I hadn't been able to sit still. We hadn't heard from Cyrus again, and I feared Matthew would get to Eliza and Annie before they made it here. I constantly wanted to call and check on them, but Eliza was stressed enough. "I can't help it." I'd considered going outside to work off my nervous energy, but I was afraid Eliza and Annie would arrive before I got back.

I was a hot mess.

Alex hissed from the love seat, "Leave her alone." He wasn't pleased with her giving me a hard time. "She's on edge and doesn't need your smart mouth making it worse."

"Listen here, bloodsucker," she started just as the door to the backyard opened and Sterlyn, Rosemary, and Griffin entered.

"You two, stop it," Sterlyn ordered. "We're all on edge."

That was one way of putting it.

"Where's Killian?" I asked. He'd gone outside with Sterlyn and Griffin to talk with the guards and wait for Rosemary. I'd expected him to come back in with everyone else.

Griffin pointed to the back door. "He's staying with the guards. He'll alert us if anything odd happens. Speaking of which, an older gray Camry is pulling into the neighborhood."

My heart leaped. They were here. "That's Eliza's car."

"Okay, we'll let Killian and the others know." Sterlyn's eyes glowed as she tapped into her wolf.

"Do we know how far away Matthew and the others are?" Rosemary folded her black wings into her back.

Sterlyn pinched the bridge of her nose. "About thirty minutes out."

My brows rose. I'd expected them to be closer, but maybe Matthew had guessed where Eliza was heading. It wouldn't have been hard to figure out. "Do you think Matthew will come here or head back to Shadow City?"

"Most likely Shadow Terrace. He's no doubt heard about what happened at Joshua's house." Alex pulled out his phone and typed a message. "I've alerted Gwen and Joshua to look out for Matthew. I'm betting he'll go back to find whatever is left of the rogue vampires. He's planning something, and it has to be about removing Ronnie and me from the equation, especially if he's heard that people want him to step down."

"But he won't find any, right?" Rosemary arched her eyebrow.

I wasn't so sure about that.

"If he does find anyone, it'll be only a handful of people." Alex stood, walked over to me, and took my hand. "I'm sure a few vampires are still loyal to him and pretending to be on our side, but I believe it's only a few. Everyone else wants to see me and Veronica in charge."

That had been another shocker that both thrilled and terrified me. I hadn't been raised to know how to rule like Alex.

The familiar sound of the Camry pulling in made my heart pound. I was so excited to see Eliza and Annie but also wary of how they'd react to me in my new form.

Alex squeezed my hand. *Everything is going to be okay. We won't let anything happen to them.*

That wasn't all I was worried about. I was also concerned that Matthew wouldn't give us much of a choice about fighting him, and we'd have to put him in jail or worse.

Footsteps grew louder as two of the most important people in my entire life approached. Not wanting to make them wait outside, I blurred to the door and threw it open.

"Ronnie," Eliza gasped. Her sea-green eyes widened as she scanned me over. Her light caramel hair was pulled into a bun, and the lines around her eyes had deepened. She was over sixty, but it was hard to tell.

Annie wore her standard red lipstick, and her wavy brown-sugar hair cascaded down past her shoulders. I noticed one change immediately—she was wearing an oversized T-shirt and jeans instead of her usual trendy clothes.

But the thing that stuck out the most was the herbal scent that surrounded Eliza. The very scent that confirmed what I'd feared.

CHAPTER TWENTY-FIVE

BETRAYAL HIT ME. Eliza was a witch. I had no doubt, especially since Alex had taught me to pick out what kind of supernaturals people were by scent alone.

Alex moved up behind me and placed his hand on my shoulder, reminding me I wasn't alone.

Needing him, I leaned against his chest, enjoying the sturdy support he provided.

"Why don't you two come inside," Alex said with an edge to his tone. *I understand you love them, but she should have told you she is a witch.*

Even though I'd been thinking exactly that, I had to remember that Eliza had Annie's and my best interests at heart. Or I hoped she did. Who knew?

"Thank you," Eliza whispered and gestured for Annie to enter the house.

As Annie breezed past me, I swore there was a faint hint of musk to her—not overly strong like Sterlyn, Griffin, Sierra, and Killian, and not enough to label her a shifter, but something.

"Annie, hey." Sterlyn smiled at my friend as she entered the living room. "How are you?"

"Fine," Annie replied robotically, and the house filled with a horrid sulfuric smell.

The magnitude of her lie surprised me, and I couldn't hold back a cough from the god-awful stench. Hell, even my eyes burned.

Eliza frowned as she walked warily past me, her focus on Alex and me, and hurt tightened my chest. Didn't she trust me?

"Are you sure you're okay?" Rosemary's brows furrowed. "Because you aren't being truthful."

A loud, high-pitched laugh escaped Annie, a sign that she was lying. "I'm seeing my sister for the first time in weeks, so I'm more than okay." This time, no smell wafted to me.

My heart warmed, and I hugged her. I had to remain very aware of my speed since Annie didn't remember this world... or, at least, while she was awake.

Eliza tensed as I pulled Annie into my arms. I breathed in my sister's familiar scent, pushing away the pain Eliza's reaction had caused. I'd never hurt Annie in a million years, and it stung that Eliza worried I would. "I'm happy to see you, too."

"These are the friends you've been staying with?" Eliza looked at Rosemary, Griffin, then Sterlyn. Her expression tensed when her gaze landed on the silver wolf.

Odd.

Hell, this whole situation was odd.

I pulled away from Annie and forced a smile, but I could feel that it'd fallen flat. "Yes." I introduced each of them. "This is Eliza, my mother." The words felt strange because, for the first time ever, I felt as if I didn't know her.

"You said you felt—" Griffin started.

Eliza cut him off. "Maybe one of you could take Annie out for a walk? She's been cooped up in the car for hours, and she could stretch her legs."

"No, I'm fine." Annie shook her head. "I can stay here."

The front door opened, and Sierra traipsed in. Her dirty-blond hair was pulled back into a ponytail, and she smelled like grease from the bar where she worked. Her gaze landed on Eliza, and her brows furrowed. She glanced around then homed in on my sister. "Hey, Annie, great to see you," she said, sounding off. "What's going on?" Her attention went back to Eliza. "Who's this?" She cupped her hands around her mouth and mouthed the word *witch* to me.

Thank God she knew Annie was clueless, or she would've said something without thinking.

"Hey, Sierra." Annie ran her fingers through her hair. "This is Ronnie's and my mom, Eliza."

"Really?" Sierra's eyes widened. "That's ... interesting."

Griffin's eyes glowed faintly as his wolf surged forward. "They've had a long drive. Maybe you could take Annie outside for fresh air and keep her company?"

"But I just—" she started, but Sterlyn cleared her throat. Sierra rolled her eyes. "Fine. I can do that. I'd like to catch up with her anyway."

Griffin frowned, and I chuckled. He wasn't happy that Sierra talked back to him but fell in line with Sterlyn.

Griffin and Sterlyn were strong in their own right, but Sterlyn was, hands down, stronger than her mate. Sometimes, it surprised me how well Griffin took it, but he was so proud of her.

"Just a few minutes." Annie frowned. "I haven't seen Ronnie in forever."

I understood that sentiment. The three of us used to be around each other every day, and my moving here had changed that unexpectedly. "Yeah, but when you go to college, it would be the same thing." I had to remind her she'd been planning to leave us, even if I'd beat her to it.

She grimaced. "Oh, yeah. We need to talk about that."

That didn't sound good.

"Come on," Sierra said and grabbed Annie's arm, leading her to the kitchen to go out the back door. "We didn't get a chance to talk before, so we've got to make up for lost time."

The six of us stood in silence and watched them walk out of the house.

When Eliza didn't speak for a few seconds, I jumped in. "So ... you're a witch." I figured cutting straight to the point would be the most efficient use of our time. "That would have been useful information to know."

Eliza's mouth dropped open. I'd never called her out like that before, not even when I was upset. I usually let her handle the tough topics, but not this time.

Not today.

"And you're a vampire... or a partial one." Eliza *tsk*ed. "After everything I've done, you wind up like this."

"Everything?" She had some nerve. She'd come here for my help, and here she was, saying shit like that. This time, I was going to stand my ground with her. "I don't know what that means, but I take it you knew I was part demon."

"I did." Eliza exhaled and rubbed a hand down her face. "When the group home workers said you were screaming about shadows, I suspected, and if I hadn't taken you in, no one would have been able to protect you."

Even though I'd had suspicions, hearing her confirm it shocked me. My chest tightened with betrayal. I had hoped she was clueless like me, but she'd known.

The entire time.

"You protected me by doing what? And what were you protecting me from?" The hurt circled my heart, squeezing. Black spots danced before my eyes. I'd never felt like this, and the person I'd trusted most before coming here had been keeping huge secrets from me. "I don't get it. You always wanted honesty, yet you hid something so important about me from *me*."

"I'd hoped your heritage would never come to light."

Eliza's shoulders sagged. "I wanted to keep you away from everything supernatural so you could have a normal life."

"Then why did you let her come here looking for Annie?" Sterlyn asked. She walked over to the windows. My gaze followed hers outside to Sierra and Annie. They were talking in front of Killian's pool. "Or did you not realize this was a supernatural hub?"

"She knew." I couldn't keep my mouth shut. I glared at Eliza. "You refused to come down here with me because you had to work. But it was more than that, wasn't it?" I needed to hear the truth. All of it, even if it hurt.

"I had to work, but yes, I knew this was a supernatural hub." Eliza rubbed her arms like she was fighting off a chill. "That's why I didn't want Annie to visit the university. I needed to keep you both away from this place, but she ran off down here. I didn't know what to do."

"You didn't want to come down here and risk someone calling you out as a witch around them." Rosemary nodded. "I can see that."

Alex placed an arm around my waist. He scowled as he asked, "Is that the only reason?"

"Leave it to a vampire to be perceptive." Eliza lifted a hand but let it fall beside her again. "No, that wasn't the only reason. People here have threatened my coven, and I didn't want to get back on anyone's radar. We moved and tried to remain hidden. We want to live a peaceful life, not start a conflict."

"Wait." My mind raced with all the information she was throwing at me. I felt like I was drowning. "You have a *coven*? Who?" I'd never seen her with anyone. She stayed home and out of sight unless she was going to the grocery store or work. Annie and I called her a hermit. How could she have a coven?

"Yes, but they don't live near me. I had separated from them before Annie's mother brought her to the coven. They asked me to take Annie, and I brought her back to my home, so that not even Annie's mother would know where she was."

"Annie's mother is alive?" Everything she said only caused more confusion. Here I'd thought her hiding that she was a witch was the worst thing she'd done, but she'd been hiding an entire *life*, not to mention key things about Annie and me. "You always made it sound like someone from the shelter brought her to you! Why did her mother give her up?"

"That's not your story to know." Eliza lifted her chin, daring someone to contradict her.

My heart dropped. "Is Annie a supernatural too? But how? She doesn't smell like one. At least ... she didn't. I can pick up a tiny hint of something now."

"Ronnie, I love you as if you were my own child, but you need to let this go." She waved her hand at me. "It's bad enough that you let your demon side loose and transformed into a vampire."

"You also smelled like a human when we met," Alex said softly. "Whatever she's doing to Annie, she did to you."

My head spun as my entire world shifted. Yes, I'd become a supernatural and found my soulmate, but Eliza was the first person I'd trusted and confided in who was an authority figure. To realize she'd kept Annie and me in the dark about who we were, even for protection, hurt.

"We need to know what you were protecting her from," Sterlyn said gently. "I'm guessing you spelled her and Annie to seem human, but there was something about Ronnie that made me feel connected to her the first time I saw her."

"Same here," Rosemary agreed. "We were responding to the demon in her."

I was still getting used to thinking of the shadow as a demon. That part of me didn't feel malicious, though, likely due to my being human once and Alex grounding me. But one thing was clear—the vampires who lost their humanity became more demon-like, which made my blood run cold.

"The reason your demon part came out so strong the night of your fourteenth birthday was that you were spiraling." Eliza's eyes, filled with sadness, focused on me. "You didn't feel loved and safe, so the demon side tried to take hold. If I hadn't brought you home with me, you would've become susceptible to its influence. I made you feel safe and spelled you to keep the demon side at bay. When Annie ran off down here, I'd hoped you would find her and bring her home quickly, but I guess he"—she pointed at Alex—"is why the spell slowly disintegrated."

"She's my soulmate." Alex's fingers dug into my hip. "I'd never purposely put her in danger."

Eliza glared at him. "Yet, you turned her."

"He saved my life." I refused to let her disrespect him. "I found a demon blade, and it cut me. I would've died if he hadn't."

"Oh, goddess." Eliza clutched her chest. "I ... I never dreamed."

"I get you not liking vampires." Griffin chuckled darkly. "Believe me. I hated Alex for years, but Ronnie has changed him. He's done everything in his power to protect her, and even I have come to think of him as a friend."

"Well, I guess I should be thanking him," Eliza said as she marched over to Alex and touched his arm. "I didn't know what happened—I just felt the spell vanish. I figured you'd done it for your own selfish desire."

Alex placed his hand on top of hers. "I would never do that to Veronica. She's the most important person to me, and her happiness is one of my top concerns."

Seeing the two of them getting along eased some of my hurt. I hadn't expected her to welcome him, not at first, but I shouldn't have doubted Alex. He was the best man I'd ever known.

Unfortunately, we still had a pressing matter: Matthew. We'd have time to discuss all of this after we'd eliminated that threat. "Do you know who's following you?" I didn't know if Eliza was aware of Matthew, and we didn't know who was with him.

She pursed her lips. "A vampire and a demon. I don't know more than that. I spelled us so we could get away, but the demon can follow the magical trail.

They'll be here eventually, but I had nowhere else to go."

"You came to the right place." Sterlyn smiled reassuringly. "You're Ronnie's family, which means you're part of ours."

"Listen, I hate to ask, but it's best if Annie doesn't learn about any of this." Eliza bit her lip. "For her safety, she needs to stay unaware of this world and the risks it poses. I'm afraid whoever is following us might try to kidnap her, and we need to do all we can to protect her."

"Why would they be after her?" She couldn't just drop a bomb like that and not explain.

Eliza sighed. "Annie is also part demon."

Shit. I hadn't expected that. "We have to tell her. If people are after her, she needs to take precautions."

"She's right." Rosemary crossed her arms and stared Eliza down. "Had we known Ronnie was part demon, she might not have almost died."

"Now listen here—" Eliza started.

Sterlyn interrupted, her eyes glowing lavender. "We don't have time to argue. Cyrus, Darrell, and Kira are coming here now. Matthew just rolled into Shadow Terrace with his demon friend."

Alex tensed. "That means whatever my brother is planning is going to happen soon. He wants to ambush us, so he can't wait too long to make his play."

"Then we gather everyone." I looked Alex in the eye. "And we head over now before he can set his plans into motion."

CHAPTER TWENTY-SIX

"WHEN YOU SAY 'EVERYONE,' please tell me that includes us," Sterlyn said, looking at Alex. "If there is a demon with Matthew, you'll need other supernaturals there to protect your kind, too. Demons made vampires, so you're a weaker version of them."

Alex exhaled and pinched the bridge of his nose. "That's why he brought the demon here. I have a feeling it isn't just you, Annie, and Eliza my brother is after." His soft blue eyes focused on me and turned navy. "He wants to hurt Ronnie by taking her family away from her like she took me from him and, as a result, hurt me in the most effective way he knows how."

"That's the problem with power-hungry supernaturals." Eliza clucked her tongue. "They'll do anything to get what they want. What happened to make him target you?"

"Like he said—me." The answer was that simple.

"I've driven a wedge between the two of them, even though I never meant to."

"It is *not* your fault," Alex hissed as he turned me to face him. "I've changed since you came into my life. You made me the person that destiny wanted me to be. I wasn't willing to be his puppet any longer. Gwen is realizing the same thing—we've had enough. As we've taken over Shadow Terrace in his absence, we've come to realize that most vampires don't want to feed from humans like the rogues do. They want to keep their humanity and have freedom. Not be tied to the darkness."

That was true. I'd been there and heard the same things. For the past fifty or so years, Matthew had Alex believing that many of the vampires who lived outside of Shadow City had succumbed to their urges and lost their humanity. But the vampires of Shadow Terrace had been around humans without succumbing to bloodlust. Many vampires in the human world had also kept their humanity.

Rosemary exhaled. "I get you don't want to tell Annie all the details, but we have to tell her something. If the demon comes after her and a wolf or angel needs to protect her, she should be aware of supernaturals. Otherwise, she'll be scared and want to get away from the very people who are helping her."

No one disagreed.

"I can talk to her while you get a plan together," I suggested. "As you all have said before, we can't go in blind. Maybe call Gwen and see if she's spotted him?" I assumed if Matthew was going to make his presence known, he'd start with his sister, especially when he realized she'd taken control of the town. If he went searching for Blade and the rogues, he'd find out they were dead or in jail.

"Ronnie, I said I don't want her to know." Eliza scowled at me, not happy that I was pressing the issue.

And I didn't give a damn. This was how things were going to happen. Eliza was done making decisions for us about this world. "I won't tell her about her heritage. That's something you should do. But if you don't, I *will* tell her eventually. Right now, I need to tell her about the supernatural world because Rosemary is right. If something happens, we can't have her freaking out. Besides, she handled it fine before. If it hadn't been for the vampire using her as his own, personal snack bar, Alex wouldn't have made her forget everything."

Eliza inhaled sharply. "That's what happened. Dear gods." She nodded. "Fine, but nothing about her heritage. Give me time to figure out how to tell her."

"Don't wait too long." Secrets only hurt us; they didn't make us stronger. I knew that finding out I was part demon wasn't fun, but dammit, I wished I'd had the information beforehand. "If we make it out alive, I want her to know before you leave here."

After a second, she agreed, "Fine." Her face turned pink, reminding me of all the times she'd been angry with Annie. Rarely had she directed that look at me.

"Like Sterlyn asked, will you allow us into Shadow

Terrace to help out?" Griffin asked. "Because if so, we need to round up our troops."

"Yes, please. We need all available and willing allies we have. Since most of the vampires back me, I can force Matthew to step down, and I'll reverse the decision of banning other supernaturals from Shadow Terrace." Alex kissed my forehead. "Let me call Gwen while you talk to Annie."

I hated to leave Eliza alone with my friends, but I wanted to talk to Annie without her presence. "I'll be right back." Not wanting Eliza to follow me, I blurred to the back door and exited before she could say a word.

When the door shut behind me, Sierra and Annie turned. Annie's once sparkling eyes seemed dull and had dark circles under them, and her usual cheerful demeanor was nonexistent.

"Hey, Sierra." The longer I put off telling Annie the truth, the harder it would be. "Do you mind giving me and Annie a moment?"

"Nope," Sierra said eagerly. "I'll go in and talk with the others." Her usual snarky humor was missing as she hurried toward the door.

Killian must have informed Sierra of what was going on via their pack link. Usually, she'd have been nosy.

Annie took a step toward me, brows furrowed. "Is everything okay?"

For a second, I nearly chickened out. Maybe Eliza was right. Why ruin Annie's life more than Eilam already had? But that would be taking the easy way out, and it wouldn't help her. "I need to tell you something."

"Okay." She tapped her foot. "What's up?"

Yeah, how did I begin? "Do you know why Eliza took you to Nashville?"

"She doesn't think I do, but two weird guys were standing outside the shelter when she picked me up from work a couple nights ago." Annie put her hands in her jeans pockets. "I noticed them because one was covered head to toe in clothing, despite it being hot as balls. I didn't think much of it until I noticed them again in Nashville. I think they were following us."

Her attention to detail had always amazed me. Annie was smart and very observant. "Why didn't you say anything?"

"You know why." She snorted. "Eliza is secretive, and I wanted to get away from Lexington. I thought maybe a change of scenery would help the dreams."

My stomach dropped. Those dreams had to be about her time here. Maybe I shouldn't have had Alex mess with her memory. "Those men were following you, and that's why you came here."

Annie rolled her eyes. "Don't be all dramatic. I didn't see them when we left today. There's no way they could find us here unless they have magical powers." She laughed but stopped when I didn't join in. Her face fell. "I was teasing, Ronnie. I don't think they have—"

"That's why I came out here." I needed to get it all out before I changed my mind. "They can follow you because they're supernaturals and have sort of magical powers." I hated to drop this on her, but we didn't have much time to get her there gently. At least, she wasn't finding out again the way I had—with a guy all vamped out on me, a guy with fangs and crimson eyes.

Annie's face remained a mask of indifference, as if I'd told her it was a cloudy day. "You're not joking, are you?" She instinctively touched her neck. "The scary thing is I believe you. Like you're confirming something that makes sense." She shivered.

My heart broke. "They're already here, and … one of the men is Alex's brother."

"Wait …" She raised a finger. "Are you saying Alex is a supernatural?"

"Yeah, he's a … vampire." Now that I'd started, I couldn't stop. "Sierra, Griffin, Sterlyn, and Killian are wolf shifters, and Rosemary is an angel."

She shook her head as if trying to comprehend. "They're all supernaturals?"

"Everyone who lives in Shadow Terrace and Shadow Ridge is supernatural. There are humans here, but they're only visitors."

"But you live here, and you're not—" Her eyes bulged as she scanned me again. "Your hair is more vibrant, and your skin is flawless. You're you, but different. Did Alex turn you?" Her face twisted in confusion. "Can he turn you?"

"Yes, vampires can turn humans." Wow, I hadn't meant to go down this road, yet here we were. "I was dying, Annie. He turned me to save me." I wouldn't go into detail. That was a conversation for when we had time because I bet she'd question everything. "But the point is, those men are looking for you and Eliza, and there might be a fight. We're going to leave you here with wolves to protect you."

"Leave me here?" Annie's voice grew louder. "What does that mean? Where are you going?"

We couldn't take her with us. "We have to meet with Alex's brother. He's back in Shadow Terrace with his friend, probably to get reinforcements, since you and Eliza came here. We're going to stop them, so they don't get to you."

I'm heading out. Alex connected with me. *Gwen hasn't seen him, but a few vampires saw him heading toward the blood bank a few minutes ago.*

Oh, hell no. *I'm coming with you.* The stupid blood bank again. I shuddered, thinking of the hidden room where Eilam had tried to force Gwen and Annie to kill me. We were coming full circle, and I wasn't overjoyed about it.

Alex's disapproval wafted through our connection. *Veronica, you need to stay out of reach so Matthew can't use you against me. I'm taking Sterlyn and Griffin with me.*

I'm going. I refused to be left behind. *Our people need to see us standing up to your brother together, especially if I'm going to be their queen.*

I must have said the right thing because Alex's feelings changed to pride and love. *You're right, though I hate it.*

I needed to join him before he changed his mind. "Annie, I've got to go." I didn't want to leave her, but she was safer here than anywhere near Matthew and the demon. "Let's get you settled inside."

We hurried toward the house, and I purposely had to make myself move slowly. Though I could smell wolf shifters close by in the woods, I wanted someone to be right next to her in case something happened.

Inside the house, everyone was standing in the middle of the room.

"Do we need to wait on Cyrus, Kira, and Darrell?" I remembered Sterlyn mentioning that the three of them were on the way.

Sterlyn shook her head. "They dropped their vehicle off at the border of Shadow Ridge and are heading straight to Shadow Terrace in their ... animal forms." She said the last two words oddly, as if asking if it was okay.

"I told her," I assured them, not wanting anyone stepping on eggshells. We didn't have time.

Sierra chuckled. "Good, because that could've been awkward."

"Let's get moving." Griffin headed toward the garage, his face set in determination. "Killian is already heading that way in wolf form—he'll be near the border, keeping an eye out for anything strange."

"Who's staying to watch over Eliza and Annie?" There was no way I was leaving them unprotected.

Eliza huffed. "I'm going with you. You may need my magic."

Annie gasped. "What? You're a supernatural, too?"

Yeah, for some reason, I hadn't told her about Eliza. "I'm sorry. I should've led with that."

"Wait, you knew!" Annie pointed at me.

I placed a hand on my chest. "I found out when you got here. I've known for less than an hour."

"We don't have time for this," Eliza said lowly. "Yes, I'm a witch, but that doesn't matter. We have two men who need to be handled."

"Another thing you failed to tell me," Annie muttered, her lips turning downward.

"Fine. Are there people close by who can watch Annie?" I wouldn't leave until I knew she was protected.

"I want to go with you." Annie stepped toward me. "I don't know why, but I can't stay here alone."

"But—"

"She's right," Eliza said, surprising me. "I can keep her close and protected when others may not be able to see what I can. Leaving her here isn't a good idea."

Right. If Matthew's companion was a demon, he could be a shadow, and I might be the only one who could see him, though Eliza thought she had a way. "But you stay back and get involved only if needed." I hated being bossy, but I couldn't lose either of them.

Are you sure that's wise? Alex asked as he pulled my keys from his pocket.

We didn't have much of a choice. *They'll just follow us in their car.*

"Then let's go." Sterlyn grabbed a bag from the floor and hurried to the garage. "I've got us a change of clothes in case we need to shift."

"I'll meet you there," Rosemary said as she headed to the back door, planning to fly.

Alex took my hand and nodded to Annie and Eliza. "You two can ride with us."

The four of us were hurrying to the car when I felt a chill in the air. I glanced up and saw the outline of something.

A shadow.

Watching us.

CHAPTER TWENTY-SEVEN

I FROZE IN MY TRACKS, my gaze locking with the apparition's red eyes.

What's wrong? Alex connected with concern. He followed my gaze, confusion lining his face.

He didn't see it.

Figured.

Neither Annie nor Eliza noticed the hovering figure, either. They rushed to the back seat of the car, where Eliza got in behind the front passenger seat. Eliza had parked her old Camry at the curb, so it wasn't blocking us in. She'd considered the possibility of needing a quick escape.

The shadow tilted its head as it watched me. This had to be the demon Matthew had brought back with him. Unlike the shadow that had haunted me, this one was clearly a person: tall, thick, and hovering. A shiver ran through me from seeing someone like myself, but I had to remember he wasn't here to get to know me. He was here to watch and attack.

Refusing to allow the figure to see my fear, I relaxed my body. *It's the demon. He's watching us.*

Get in the car, Alex commanded as he reached the driver's door. *We've got to move.*

The alarm in his voice broke me out of my stupor. He was right. Standing here, staring at the thing, wasn't doing any good.

As the garage door opened so Griffin, Sierra, and Sterlyn could leave, I turned to head to the passenger seat, but with each step, the air cooled around me as if the demon was getting closer.

The hair on my arms stood on end, and I spun around in time to watch the demon close the short distance between us.

"Veronica!" Alex yelled. "What's wrong?"

"The demon." I didn't need to focus on answering questions but rather on determining a way to make it leave. Or kill it. But how?

A familiar hand touched my shoulder as Eliza appeared beside me. She lifted a hand, and the area around her eyes tensed as she said, "*Expellere!*"

The wind churned around us, and the demon startled back.

Eliza extended her hand, and the wind surged. The demon's red eyes brightened.

"We need to go," Eliza said through gritted teeth. "Spells take a lot out of me, so I can't do this long."

Shit. I wasn't sure what we would do once she

stopped. The wind was holding him back in shadow form, but what if he turned solid?

I blurred, opening the back passenger door for her. "Get inside."

She continued to concentrate on the demon as it desperately tried to get to us.

Sterlyn stepped out of the garage. Her gaze followed the gust of wind. She must have seen something because her mouth dropped open. "Go. We'll be right behind you."

Leaning over the back seat, Annie helped me guide Eliza back into the car since her full concentration was on the demon and her powers. She didn't fight us as we nudged her inside.

"Now you get in." Annie's voice quivered, the only hint that this situation was getting to her. "I can buckle her."

Not wasting another second, I slammed her door and jumped into the passenger seat. As soon as I shut my door, Alex spun out of the driveway and rushed out of the neighborhood.

As we drove past the thick cypress trees that surrounded the neighborhood, wolves ran from the tree lines. From what I could count, there were at least thirty.

I turned, watching in horror as they ran past Griffin's Navigator toward the demon.

"Ugh," Eliza groaned in pain and exhaustion.

"Eliza!" Annie yelled, and I turned around in my seat.

Sweat sprouted along Eliza's forehead, and her skin

was pasty white. Her eyes grew heavy as if she couldn't keep them open. "So tired. Fighting off a demon takes so much out of me."

"Is there something I can do?" I felt useless and racked my brain for how in the hell I could help her.

Her head sagged, and I watched in horror as the wind keeping the demon at bay slowed.

"No!" I shouted, and my hands and feet began to tingle.

What are you doing? Alex asked, glancing at me. *Veronica.*

Annie's ear-piercing scream confirmed that she was in trouble.

"Where's Ronnie?" Annie cried. "She was right there a second ago."

My vision wavered, and I looked down at the outline of my body.

I'd transformed into my own shadow.

A loud, pained howl stabbed my eardrums, followed by another from a different wolf.

The demon was attacking Killian's pack, and I couldn't sit here and let it continue when I had the best chance of taking the demon on.

I've got to help them. I floated out of the crack in the window, leaving the car. *I'll meet you in Shadow Terrace.*

Damn it, Veronica, Alex hissed through our connection. *I can't leave you here.*

Griffin's Navigator barreled underneath me.

Get them to Shadow Terrace and safe. If he stopped, Annie and Eliza would be compromised, especially with how weak Eliza was. *And see if we can help Eliza recover. If you stop, that will put us more at risk, because I'll be desperate to protect them.*

Frustration and anger wafted through our connection, but the car continued to move. He connected, *I'm not happy, but get your ass over there now. Make him chase you, anything; just don't fight him head-on. Rosemary is our best weapon against him.*

I hadn't thought of that, but he was right. Rosemary was pure angel and should have strength equivalent to a full demon.

Okay, promise. I'd do anything as long as he protected the people I loved, including himself.

The Navigator stopped, and Sterlyn jumped out. I rushed toward her and stopped right in front of her. I needed her to get over to the blood bank. Splitting up would only weaken us. "Hey, go on. I'll get the demon to follow me."

Sterlyn stopped and looked at me. "Are you sure?"

"Yes, go on." I didn't have time to explain as another pained whimper filled the air. "I'll get him. If we engage here, we won't win."

She nodded as Griffin's door opened. "I'll tell him. Just be careful."

It was crazy how much my family had grown in the past month, but I wouldn't have it any other way. "Promise."

Trusting her, I trod the air, rushing to the demon. As I took the turn that led back into the neighborhood, vomit inched up my throat.

The demon had ripped the head off a wolf, while another lay on the ground, its neck in an unnatural position. The demon had another wolf in its grasp and seemed to be choking it. In my shadow form, I could see the demon's sinister smile as it enjoyed the pain and torture it inflicted on its victim.

Even more heartbreaking, the other wolves could only watch in horror as one of their own died. They thrashed, clawed, and nipped at the air where they thought the demon was, but they fell right through the shadow. They couldn't hurt the demon.

I had to do something before anyone else died.

"You're hurting wolves that can't even see you?" I needed the asshole to pay attention to me. "That's a little unfair, don't you think?"

The shadow's head jerked up, its gaze locking on me. The demon released the wolf and turned to me.

Okay, I had its attention. Now I needed to capitalize on it. "Come on and fight me."

Within seconds, the demon was in front of me. It moved quicker in this form than I could on both feet. The realization that I was at a major disadvantage settled heavily in my chest.

Maybe I hadn't thought this through.

"I don't want to fight you," the demon said, its voice resonating deep inside me. "I came here to bring you home."

This had to be a joke, but was that why I'd initially felt excited? Did we have some sort of familial bond? "I am home." How could I possibly know him?

"Sweet child." He laughed. "You won't know what you're missing until I take you there. It's a place where you can embrace who you are. Since we aren't full demons, we can't stay there for long, but we can go in long enough to understand what we are. Unfortunately, I wasn't around to raise you, although you were supposed to die with your mother."

Wait. None of that made sense. "How do you know my mother, and what do you mean since we aren't full demons?" Hysteria edged its way inside me as his words circled in my head.

"Oh, I knew her in the best ways possible." His red eyes brightened as if the memories brought him happiness. "Sexually and violently. I didn't want you to be born for so many reasons. You were more human than demon, which can be problematic, but I never considered having a vampire turn you. Now, with time, you can be as strong as me, and we can wreak havoc on the world."

My world flipped around me. "You're my *father*?" I'd known that my mother had died in a car wreck, and I'd been born early because of that, but I'd always wondered about my father. No one had ever known anything about him.

Veronica, Alex connected, his love and concern filling me when I desperately needed it. *What's wrong? I'm turning around.*

No. Don't. I couldn't let this man take anyone else away from me. *He's not attacking me. The demon … I think he's my father.* The last word was difficult even in connection.

What? Alex felt as surprised as I had. *How do you know?*

He's talking to me.

"Yes, I'm your *father*." The demon said the word like it was filthy.

"If you tried to kill my mom and me, why are you here?"

"I already explained." Somehow, he rolled his eyes, even in this form. "I thought you'd be too weak, but you aren't—not anymore. Good thing I found out about you after you became a vampire, or I would have come back to kill you."

Wow. Did he think that was comforting? And here I'd thought Matthew and Azbogah were the biggest douches I'd ever met. Now there were three. I opened the connection between Alex and me, wanting him to hear everything. "Let me guess. Matthew told you about me?"

A whimper from below drew my attention. The wolves were on edge, and two were checking the dead.

My throat tightened, and I swallowed down bile. I was responsible for their deaths.

This demon was here for me. If not for me, they would still be alive. All these people were at risk again because of my presence.

"The vampire king is an idiot—he had no clue. But you look like your mother, and you have my magical energy. He wants me to kill your family in front of you and let you feel what it's like to lose the people you love; then kill you to put his brother back in place. But I won't kill you, seeing as you could be useful to me."

"This has nothing to do with you loving your daughter?" I already knew the answer, but I needed to hear him say it. That would be the final nail in the coffin. "And what about *your* parents if you aren't full demon?"

"Love?" He snickered. "Love is a weakness. My bitch of a mother died just like she deserved, by my father's hand. You'll learn that hate, revenge, and terror are the building blocks for a long and joyous life. When you see the life leave someone's eyes, or force someone to watch you kill their family member, you feel so powerful. And when they beg for mercy, you'll feel like a god. Nothing compares to that. You'll understand, once we help Matthew corrupt the vampires here."

This man was a monster. "I'm not interested." I was done engaging with him.

Don't antagonize him, Alex connected with me. *Play along.*

But I refused to even pretend to be like him. The thought made my skin crawl.

"Excuse me?" His smile dropped, and his shadow darkened. "Did you think I was giving you a choice? That's cute. But you see, you're mine. I own you."

His maliciousness slammed into me. I'd been wrong about Matthew and Azbogah. This guy was worse than anything I'd ever encountered. His evilness coated my body like sludge.

"No." No one owned me, not even Alex. I was my own person, and I wouldn't bow to anyone's will. "You don't."

"We'll see about that."

Something warmed the palm of my hand, and I grasped the dagger tightly. It always appeared when I was in danger. I'd hidden it away in my and Alex's room, but as always, it had found me when I needed it.

The demon surged toward me, and I swung the dagger upward. It sliced through the shadow.

He hissed and grabbed his shoulder, where bluish-black blood trickled down his arm. "You bitch."

How fatherly of him. His attitude made it easy to ignore any connection we had.

A wolf growled, and I glanced down. Every single wolf was now looking at the shadow.

Maybe injuring him with the blade had made him visible.

"How did you get that?" His eyes narrowed. "That belonged to my father, and he won't be happy that you have it."

"Oh, you want this?" I waved the dagger. Maybe if I injured him again, I could level the playing field more.

"Yes." He held out his hand, expecting me to hand it to him. "Now."

The asshole was cocky, but that would work in my favor. I pretended to hand it to him.

He must have predicted my next move because he twisted my wrist and removed the dagger from my hand. "I was going to use you, but you're more of a problem than you're worth, so this ends now." He struck out with the dagger, but it disappeared from his grasp and reappeared in my palm.

His eyes widened as he looked at his empty hand.

Using the moment to my advantage, I stabbed him in the other shoulder. I pulled the dagger out at an angle to damage him as much as possible.

A loud rumble emanated from his chest, and he lunged at me.

CHAPTER TWENTY-EIGHT

I JERKED BACK and to the side, and the demon missed me by inches. I could see the strain on his shadow face from all the hate he was channeling.

He wouldn't think twice about killing me.

Hell, he'd tried before. Luckily, he'd been too arrogant to stick around and make sure I was dead.

The past didn't matter now. He'd killed my mother and attempted to kill me—that was all I needed to know.

"I'll fix the little problem of you being alive now," he hissed, his sibilance reminding me of the way the vampires spoke when their fangs were extended.

Needing to lead him away from the wolves and toward Shadow Terrace, I turned and moved as quickly as possible toward Alex. *I'm on my way,* I connected with him.

About time. His displeasure was easy to read through our connection. *We're in Shadow Terrace, getting close to the blood bank.*

I tensed in anticipation of the demon grabbing or hurting me, but I refused to slow down. *Any updates there?* I didn't turn to see how close he was. That would only slow me down.

It's not good. Alex paused. *The remaining rogue vampires and my brother are holed up in the blood bank, refusing to let any blood out. It's not an issue now, but in the next few days, when we run low on supplies, the vampires will eventually succumb to their natural urges and attack the visiting humans.*

Of course, that was the jackass's plan: Barricade the blood and starve everyone. *We can't let that happen.*

We'll find a way in. Worst case, we can use the underground tunnel. Alex's dread filled our bond because he knew what I did: Matthew was banking on that, and there was no telling what kind of traps or guards they had down there.

We'll figure out something else.

We had to.

The wind picked up, moving me toward the Terrace, but that meant it was helping the demon as well. I came close to laughing. I had no clue what my father's name was, but that was for the best. Putting a name to his shadow face would only humanize him, and I didn't need that. He was a monster, and I needed to keep that in perspective.

Unable to stop myself, I glanced over my shoulder, wondering why he hadn't reached me.

He was fifty yards away and moving slower than before. His shadow looked more solid, and the wolves could see him. Obviously, the dagger had hurt him, weakening his magic.

Maybe I could reach the blood bank before he caught up with me. Reinvigorated, I pushed myself harder to widen the distance between us.

I faced forward and focused on reaching Alex. If I got to him, we could end this conflict before war broke out.

I noticed there weren't any birds around, and when I reached the trees, I didn't hear squirrels scurrying in the redbuds and cypresses. The world sounded as if it had stopped moving.

That couldn't be a good sign.

The bustling town of Shadow Terrace had humans walking the cobblestone streets as if everything was normal. Little did they know that ten miles away, vampires were gathering to get access to their food so they wouldn't turn on the visitors. A shiver ran down my spine even in shadow form.

If we couldn't resolve things quickly, we might need to evacuate the humans.

Hopefully, things wouldn't come to that as Matthew had planned.

The blood bank came into view. The three-story beige stone building reminded me of a mental hospital. There were no windows except for two small ones next to the main door, through which no one could enter without permission. Of course, there was the hidden basement we'd become aware of due to Eilam kidnapping Annie and Gwen. If I were a betting person, I'd put my money on Matthew hiding there. It was all concrete walls, with a back exit that let out a couple of miles away.

That thought unsettled me. Taking over the bank seemed like it had been a thought-out plan, not something thrown together. He must have been planning this for some time.

My soulmate stood out front with Sterlyn, Griffin, Sierra, Rosemary, and Killian in his wolf form. That wasn't an issue for conversation, since he could pack link with the other three wolf shifters. I damn near cried when I realized Annie and Eliza weren't with them.

I'm getting closer, and I can see you. I scanned the area. Gwen and Joshua walked from the other side of the building toward Alex, past forty-five vampires. *Please tell me those vampires are on our side.*

Yes, these are vampires that Joshua and his friends trust. Alex turned to me, but his face wrinkled in confusion as he searched the sky.

He still couldn't see me. That was a good thing. Maybe I could get inside the blood bank and spy on Matthew without him knowing. *I'm almost there.*

You must blend in with the sun. Alex ran a hand through his sun-kissed brown hair, messing it.

Shadows are always around; sometimes, the sun hides them from view. I didn't know why, but those words came automatically. I'd never thought of that before, but it made perfect sense. *Where are Eliza and Annie?*

I left them in the car, half a mile away. I didn't want them to be too close and easy targets, Alex explained as I reached the group.

"Rosemary can't get through the doors." Sterlyn shook her head, not yet aware of my presence. "We'll have to try the tunnel. I don't know another way."

Gwen reached the group a few seconds after me. "That's not smart. That's what Matthew is trying to force us to do. Think about it."

"What other option do we have?" Griffin growled. "I'm not happy about it either, but the window is shatterproof, and the door is made of angelic material so no one, not even the angels, could get in. How the vampires got it is a separate issue that we'll address later, after this shitshow."

"For once, I agree with everything he said." Sierra waved her hand at Griffin. "How are we doing this?"

Yeah, they weren't going to do it at all. I spun around and was relieved to see I'd lost the demon. I didn't doubt he was on his way, but I'd moved much quicker than him. I should have time to slip in and open the doors from the inside. *Don't do anything. I'm handling it.*

"No!" Alex yelled and waved a finger like a weapon. "You are not."

"That's not a legit answer to my question." Sierra patted her chest.

Alex rolled his eyes. "I wasn't talking to you. I was talking to Veronica."

"She's here?" Joshua glanced around, searching for me. "She must be in that form."

"Shh ..." Gwen placed a finger to her lips. "No one knows about that. Remember?"

Oh, great. They were going to out me before I got

inside. *I promise I'll just slip through the door and open it. I'm not trying to be a shero.*

I don't even know what that is. Alex dropped his head. "She's going inside."

"That's an excellent idea." Sterlyn smiled. "That solves our problem, and they likely won't see her."

"Well, I can too." Rosemary puffed out her chest as her eyes focused directly on me. "But that doesn't matter. No one in there should be able to."

"You can too?" Griffin's eyebrows shot up. "Must be the angel connection."

I didn't need to waste any more time. My demon parent would be here soon. I floated to the window and flowed through the small crack between the glass and the frame. As my body slipped in, I felt claustrophobic as if I were being squeezed. When I'd slipped out the car window, I'd had no clue what was happening, and my fear must have overridden this sensation, but now that I was purposely doing it, it felt tighter than a constricting seatbelt.

I got inside and didn't see anyone in the cement hallway.

Odd. You'd think that a guard would be here, watching in case someone got through.

I'm going to check things out real fast. If no one could see me, it was best to make sure we weren't walking into a trap.

Unsurprisingly, Alex's anger slammed into me. *Veronica, you said you would just go in to open the damn door.* Even through our connection, his tone was frosty.

I know. You're right. I wanted to protect the people I loved, but if the demon caught up, he could kill them. If they lived, Alex would rush off to the tunnel without a second thought, and even if I didn't get myself into trouble, he would be in danger. I had to use my brain.

Despite everything inside me screaming to check things out first, I turned to the door and attempted to unlock it, but my hand slipped right through it.

Dammit, I couldn't grasp it. I was too unfocused to solidify completely. There had to be a way to turn it. I was able to hold the dagger.

As if the dagger had heard my thoughts, the handle warmed in my hand, heating my blood. My hand tingled where I grasped it, and that gave me an idea.

Is everything okay? Alex connected.

Yeah. I rubbed my fingers together, preparing myself. *I'm unlocking the door.* Or I hoped I could.

Inhaling deeply, I focused on my fingers. As I reached for the handle, my fingers tingled like my hand holding the dagger.

I prayed that meant something good.

I touched the bolt lock and felt cool metal against my hand. Not wanting to celebrate too early, I concentrated. The lock clicked open, and I exhaled as a weight lifted off my shoulders.

The door opened, and Alex blurred inside. His blue eyes searched for me.

I'm here. I willed myself to turn visible, but not completely solid.

His mouth dropped. "I see you."

"So do I." Griffin shook his head. "Creepy."

Two silver wolves rushed into the blood bank, taking me by surprise. This had to be Cyrus and Darrell, who had been with Kira. Just as I thought of her, a red fox trotted in behind them.

Cyrus growled as his eyes focused on me; then he stopped. Sterlyn must have told him who I was.

The most important thing was the entire crew was on their way.

Rosemary stepped into the blood bank between Sterlyn and Sierra. "Mom and Dad are on their way since a demon is involved. They should be here soon, but we shouldn't wait. I have a feeling Matthew didn't expect us to get inside this way, since no one is guarding the door."

"I agree. We need to take them by surprise while we can." Sterlyn nodded, her body coiled with tension. "Let's move."

They'll be in the secret room and underground tunnel.

Gwen entered the building. "Alex, I'll coordinate the rest."

"Come to the hidden room you were chained in. Give everyone a heads-up about the layout, and don't be too far behind." Alex grimaced. "I'm sorry."

"Me too, but I have to face that day eventually." Gwen's face turned a shade paler. "Might as well be today. I'll go talk to the vampires."

"We don't need to talk," Rosemary whispered. "It'll be more complicated with me and the vampires, since we can't pack link, but we need to be quiet."

No one else said anything, and we all headed toward the dreaded location.

I floated ahead of the group since no one could see me. I pulled my visibility back as I headed down a long hallway that led to this floor's draining room, passing by the two shut doors on either side that held freezers where blood was stored. Alex had explained that the main food supply was kept here, and houses were stocked for several days at a time. We didn't want to provide too much food at once and risk running through our supply too fast.

As I floated closer to the draining room, the metallic scent of blood increased. When I'd toured the bank last week, I'd learned there were three floors with this same layout. Each specialized room could drain up to fifty humans at a time. There was a recovery ward, where the humans were fed cookies and orange juice to get their sugar back up after losing so much blood. After they recovered, the vampires made them forget the entire night.

We now knew the golden rule—no kids were to be touched—had been ignored. Every person brought into the bank had to be eighteen and older. The vampires took the adults from the inn and manipulated the kids' minds to put them into a deep sleep. That was one reason the vampires wanted Alex and me to step into power. They didn't like using children like that. Taking blood from the town's adult tourists helped vampires survive, while retaining their humanity, and each human was to be respected and preserved.

That was until Matthew and Blade went into business together.

Outside the draining room, a spiral staircase led to the top two floors, but Matthew and the others wouldn't be there. They'd be in the basement.

You'll need to unlock the door to the draining room. Alex lifted his hand, signaling the others to stop.

I floated through the locked double doors and entered the draining room. *On it.* Just like with the front door, I focused on unlocking the doors so the others could get in. When the door clicked, I opened it slowly, making sure not to make any sound.

Our group slipped through and walked past fifty empty tables with tubes traveling from temperature-controlled boxes holding the bags to the IVs that would enter the humans' arms.

We made our way slowly to a stone door. It remained broken from when Alex and the others had located the hidden entryway to the secret basement. Apparently, there was no need to pretend anymore.

"What if they get in the front door?" an unfamiliar voice asked from down the stairwell.

Matthew laughed sinisterly. "Don't be stupid. Andras is taking care of the girl, and they have no way to get inside."

The bastard had expected my demon father—Andras —to kill me. Granted, Andras was trying to now, so Matthew wasn't too far off the mark.

Raw rage swirled around me from Alex.

"But that's his daughter, right? Azbogah figured it out from that dagger she has," the man pressed.

"Yes, and luckily, he knew where to find the demon that would be willing to come here and get it back. The dagger belongs to his family." Matthew sounded so smug. "Demons love enormous cities, you know."

The vampire grunted. "You can't trust a demon. Are you sure—"

"Shut up," Matthew growled. "I am your king, and you'd best remember that."

Before I realized what was happening, Alex had blurred past me.

No. He was too angry and not thinking straight. I tried to catch him, but he had too much of a lead.

"Not if I have anything to do with it, *brother*." Alex hissed as his fangs extended and his eyes turned crimson.

The basement was just as I remembered it, with a floor and walls of pure cement. A maroon rug lay in the middle of the room, with a loveseat on the edge. Matthew sat in the middle of the loveseat, and a strange vampire stood beside him.

The horrible night I'd come here to rescue Annie raced through my mind, but I had to push the memory aside. I needed to help Alex.

"What? How?" Matthew stood from the couch. His skin was pasty white, and a vile, putrid energy poured off him. He was covered from head to toe in dark clothing, his face the only skin visible.

"I told you," the tall male vampire said. His skin matched Matthew's, but a little warmth was left inside him; he wasn't completely gone. "We can't trust a demon."

You're visible, Alex said, his concern lacing through me.

It didn't matter. I was here now, and I'd fight beside him. There was no chance this would end amicably. Matthew had gone too far.

"Your plan wasn't foolproof." My voice was hoarse from not being in human form. "Andras wanted to keep me alive to do his bidding."

"I don't care." Matthew smirked. "I'll enjoy killing you myself."

"How could you do this?" Alex asked, tense, ready to fight. "You've turned savage."

"The way we were intended to be." Matthew spread out his arms. "Humans are meant to be our food, and we are not meant to fear anything. I'd hoped you would see that, but I've given up. You're a barrier, and once you and Gwen are eliminated, everyone will fall in line. I'll make sure of it."

"Not if I kill you first." Alex blurred toward his brother.

All chaos broke loose. Sterlyn and the others charged into the basement, and I lifted my dagger. I couldn't let Alex kill his brother.

But as I raced across the room, something grabbed my arm and jerked me to a halt. A deep chuckle caused goosebumps to sprout across my body as I was forced to turn and stare into the face of someone who looked similar to me.

Andras was here and in human form.

CHAPTER TWENTY-NINE

THE SIMILARITIES between us were uncanny. We had the same copper hair, but his was in a buzz cut, and we had the same heart-shaped face, but his eyes were milky white.

My emerald-green eyes must have come from my mother, which was a relief. At least, I hadn't inherited everything from him.

He sneered, towering a foot over me. "Did you really think you could get away?"

I hoped his appearance in human form meant he was weaker than he let on and couldn't hold his shadowy form.

I shook my head, lifting my chin. I didn't want to cower before him, but dammit, that's what I felt compelled to do. "No." I let the truth speak for itself.

"At least you aren't stupid like him," Andras said, nodding at Matthew. "That idiot thought he could tell me what to do and how to do it."

Even though I shouldn't have taken my gaze off the demon, I couldn't help but glance over to check on Alex.

Alex and Matthew were in hand-to-hand combat, but Matthew had an edge, probably because he was filled with human blood, had lost his humanity, and didn't have any reservations about killing his brother.

Our friends had sprung into action; Griffin, Killian, and Sierra were charging toward Alex, while Sterlyn and Rosemary raced to reach me.

The silver wolves and fox attacked the unknown vampire that had been standing next to Matthew. Maybe this battle would be short after all.

Seeing Alex receiving help eased my concern. Those three wouldn't let anything happen to him. Against all odds, we'd become family.

"And did you really think we wouldn't help her fight you?" Rosemary asked, parroting Andras's words.

Sterlyn pulled her knife from her pocket and struck at his heart.

In a flash, Andras released his hold on my arm and spun, catching Sterlyn's wrist. He smirked and shoved her. She flew across the room and landed on her ass.

Her body jarred as she hit the hard cement floor and crumpled.

Shit, he'd hurt her without breaking a sweat. If this was him injured, I'd hate to see him at full strength.

Not wasting a second, Rosemary's wings exploded from her back, and she lifted off the ground, then barreled toward Andras.

The demon seemed unconcerned as his physical

form dissipated into a shadow. He inched upward, and Rosemary stopped her flight seconds before she would have crashed into the concrete wall where he'd been standing moments before.

He was a good fighter, and unfortunately, none of us knew how to fight a demon.

I watched in horror as Andras sped across the room to the entrance of the underground tunnel.

Hell no. He wasn't getting away that easily.

As I blurred after him, Sterlyn yelled, "Ronnie! Wait."

I wanted to ignore her and keep moving forward, but Sterlyn had amazing instincts when it came to combat. Forcing myself to stop, I pushed down the urge to chase after the man who'd taken away my mother before I was even born.

Sterlyn reached my side and exhaled. "Thank goodness you listened."

"I didn't want to." Everything inside me screamed to go after him. "If he gets away, he'll just come back."

"I have a feeling he's not running away." Sterlyn gestured to the door. "Remember when we said the tunnel is probably a trap?"

Holy shit. She was right. He was probably getting reinforcements, and I'd nearly run straight into them.

The door opened, and fifteen vampires charged into the room. Each one held a gun, ready to shoot.

This was worse than I'd realized.

"They have weapons," Sterlyn yelled, alerting everyone in the room. "Watch out."

If I'd gone out the door, I'd have been captured or shot. The demon knew how to hurt me, even in shadow form.

Rosemary flew past and landed in front of us. She spread her wings wide, hiding us from view. She would get herself shot, or worse.

A blood-curdling scream caused all of us to turn around. A silver wolf landed on all four feet, and the neck of the vampire next to Matthew gushed blood. The vampire clutched his neck to stop the bleeding, but the liquid slipped between his fingers and poured down his arms.

In the last month and a half, I'd seen more blood and destruction than in the first nineteen and a half years of my life. The supernatural world was bloody and violent ... at least, here in Shadow Terrace. We needed to find a balance to bring peace to the masses.

"Attack!" Matthew yelled as he fought Killian, Sierra, Griffin, and Alex. Despite having four against him, he was standing tall, his only visible injury a gash on his cheek.

Dammit, we had to figure a way out of this. The best strategy I could think of was to injure them all.

I focused on my body, turning myself over to the shadows. If they couldn't see me, I'd be the best weapon we had.

Or I hoped to be.

Footsteps pounded overhead. The cavalry was arriving. Thankfully, Gwen and the others had quickly coordinated and were almost here. We needed all the backup we could get.

My body tingled as the transition was underway. The weight on my legs vanished, and I floated into the air. I rose above Rosemary's head just as a tall vampire with shaggy blond hair pointed his gun at her.

I surged forward to smack the gun from his hands. A foot from him, something slammed into me, knocking me to the ground.

Pain exploded in my side as I hit the cement floor. Andras floated above me, his red eyes glowing brightly.

"I will let you watch everyone you love die first. Then I'll kill you slowly," he vowed, enjoying the advantage he held over us.

The gun fired, and my gaze landed on Rosemary. She was standing in front of Sterlyn but had folded her wings around herself a millisecond before the bullet hit her. The bullet clanged to the floor, and I exhaled with relief. That would've been a shot right through the chest.

"Idiots!" a vampire called in the back. "Angel wings are impenetrable."

Yet another thing I hadn't known, but I was so damn grateful. That was why she'd stood in front of us to protect us.

The silver wolves appeared next to Rosemary as fur sprouted along Sterlyn's body. I watched in amazement as her clothes ripped off her, and her bones cracked as her body shifted into her animal form.

"Careful not to hit the king," the blond vampire shouted as the fifteen fighters charged.

Gwen and her vampires ran into the room, and I exhaled in relief when I saw they had guns, too. Even though weapons weren't ideal, they put us on equal ground.

Wanting to help them, I floated off the floor, but Andras hovered in front of me.

He shook his head. "You aren't doing anything."

Like hell, I wasn't, but I had to play the part of a scared little girl. "They're my friends."

"Exactly." Andras got closer to me, so damn cocky despite getting stabbed twice. "Like I said, you're going to watch. I'll start with the one you love most." He turned and floated toward Alex.

No. Hatred consumed me as the dagger warmed in my hand. I flashed after him, moving faster. Pushing the surprise away, I stabbed him in the back, straight into his heart.

Dark blue blood poured from the wound, and he spun around, his red eyes already dulling. "How?" he rasped and fell to the floor, changing back into solid form.

"I will always protect the ones I love." The fact that he was my father had no influence over me. He'd made it clear he didn't care about me and would use me to his benefit. He would never do anything good.

He crumpled onto his chest, and my hand inched forward and yanked the dagger out.

Part of me hurt, watching the man who'd helped create me slip into death, but I had to remember what he was.

A demon that enjoyed inflicting pain and terror.

If I hadn't killed him, he would've gone after Alex. And Alex was someone I couldn't lose ... ever.

Gunshots blasted as the vampires shot in a craze. I watched as Griffin and Killian raced toward Sterlyn. I had to help too, or there would be deaths on our side.

I rushed toward the fifteen vampires and zeroed in on the blond firing at Sterlyn. With each shot, Rosemary jumped in front of her, protecting her distant cousin.

If another vampire joined in, Rosemary wouldn't be able to deflect all the bullets. I flew past Rosemary and raised my dagger. My hands trembled, not wanting to kill another, but I didn't have a choice. If I didn't help, then my friends would die.

As if the vampires had figured out they needed to focus the attack on Rosemary, a guy turned in the angel's direction.

Shit! Turning myself over to my vampire and demon side, I let them take control. I had to rely on them to guide me, or I wouldn't help like I needed to.

As the blond vampire raised his weapon to shoot again, I slammed into his chest, and he stumbled back. His soulless hazel eyes widened in surprise, searching for his attacker.

He frantically swiped the air. "What the hell? Who's there?"

"What are you talking about?" a vampire with sharp cheekbones asked as he fired at Rosemary.

"Something hit me," the blond vampire yelled. "But I don't see a damn thing."

I was wasting time. With the butt of my dagger, I

smacked the blond vampire in the head, and his eyes rolled back as he passed out.

"What the—" The sharp-cheeked vampire started and looked at his unconscious friend.

That was all the distraction Sterlyn needed. She leaped on the sharp-cheeked man and sank her teeth into his neck then ripped out his throat.

My stomach churned, but I pushed the nausea aside as a dark-haired vampire swung his gun toward Sterlyn.

No. Way.

I lunged, trying to reach her before he could pull the trigger. Someone bumped into me, and I stumbled to the ground. However, they didn't even seem to realize we'd collided. Right when I'd practically lost hope, another massive silver wolf jumped in and clamped its jaws around the dark-haired vampire's gun hand. The vampire shrieked, and the gun tumbled from his grasp.

Rosemary flew over and swiped the gun from the floor. She turned and fired at the vampires surrounding us as Gwen and her vampires surged forward.

Screams echoed off the walls as the stench of vampire blood filled the room. It didn't smell as sweet as a human's. Alex had told me that soulmates enjoyed each other's blood because of their connection, but all other vampires' blood smelled like decay. He had described the smell perfectly. When I tasted his blood, it was sexually exhilarating but couldn't satisfy my hunger.

Within seconds, the fourteen vampires lay dead at our feet. The blond vampire was the only one alive and still passed out.

"Alex, no!" Gwen screamed, forcing me to turn around.

My world stopped.

Matthew had Sterlyn's knife pressed against Alex's throat. Blood trickled down Alex's neck and onto his shirt. Matthew's eyes gleamed wildly as his face twisted with pure hate.

Sterlyn must have dropped the knife when she'd shifted.

"You need to give up," Rosemary said threateningly. "All your people are dead, and you have no one else on your side."

"I'm the king," Matthew sneered. "All the vampires have to follow me."

"No, they don't," Alex gritted. "They can choose their leader."

"That's just another stupid idea that bitch put into your head." Matthew dug the knife in deeper. "This isn't a democracy, dear sweet brother. Bloodline and birth order mean everything."

Alex winced. If we didn't do something quickly, Matthew would kill him. I materialized, wanting Matthew to focus his hatred on me, instead of his brother. "Times have changed."

As I expected, Matthew glared at me. He rasped, "Not for vampires. And once I kill Alex, they will fear me and cower once more."

"What about me?" Gwen stepped toward him, lifting her chin. "Will you kill me, too, to eliminate all your threats?"

Matthew laughed. "Are you serious? No one would follow you."

She jerked back like she'd been slapped. "Because I'm a woman? I'm on the council."

"I pushed for you to be on the council, knowing you'd vote my way." Matthew sighed in disappointment. "Did you really think I wanted to hear your ideas? You're weak and always have been. I took care of you to humor Alex. He's always held a soft spot for you, and softness makes you weak and replaceable."

Joshua stepped around our group of vampires. He stared at me and flicked his eyes toward Matthew. He mouthed, "Distract him."

"Isn't that funny?" I snorted and placed a hand on my chest. "You think they're replaceable, when we've killed the only vampires who supported you." I got closer to make him nervous. I'd love to be the one to kill him, but Joshua had the right idea. Matthew expected me to do something stupid. I had a feeling he was banking on proving that love caused death.

"Yes, I do." Matthew grinned. "One more step, and I'll kill Alex even sooner."

I love you, Alex connected. *You've made me a better man and happier than you'll ever know.*

Stop. You are going to live. I stopped and forced my bottom lip to tremble as if I was scared. It wasn't hard because there were no guarantees Joshua could pull this off. But it was our best bet. *Be ready. Joshua is about to attack.*

Alex's eyes lightened to sky blue when he saw Joshua edging out of Matthew's direct sight.

The vampire king was so angry and full of hate that he was focusing on me, Gwen, Sterlyn, and the wolves. Lucky for us, he was cocky enough to think the vampires on our side wouldn't attack him.

"Please." My voice broke of its own accord. All I could do was hope and pray this plan worked. Everyone's attention was on me and Alex, which helped keep Matthew from noticing Joshua. "Don't hurt him. Hurt me instead."

A cruelness settled over him as he considered my words. "You know what? Okay. Watching you die will make him not want to feel anything anymore—he'll beg to lose his humanity. That's actually an excellent idea."

What are you doing? Alex tensed. "Don't listen to her."

"Too late." Matthew laughed evilly. "Let's switch."

"No!" Alex yelled and grabbed his brother's hand as if to finish the job himself.

Chaos erupted, and I blurred to Alex. There was no way in hell I would allow him to sacrifice himself for me.

I slammed into Matthew's side. He stumbled back as Gwen appeared beside me and yanked Alex out of Matthew's grip.

The six wolves stood in front of Matthew, snarling, and baring their teeth, making it clear that they would protect everyone here.

"Fine." Matthew lifted his hands. "I give up. I see that I can't win."

"You don't mean that," Alex hissed as he came to me and wrapped his arms around me. "You will never give up."

Joshua materialized in front of us and stabbed Matthew in the chest. He said lowly, "That's for everything you've done to me, my friends, and every human here."

Matthew's eyes bulged with the realization that death was imminent. "Fools. You'll never truly win." Blood trickled from his mouth as the life left him, and he crumpled to the floor.

Everyone stared in silence until his heart stopped beating.

Alex's heartbreak poured through our bond, deep and suffocating, and I wished I could take the pain away. *I'm so sorry. If I could...*

No. He wasn't the same person. Alex kissed my head. *It's better this way. He wouldn't have stopped. Joshua did the right thing.*

"Ronnie!" someone yelled from the doorway. It took me a second to figure out who it was, since I'd seen her in fox form. "Ronnie!" Kira stepped through the doorway in human form, panic clear on her face. "Eliza and Annie need you."

"What's wrong?" But I realized what it was.

Andras's body was gone.

CHAPTER THIRTY

PURE TERROR THREATENED to freeze me, but I couldn't let it. Not with Eliza and Annie at stake. "How is that possible?"

"What do you mean?" Alex asked, studying the area where Andras had been.

Right, he'd been fighting Matthew when all that had gone down. "I stabbed Andras in the back, right where his heart should've been. He was lying right there."

"Stabbing a demon in the heart doesn't kill them," Rosemary explained. "When angels turn away from what little humanity they have, stopping their heart doesn't kill them. Separating their head from their body does."

That would've been nice to know an hour ago. I would've made sure the bastard was dead. I wouldn't make that same mistake again.

"You need to hurry," Kira insisted and ran out the door.

Let's go, Alex connected and sped after her.

My desire to save them propelled me forward. Within seconds, I was back outside, following Alex to their car.

Unfortunately, I didn't need to chase after him much longer because of Annie's ear-piercing scream.

Andras had found them.

Tapping into my demon and vampire, I surged forward.

Veronica! Alex connected, and his desperation surged through me. *Wait.*

I'm sorry. He was chasing me. He'd be, at most, only a couple of minutes behind me. It wasn't like I was going far or anything. *I have to get to them.* I didn't slow, finding the strength inside me to push full speed ahead.

I ran over the top of the hill, and my old Mazda came into view. Andras was in physical form and had lifted Annie off the ground by the neck.

Hands lifted, Eliza stood next to the driver's side. "Stop," she commanded. "Please."

"You're next," Andras sneered. "You hid my daughter from me."

"Your *daughter*?" Eliza asked in confusion. "But—"

"Speak of the devil—there she is." Andras turned to me, beaming with maliciousness. "I wondered how long it would take the fox to rat me out. I'm impressed by the speed in which you got here, but I shouldn't be surprised. Bleeding heart and everything." He rolled his eyes and wrinkled his nose in disgust. "I'd expected better from my daughter, but alas, I had the right instinct when I first learned about you."

He was trying to mess with me, but I wouldn't let him. "Let her go. It's me you're after."

"And that's why I won't let her go." Andras lowered his head. "I will kill these two and then your mate, and when you beg for mercy, that's when I'll know you've had enough."

What was up with these assholes wanting to kill everyone I loved? Was it written into their genetic code? "You won't hurt any of them."

"Wait." Eliza rubbed her forehead. "This is your father?"

"He doesn't deserve that title." To me, the word *father* implied family. This man wasn't my family. He just happened to be part of the process of creating me.

Alex caught up to me, and I could hear the rest of the group coming. They'd be here in seconds. There was no way one demon could take us all down.

But maybe he didn't plan to.

The thought chilled me, turning my palms sweaty.

"Say goodbye to your friend." Andras tightened his grasp on Annie's neck, and she struggled to breathe.

No.

A flash of black darted against the sky and slammed into Andras. He fell to the ground, taking Annie with him. She yelped as they struck the cobblestones.

Yelahiah stood over Andras, her purple eyes shining. She snatched the wrist of the hand holding Annie and squeezed as she commanded, "Let the girl go."

His eyes flashed with anger, and his face twisted in pain. After a few seconds of their standoff, Andras released Annie and rasped, "You will pay for that, angel."

The sunlight hit her amber hair, adding to her already majestic beauty.

Sterlyn and the shifters reached us just as the demon tackled Yelahiah in the stomach, forcing her to stumble backward into a redbud tree trunk.

"Mom!" Rosemary cried and flew past me.

Andras didn't bother to turn toward the oncoming angel. He punched Yelahiah in the face. Her head snapped back against the tree, but she kicked Andras in the stomach, and he took several steps back.

Now that Andras was preoccupied, I raced across the clearing to Annie. I wrapped my arm around her waist and helped her to her feet. We needed to get her out of here before something worse happened.

Let me help. Alex blurred to Annie's other side, taking some of her weight off me.

A whimper forced me to turn, ready to fight, but I found a silver wolf standing in front of me. He was slightly smaller than Sterlyn but larger than Darrell. This had to be Sterlyn's twin, her beta.

He hunkered down, and I wasn't sure what he wanted.

He wants us to put Annie on his back and let him take her away from here, Alex connected. *I've seen wolves do this before.*

That was probably the safest thing to do for her—that way, she wouldn't be in the demon's sights. *Okay. It should be fine, right? Sterlyn trusts him?*

Yes, and Cyrus is one of the strongest fighters here, besides those two angels and Sterlyn, and he can see the demon form. He's one of the safest people she could be with when she's away from you and Eliza.

I found Eliza standing in front of the car. She watched the fight unfold, her hands raised, waiting for the right moment to strike. She was fine for now; I had to focus on Annie.

Agreeing with him, we led Annie to the silver wolf.

"Is that a wolf?" she asked, her voice raspy.

I needed her to remain quiet, but if I didn't answer her, she'd get louder and more persistent. "He's a wolf shifter. He'll take you somewhere safe."

"Wait ... that's a man?" Her mouth dropped as she looked at the animal.

We didn't have time for this. "Please, let him take you somewhere safe. I'll be there to check on you in minutes."

"Okay." Nodding, she suddenly found the strength to walk the rest of the way to him. She climbed onto his back and wrapped her arms around his neck.

Cyrus rose and nodded his head toward me, then took off toward the blood bank.

Now I needed to get Eliza out of here. I spun around and found Sterlyn, Griffin, Killian, and the other silver wolf around her. Of course, my friends would protect the person I considered my mother.

"Agh!" Rosemary flew across the road and hit the grass so hard she left an indentation in the earth. Her long mahogany hair was in disarray, and when she tried to stand, she fell back onto her ass.

Yelahiah fought the demon hand to hand, each one punching the other as if trying to prove something to themselves. Yelahiah flapped her black wings, lifting into the sky.

That was the opportunity Andras had needed because he transitioned into his shadow.

"He disappeared," Alex hissed.

But that didn't faze Yelahiah. She spun faster and faster until she looked like a tornado and dropped from the sky toward Andras.

I needed to do something while he was focused on someone else. Trying not to overthink, I blurred toward the demon.

I held the dagger outward, ready to stab Andras again. When Yelahiah reached him, she flew right through him and slammed into the cobblestone road, cracking it.

Dammit, we had to kill him before he hurt anyone else. I swung my arm, aiming for his neck, but Andras spun around and caught my wrist.

"At least, you tried." He laughed. "I respect that. But your grandfather, Wrath, taught me everything I know. This is your game-over." Andras grabbed my head and pulled.

My neck screamed as it stretched.

"No!" Alex cried and ran toward us, but it was too late.

My bones cracked and popped, and dizziness consumed me.

"*Fulgurites!*" Eliza screamed.

Something cracked through the air, and static built inside me. Andras was slowly ripping my head from my body, but I hadn't expected to feel that sensation.

Light blazed and crackled through my near-black vision and hit Andras's chest half an inch from my face. Eliza had called lightning.

He released me, and his body shook and buzzed from the charge.

As I fell away from him, his body materialized from the spells Eliza was casting upon him. I looked up, letting my fuzzy vision focus on my foster mother. Blood trickled from her nose, but she held her hands firm.

I grabbed my aching neck, confirming my head was still attached to my body. Despite Andras's hold being gone, I was still in intense pain.

"She's free," Rosemary slurred as she slowly got back onto her feet.

"Fire!" Alex commanded.

Gunshots rang all around me, assaulting Andras with bullets as Eliza's lightning continued to strike.

"That's not enough." Yelahiah flitted her wings, taking to the air. "A demon must be beheaded."

Adrenaline burst through me. *Get them to stop shooting.*

Why? Alex said, "Hold your fire!"

I stepped toward Andras. I would end this once and for all.

Let Yelahiah do it, Alex pleaded, aware of my plans.

But I knew it had to be me. The dagger's heat surged throughout me as I aimed for the fried demon.

Eliza dropped her hand. The lightning disappeared as she passed out, hitting the ground.

Andras's head turned my way. He was still impacted by the onslaught, so I had to move fast. I swung my dagger and expected him to catch my hand again, but I felt it cut through flesh and bone. His eyes widened moments before his head rolled from his body onto the stony ground.

Everyone was silent, and the world stopped moving.

Until pain rocked through me, and I crumpled.

"Help her." Alex cried, his voice growing closer. He dropped beside me, taking my hand in his. "Baby, stay with me."

I wanted to. Hell, I was trying, but my vision darkened again. Andras had inflicted worse injury than I'd thought.

"Someone help her!" Gwen screamed and dropped to my other side. "Help my sister!"

Howls filled my ears as the world blurred.

At least I'd saved everyone I loved.

ROSEMARY'S VOICE trickled into my consciousness. "She'll be fine. I promise. Mom and I healed her. She just needs to recover from the shock."

Wait. I wasn't dead?

"What about Wrath?" Sterlyn asked with concern. "We killed his son."

Wrath. My grandfather. No wonder Andras had been filled with such rage and violence.

"It'll take centuries for the Prince of Hell to realize one of his sons is dead," Rosemary assured her.

Dread laced through me. My grandfather was the Prince of Hell? I wasn't sure what that meant, but it couldn't be good.

I inhaled deeply, smelling Alex's delicious syrupy scent. My hand was wrapped in his, and I moaned.

I'd never tire of waking up with him.

Veronica. His relief was immeasurable. *Thank the gods.* "She's awake."

I opened my eyes and found my soulmate leaning over the bed we used at Sterlyn and Griffin's house. The strain of exhaustion was etched into his face. "Hey, you," I said, hoping to lighten his look.

Do you know how much you scared me? Alex growled. *Running off multiple times, and I could do nothing about it? Now I understand everything Griffin has gone through. I feel more kinship with him than ever.*

If only I was a badass like Sterlyn. I was more half-assed compared to her. *I'm sorry. But Andras is dead. Right? And everyone is okay?*

Yes, except for the vampires who died in the blood bank. Joshua and the others are there, taking care of the bodies.

Annie stepped into my room with tears streaming down her cheeks. "Ronnie, thank goodness." She ran to my bedside and hugged me. "We were all so worried."

"I'm sorry." I hadn't meant to worry everyone. "I just —" I stopped, unsure what I could say to make it better.

Eliza stepped into the room, followed by Gwen, Sterlyn, Griffin, Killian, Rosemary, and Sierra. Everyone I considered my family.

"You had unresolved issues to handle." Eliza frowned. "And I hate that I added to the burden."

"Please." Sierra snorted and rolled her eyes. "She's a beast at handling things. I've never seen anyone so resilient before. Like, oh, there are vampires, angels, demons, and shifters? Please, I've seen worse. For example, Griffin's horrible mullet-like haircut."

"It is *not* a mullet. It's equally long in the front and the back." He gestured at his freshly gelled hair.

"Yeah, man." Killian smacked his back. "Let's go with that."

"Now listen here—" Griffin rasped.

Sterlyn leaned her head on her mate's shoulder and stared at him adoringly. "Don't listen to them. They're just jealous. I, for one, love everything about you."

A tender smile spread across his face. "And that's all that matters."

"Is that what a healthy relationship looks like?" Gwen's face scrunched. "Because that's how Alex and Ronnie act, too. Maybe I should be taking notes?"

"Please, no." Sierra shivered and rubbed her hands on her arms. "I can only handle so much mush, and I gotta say these two couples have me maxed out. I don't want anymore."

For the first time in a while, things felt normal. Well,

as normal as they could be, given I'd learned I was the granddaughter of a high-ranking demon.

Rosemary stood next to Alex and examined me. "You seem better. Are you in any pain?"

"No, I'm good." The pain I'd felt before blacking out would always haunt me. "Thanks to you and your mother."

"Speaking of which, I need to get back to Shadow City." Rosemary's nostrils flared. "Azbogah is causing issues because Mom left without notifying anyone, which is stupid. That's why Dad stayed behind, to head off any trouble. I need to get back there to help calm things down."

"Okay." I hated that she was leaving, but I understood. "But real fast—what is the Prince of Hell?"

Rosemary's face fell. "You heard that. It's nothing you need to worry about. We'll figure out how to handle him if he tries to see you. We're safe for now and have time to determine a strategy."

"Let's enjoy a sense of normalcy before our world gets turned upside down again." Sterlyn tried to smile. "We'll do research to figure out what we're up against, but we need to focus on settling things down with the council and our towns."

She was right. I glanced at Rosemary. "Will you please tell your mother thank you? I'm not sure we would've made it if it weren't for you two."

"I will." Rosemary gave me a small hug, catching me off guard. She'd never shown me affection before.

"Do you all mind giving Ronnie and me a moment alone?" Eliza asked, avoiding my gaze.

Alex nodded. "Sure." *Are you okay with that?*

Yeah. I didn't want him to leave, but if Eliza wanted to talk, I wanted to hear what she had to say. *But stay close.*

Forever. Alex leaned over, kissing my lips softly. *There's no way I could ever go far.*

I cupped his cheek. *I love you.*

And I love you. He kissed me again before walking out with everyone else, including Annie.

Awkward silence descended, but I remained quiet. She'd asked to speak with me after all.

Eliza cleared her throat. "I was wrong. I should've told you from day one what you are, but I thought, by not telling you, I was protecting you."

I understood that all too well. It had been hard at first, but I'd gotten Alex to make Annie forget her time in Shadow Terrace for the same reason. And now she was having nightmares. "I know. I'm sorry if I was too hard on you."

"You weren't." Eliza sat on the edge of the bed and faced me. "And I will tell Annie about herself. I see now that keeping this world hidden from her has put her at risk, too. Had I just told you two why I didn't want her to come here, maybe this never would have happened."

Grimacing, I shook my head. "Don't get me wrong. I wish Annie hadn't gone through hell here, but I can't regret meeting Alex and my friends. Alex makes me happier than I've ever been, and Sterlyn and the others, they're amazing friends."

"Yeah, I've noticed that." Eliza chuckled. "When I first got here and saw what Alex was, the last thing I wanted was for you to be with him. But that changed in hours, after seeing how he protects you and cares for you. Granted, we were fighting crazy-ass vampires, but he loves you."

"I know." There was no doubt in my mind. He was my other half.

Knowing she needed to hear it from me, I lifted my left hand. I'd wanted to tell her as soon as she got here, but we'd been in danger. Maybe now was the perfect time. "He asked me to marry him."

Her eyes latched on to the ring, and a sad smile spread across her face. "And I take it you said yes."

I nodded, at a loss for words. "But he's refusing to plan it without your blessing. He was planning to ask you when we came to visit."

"Ah ... I like that. Very old-fashioned." Eliza moved her head side to side. "And, of course, I'll give it to him."

A weight lifted from my chest. I hadn't even realized I'd been that worried. "One last question."

"Yes?" she asked.

"Were you able to see the demon? You were able to hold him off, but it was also like you couldn't see him." I wasn't making sense, but that had been bothering me.

She exhaled and pursed her lips. "I couldn't see him, but I could feel his negative energy. It clashed with nature, so my magic sensed him. I could see him through my magic if that makes sense."

The crazy thing was that I understood. That was how far I'd come, living in this world.

"Enough of that—let's handle happier matters." Eliza beamed. "Alex, will you come join us?"

The door opened, confirming Alex hadn't been far. I'd bet he'd overheard the entire conversation. He entered the room with a huge smile on his face.

Eliza tilted her head. "Do you have something to ask me, boy?"

He nodded. "I'm completely in love with your daughter, and I want nothing more than to marry her. I was hoping to have your blessing."

"You have it." She climbed to her feet and placed her hands on his shoulders. "It didn't take long for me to see how much you love her."

"She's my soulmate in every way." Alex's soft blue irises focused on me. "And she makes me a better person."

Eliza turned to me. "And I think you do the same for her."

"Eh." I winked at Alex. "I guess."

"We've got a wedding and coronation to plan, people!" Sierra shouted from the other room. "Mayday. Mayday. It's time to get serious. I think it should be epic and done all at one time."

It hit me that she was right. Alex was the vampire king, and I would be his queen. That was a whole lot of pressure, but it felt right—as if we were destined for it.

Sierra burst into the room with a notebook and magazines. "I've been anticipating this moment! The time has finally come." She jumped onto the bed, scattering the bridal magazines everywhere. "Sterlyn! Annie! Get your asses in here. We need your opinions too."

"She realizes it's Ronnie's wedding, not hers, right?" Annie asked as she came in, sounding baffled.

"You'll soon learn Sierra has her own type of logic." Killian sighed from the doorway. "So ... have fun."

This moment felt right. Everyone I loved was nearby, and I would soon marry the love of my life.

Everything was perfect.

ABOUT THE AUTHOR

Jen L. Grey is a *USA Today* Bestselling Author who writes Paranormal Romance, Urban Fantasy, and Fantasy genres.

Jen lives in Tennessee with her husband, two daughters, and two miniature Australian Shepherd. Before she began writing, she was an avid reader and enjoyed being involved in the indie community. Her love for books eventually led her to writing. For more information, please visit her website and sign up for her newsletter.

Check out my future projects and book signing events at my website.

www.jenlgrey.com

ALSO BY JEN L. GREY

Shadow City: Silver Wolf Trilogy

Broken Mate

Rising Darkness

Silver Moon

Shadow City: Royal Vampire Trilogy

Cursed Mate

Shadow Bitten

Demon Blood

Shadow City: Royal Vampire Trilogy

Ruined Mate

Shattered Curse

Fated Souls

The Hidden King Trilogy

Dragon Mate

Dragon Heir

Dragon Queen

The Wolf Born Trilogy

Hidden Mate

Blood Secrets

Awakened Magic

The Marked Wolf Trilogy

Moon Kissed

Chosen Wolf

Broken Curse

Wolf Moon Academy Trilogy

Shadow Mate

Blood Legacy

Rising Fate

The Royal Heir Trilogy

Wolves' Queen

Wolf Unleashed

Wolf's Claim

Bloodshed Academy Trilogy

Year One

Year Two

Year Three

The Half-Breed Prison Duology (Same World As Bloodshed Academy)

Hunted

Cursed

The Artifact Reaper Series

Reaper: The Beginning

Reaper of Earth

Reaper of Wings

Reaper of Flames

Reaper of Water

Stones of Amaria (Shared World)

Kingdom of Storms

Kingdom of Shadows

Kingdom of Ruins

Kingdom of Fire

The Pearson Prophecy

Dawning Ascent

Enlightened Ascent

Reigning Ascent

Stand Alones

Death's Angel

Rising Alpha